Through The Crystal

Becky Coelho

© 2007 by Becky Coelho.

All rights reserved. No part of this book may be reproduced, stored in a retrieval system or transmitted in any form or by any means without prior written permission of the publishers, except by a reviewer who may quote brief passages in a review to be printed in a newspaper, magazine or journal.

First Printing 2007

Although portions of this novel were suggested by real events and/or performers at those events, most characters appearing in this work are fictitious. Any resemblance to real persons, living or deceased is purely coincidental.

The lyrics from the song "My Jesus" © are used by permission of Ardent Records, all rights reserved.

The lyrics from the song "You Never Let Go" © are used by permission of Music Services, all rights reserved.

The lyrics from the song "Cry Out to Jesus" © are used by permission of Music Services, all rights reserved.

Other works by Becky Coelho
    Born In December © 2006

ISBN 978-1-4303-2855-1

+++

Prologue for Through the Crystal

Becky Coelho has a tremendous gift. Her gift is with words, and I am privileged to recommend her book "Through the Crystal" to anyone who has a desire to find meaning and purpose to their lives. Anyone who works with young people needs to read this book, and allow the lives described in this book be a "heads up" to share with others along your journey. Becky's gift comes from God and I pray that God will use her words to inspire all who read "Through the Crystal."

Bruce A Rice
Executive Director
Great Commission Broadcasting Corporation
Quincy, IL

For Matt

Chapter One

The wild day lilies were swaying in the hot summer breeze along the long rutted lane. The car rocked to and fro although it was going very slow. John had his head stuck out the back window, straining to see the old farm house beyond the stand of trees near the curve ahead. Jenny sat back in her seat as if in a pout. She didn't want to come see her grandparents because it was going to be so boring here on the farm for the young teenage girl; and she was missing a party with her friends back home.

Barbara and Bob tried to bring their family to visit his parents at least twice a year. Bob recalled his days on the farm with a melancholy nostalgia. He misses the quiet security of the west central Illinois farm community. He couldn't wait to finish high school so he could leave the rustic rural community. He went to college, earned his M.B.A. and acquired an excellent position with a major firm in Chicago. He met Barbara Robbins while attending Northwestern. They married shortly after graduation and started a family near Bob's job in Chicago. Now, that their two children are getting older, they long for the safe atmosphere in which his children can grow up alongside their loving, hardworking Christian grandparents. Little do his children know that he and Barbara had been talking of moving the family back there.

The car had barely come to a stop at the edge of the lawn when John threw open the door and started running toward the barn. He knew Poppy would be there working either with the animals or on one of the old tractors. Grammy came running out of the house drying her hands on her homemade polka dot apron. Bob reached out and grabbed the small, gray-haired woman around the waist and lifted her off her feet, spinning her around. Although she was protesting through her bursts of laughter, Bob finally put her down. She grabbed Barbara not only to greet her, but also to keep herself from falling from the dizziness that Bob had caused. They were all laughing and simultaneously greeting each other with all sorts of questions about their health, their jobs, the children's school and the trip here.

Jenny slowly got out of the back seat of the car and leaned against the back fender of the car. She stared out over the cornfield to the woods beyond.

"There is nothing for miles around here," was her first thought. Jenny knew she was just going to die from the boredom on *Old MacDonald's Farm*. She rolled her eyes as she turned around to follow the adults into the house. She shuffled right on through the kitchen through the dining room and plopped herself down in an overstuffed chair in the living room.

"It's so good to have you here," Grammy started. "Are you planning to stay the whole weekend? They are going to have fireworks over the river on Sunday night. I do want to take the kids to see that. Can you stay? How long do you have off for the holiday?" Grammy talked so fast and fired question after question without waiting for the previous one to be answered.

"Mom," Bob began as he pulled out a chair for his mother. "Sit down, Mom. Barbara and I have something to talk over with you and Pop."

Grammy stood there with her mouth open to ask another question but instead she knitted her forehead and waited for Bob to continue. But, as she grabbed for a pot holder for something to hold on to, she just had to plead, "Son, you just have to stay until Monday. You've got to stay for the fireworks."

"Mom, we are planning to stay for the fireworks," Bob said as he guided his mother into the chair. "As a matter of a fact, we'd like to stay longer, if it is all right with you and Pop."

"Of course, son," Grammy said putting her hand on Bob's arm. "You and your family are welcome here for as long as you want. This is your home."

"We'll talk to you and Pop tonight after supper," Bob said. Then, in a whisper, he continued, "After the kids are in bed."

Grammy started to say something when Bob put his finger to her lips and looked toward the living room where Jenny was sitting. She nodded her understanding.

"Well, I have to check on this roast for supper," Grammy said changing the subject and jumping up and going to the stove.

Bob heard Barbara ask if there was anything she could do to help with supper as he was walking into the living room. He asked Jenny if she would help him bring in the luggage from the car.

"Why can't John help?" Jenny whined.

"He is helping your grandfather with the chores." Knowing how prissy Jenny was, Bob then added, "Would you rather go down there and help them?"

Jenny just shrugged her shoulders and shuffled back through the kitchen to the car. Jenny was having trouble carrying two suitcases on the stairway. Grammy came up behind her and grabbed the larger of the two and bounded up the stairs, talking all the way.

"Now child, you know you shouldn't try to carry two of these heavy things at once. Take your time." The next words Grammy said were muffled as she had already rounded the landing and went into the North bedroom. Jenny was so frustrated that she had been shown up by an old lady. Jenny followed Grammy into the North bedroom and dropped her mother's suitcase onto the four-poster bed that her parents would share. Jenny always imagined that Lincoln must have slept there when Grammy was a child. The pictures of Poppy's parents hung in drab oval frames above the bed. Their stares seemed to follow Jenny as she walked across the room and made her skin crawl. Bob startled Jenny as he walked into the room with his suitcase.

"Oh!" She cried as she jumped when he walked up behind her. "You scared me!"

"Sorry," Bob said as he put his suitcase on the burgundy velvet fainting couch across from the bed. "Are Grandpa and Grandma Madison staring at you again?" He teased Jenny as he ran his fingers up her back.

"Stop it," Jenny snarled. "They give me the creeps."

"You had to know them," Bob said. "They were really great people."

Grammy had opened the room earlier in the week to air out. The perfume of the climbing honeysuckle floated through the windows. Bob took a deep breath before letting out a refreshing sigh.

"Ah!" he sighed. "I remember waking up to the smell of the honeysuckle. Doesn't is smell good, Jen?"

"I guess. It's so hot in here," Jenny complained. "Why don't they have air conditioning?"

"It's not bad up here, Jen," Bob said. "It'll cool down even more once the sun goes down and the breezes kick up off the river."

"I'll die," Jenny said as she fell across the bed.

"I don't think you will," Bob said. "Let's get the rest of the things and you can relax. Maybe Mom will have some lemonade downstairs."

"How wonderful," Jenny said sarcastically as she got up to go downstairs.

After bringing all of the other bags up, Jenny finally came up with her suitcase and small vanity bag. Grammy met her at the top of the stairs.

"Jenny, this year you will have the East room," Grammy said with a smile on her face.

Jenny perked up when she heard that. The East room was the most beautiful room in the house. No one ever used it. The windows went from the floor to the ceiling and they were draped with sheer beige lace curtains. The French doors led out onto a small balcony over the front porch of the house. There was a table and two chairs made of whicker on the balcony with a bouquet of flowers on the table. The room was bright and airy. There were smaller windows to the north and south also. Between the south windows was a large vanity dresser with a beveled mirror and a velvet padded seat. Across the room on the south was a chest with a pitcher and bowl sitting on it and a towel and hand cloth hanging neatly nearby. The large canopy bed was against the West wall looking out toward the French doors. The canopy, bedspread and shams all matched in a pattern of small pink roses hand-embroidered by Grammy's mother many years ago. An old wooden rocking chair sat empty next to the bed. The walls were papered in a pale green pattern matching the throw rugs on the oak hardwood floor.

Jenny couldn't believe that she was allowed to stay in this room. Many times she and John were scolded for even entering the room without permission. She gingerly sat her suitcase on the floor near the closet door. She walked over to the vanity and placed her vanity bag on the chest. She didn't know what to do first. Grammy stood in the doorway, not saying a word, just smiling.

Back downstairs, Barbara was slicing the roast and Bob was whipping the potatoes. John walked in behind Poppy and followed him into the downstairs bathroom to wash up for supper. Grammy came downstairs giving orders and carrying platters of food to the dining room table. Jenny even helped set the table with silverware and napkins. Soon all was ready for the family to sit and eat.

Poppy came in and took his seat at the head of the table. John rushed up to sit to his right. Jenny sat next to John with their parents across from them. Grammy sat at the opposite end of Poppy, closest to the kitchen. Poppy lowered his head and folded his hands. The others followed his example and Poppy said a rather long prayer thanking God for the blessings before them, the healthy animals, that the family had a safe trip; he then began to ask for continued blessings on the farm and family. John's stomach was almost ready to start growling when they all answered with a devout "Amen". Poppy started filling his plate with the roast and then passed dish after dish around the table. Soon everyone's plate was full.

"The children are staying long enough to watch the fireworks with us, Hank" Grammy said to Poppy. "They are all settled in already, too." Poppy acknowledged her with a slight nod.

"We got all the cows fed and the sheep put in for the night and I even collected about a dozen eggs," John bragged. "After supper, Poppy and I can go close up the chicken house."

"You're a good little helper," Grammy complimented. "I don't know how Poppy gets all his work done when you aren't around to help him."

John just beamed. It was quite a compliment for the 12-year-old boy. Poppy nodded in agreement and reached over and tousled John's chestnut hair. John just grinned.

After supper, John went with Poppy to finish up the chores. Barbara and Jenny helped Grammy clean up the dishes. Bob went upstairs and put his and Barbara's clothes in the closet. Afterwards, he went into his childhood bedroom and put all of John's clothes away. Bob loved his room. It still had his Cardinal pennant on the wall from his old high school. His Hamilton High School letterman's jacket was still hanging in the back of the closet. Grammy had put it in a plastic cleaner's bag. Thinking about it a second, this was a great place to grow up.

After tucking John in bed and saying goodnight to Jenny, Bob and Barbara went down to the dining room to talk to his parents. Poppy was leaning back in his chair sipping on a cup of coffee.

"Now son, what's wrong? If there is something troubling you, you can tell us about it," Grammy rambled.

"Mom, Pop, we want to move back here. It is getting crazy in the city. I am afraid for the kids. There are policemen stationed at their schools, the kids walk through metal detectors when they go into the building. At Jenny's school, they have canceled all sporting events because of problems. Neither of the kids will have the opportunity to play any sports or participate in any extracurricular activities. It's a shame. They will lose out on so much." Bob leaned back in his chair. "Twice already there have been threats against teachers and shots fired at the school from passing cars. We are losing a lot of our good teachers because they are afraid to come through the area to get to the school. I've had enough and I want my kids to feel safe at school."

"The children don't have anywhere to go that is safe anymore. The gangs have taken over the parks and the mall. We don't even shop in any stores in the area. Bob picks up groceries on his way home from work." Barbara sighed heavily before continuing. "It is so different from when I was a child. Everything has changed."

"I can work from home if I have to. I can e-mail and fax everything to the main company from any where we live. I want the kids to enjoy their childhood as much as I did," Bob said.

"As I recall young man, you were in an all fired big hurry to get out of the boon docks," Grammy said. "I guess you never know what you have until it's gone. You remember that, Robert?"

"Yeah, Mom, you're right. So, what do you think? Can we move back here? We'd kind of like to look for a house while we're here now." Then, Bob directed the next question to his father. "I would like to leave Barbara and the kids here while I go back and try to sell the house and get everything settled with my job. Is that all right with you?"

Poppy nodded as Grammy said, "Of course, Bob. Barbara and the children can stay for as long as it takes. And there is no need to look for houses here until you get your house sold in Chicago. Take as long as you need."

"Thanks, Mom, Pop. That takes a big load off of my mind," Bob said with a sigh.

Barbara and Bob said goodnight to Poppy and Grammy and went up to bed.

Grammy said, "Hank, it will be good to have them here," Poppy just nodded.

Chapter Two

John woke up to the sun blasting in his eyes. He sat up, rubbed his eyes and looked to see it was already 8:30. John jumped out of bed and pulled on a pair of shorts, grabbed his socks and shoes and went flying down the stairs. He was heading out the back door when Grammy yelled at him.

"Hey boy!" she cried. "Come back here and sit down to breakfast."

"I can't Grammy", John said as he paused long enough to pull on his socks and shoes. "Poppy needs me. I told him to wake me up when he went out this morning."

"You sit down here young man. Poppy will be in here in just a couple of minutes to eat, too. Then you can go out with him." Grammy turned toward the stove and saw Poppy walking toward the house through the kitchen window. "See, here he comes now."

As Poppy walked through the door, John was all over him. "Why didn't you wake me up Poppy?"

"Poppy wanted to let you sleep your first morning here" Grammy said, not giving Poppy a chance to answer.

Poppy sat down after pouring himself a cup of coffee. He sat stirring his coffee although he didn't add sugar or milk to it. He smiled at John's enthusiasm. John started shoveling cereal in his mouth.

"Slow down boy," Grammy scolded. "There's plenty of time to eat properly. If you get yourself sick, you won't be able to help Poppy at all."

John laid down his spoon and chewed the mouthful of cereal. After swallowing he took a big gulp of cold milk. John's eyes were fixed on Poppy, watching his every move. He picked up his spoon and started stirring his milk just like Poppy was stirring his coffee. Grammy saw this.

"Don't play with your food, John," she scolded again. "Poppy, here's your breakfast. Eat up."

Poppy laid down his spoon and took a sip of his coffee, then started eating his eggs and ham. Grammy put a plate of homemade biscuits on the table. Poppy reached across and took a couple and smeared butter and grape jelly on them. Then he handed one to John. Without saying a word, Poppy took a bite out of his biscuit. John did the same with his biscuit.

With grape jelly oozing out of the corner of his mouth, John said, "These sure are good, Grammy."

Barbara and Bob came into the kitchen and sat down at the table. Grammy handed them both plates of ham and eggs. Barbara poured cups of coffee for them and added a drop of milk to each cup.

"What are your plans for today, Pop?" Bob asked.

Before he could answer, Grammy said, "Poppy and John are going to give the calves their shots this morning. This afternoon George is coming over to help shear the sheep."

"Sounds like a busy day," Bob said. "Need any help?"

Poppy nodded as he took another bite of ham. Bob remembered how hot and dirty they got shearing the sheep. He knew John would not last an hour in the barn.

Grammy said she was going into town to get groceries and asked if Barbara and Jenny wanted to go with her. Barbara said that she would love to look around the town. She wanted to get a paper to see what might be on the real estate market. The adults had agreed not to say anything about the move to the children just yet.

Jenny walked into the kitchen and sat down next to her mother. She poured herself a glass of milk and drank it quietly. Grammy offered her a plate of ham and eggs but Jenny said she did not eat breakfast and that milk would be fine for her.

"You need breakfast" Grammy started. "It's the most important meal of the day. You'll be starving by noon."

Poppy got up to head out to the barn and John swallowed his last bit of milk and ran after him. Bob said he had a couple of phone calls to make before he would go down to help the men. When Jenny heard of the plans to go into town, she rushed back upstairs to put on one of her nicer shirts and a pair of jean shorts. She looked in the mirror and saw that her legs looked so white in the shorts. She decided to quickly change into a pair of long jeans. She would have to lie out in the sun to get her legs tan enough to wear shorts. Grammy and Barbara were heading toward the car when Jenny came running out the back door. It amazed Jenny that Grammy didn't lock the house when they left.

After a ten minute drive through the farm land, Barbara turned the car onto the main highway to Hamilton. The town was situated right on the Mississippi River across from Keokuk, Iowa. Jenny had never been across the bridge, but Keokuk looked larger and more interesting than Hamilton. Barbara pulled the car into the parking lot of the local Wilson grocery store. It was the biggest market in town, but Jenny thought it was one of the smallest stores she had ever seen.

Inside the store, Jenny walked a few steps behind the older women. God forbid she should be seen with them. She stopped at the magazine section and picked up a teen magazine and began to read an article. Out of the corner of her eye, Jenny saw one of the stock boys working down the aisle from her. He looked about her age. He was tall and kind of cute. Jenny smiled at him when he looked her way. He smiled back as he picked up an empty box and walked passed her to the back of the store. Jenny was disappointed that he did not stop and talk to her. She figured he was just a country bumpkin anyway and went back to reading her magazine.

On the way home from town, Grammy was telling the girls all about the picnic and fireworks planned for the fourth. She was planning on making fried chicken to take to the picnic. Barbara was going to make a German chocolate cake. Jenny suggested that Grammy bring her potato salad, too. The menu was planned then, which also included fresh lemonade and Cole slaw. They would go late in the afternoon to get a good spot so they could see the fireworks over the river.

John was sitting on the back step of the house when the women came home.

"What's wrong John?" Grammy asked.

"It's so hot in the barn. I feel kind of sick," John explained. His face looked flushed and beads of perspiration glistened on his forehead.

"Well, come in and have a cool drink" Grammy ordered. Barbara suggested that she and Jenny take some cold drinks down to the men shearing the sheep. Jenny grumbled about going down to a stinky hot barn, but she conceded and followed her mother. The sound of the motor running the shears was deafening. Barbara tapped Bob on the shoulder to get his attention and let him know about the drinks. Bob, in turn, told Poppy and the other men. George, the head shearer, who lived at the next farm, turned the motor off and all of the men walked out into the fresh air. Barbara and Jenny poured glasses full of cold lemonade for each man.

"Thanks a lot", said a dirty-faced youth to Jenny when she handed him a glass. His smile appeared whiter than it was against his dusty face.

"You're welcome," Jenny said, somewhat interested in the disgustingly dirty kid.

The boy reached into his back pocket producing a large handkerchief and wiped his face as he pulled off his cap. Jenny was quite surprised and pleased at what she saw. The boy had dark brown eyes and sandy-colored hair. When he took a drink of the sour lemonade, deep dimples twinkled in his cheeks.

"I'm Jenny Madison."

"I know," the boy said. "I'm Todd Kramer, George's son. I've been wanting to meet you ever since Hank told us you were coming."

Jenny blushed. Bob saw the two teens talking and poked George in the ribs with his elbow. The two older men smiled and finished drinking their lemonade.

On the way back to the house, Jenny asked her mother all about Todd. Barbara said that she didn't know too much about him except that he was 16 and would be a junior at Hamilton High next fall. Jenny smiled because he was the same age as she. She planned to check him out more later on.

When they walked into the kitchen, Grammy had a stack of plates sitting on the table and the stove was full of pots steaming with food. It looked as though she was cooking for an army.

"Gee, Grammy", Jenny said. "You trying to get us all fat with all that food you're cooking?"

"Jenny," Grammy grinned. "This isn't just for the family. George, his son and Mr. Carson will be joining us for supper. We will set up the table out on the lawn. Go get the big yellow tablecloth out of the pantry and put it on the table for me. Then come back in and get the plates."

Grammy continued giving orders to stir this or get that out of the refrigerator. Barbara and Jenny were running into each other in the kitchen trying to keep up with the orders. Finally, Grammy ordered Jenny to go down to the barn and ask the men when they would be ready for supper. Jenny took a quick look in the mirror in the downstairs bathroom and fluffed her hair a bit before she headed for the barn. After all, she wanted to look nice for Todd. Just as she was rounding the corner of the barn, she realized that she did not hear the motor running. The men were bailing the last of the wool and stacking it onto the truck.

"Grammy wants to know when you will be ready for supper." Jenny asked them.

"We'll be heading up in a few minutes" Bob told her. Then to Todd and Mr. Carson, Bob said "You two go ahead and go up. We all can't get in to get cleaned up at the same time."

Mr. Carson threw his bale onto the truck and started walking toward the house. He was more than twenty yards away from the barn before Jenny and Todd turned toward the house.

"We're having pork chops and mashed potatoes," Jenny said. Then she realized that was a stupid thing to say.

"I love Mrs. Madison's pork chops," Todd said. Jenny smiled in return. The two teens walked the rest of the way in awkward silence.

Jenny helped her mom and grandmother put all the dishes on the long table in the yard. Todd and John carried two long benches and put them on either side of the table. There was enough room for all of them around the table. Poppy, Bob and George came up to the house ready to eat. Grammy smacked Bob's hand as he reached for a roll.

"Go wash your face and hands," Grammy snapped.

Once everyone was seated around the table, Poppy lowered his head, once again giving his extra long grace. Jenny thought to herself that although Poppy didn't talk much, he sure did pray a lot. Following the "Amen", the old man started filling his plate and passing the dishes around the table. Jenny blushed as her hand grazed Todd's hand as he passed her a bowl of carrots. Todd just smiled. The same thing happened when he passed the next bowl. He was placing his hand just in the right place so that Jenny had to touch it when he passed her the bowls. Todd enjoyed seeing the pink rise in Jenny's cheeks each time. He just smiled, showing off his dimples and twinkling brown eyes. Bob and George noticed what was going on between the two kids and just chuckled at them.

As the neighbors were beginning to leave, Grammy asked them about the picnic tomorrow.

"Will we see you at the picnic" she asked. "George, you have Margie call me so we can plan our menu."

"I'll do that Ruth," George said. He started the truck and drove off. Todd waved as they rounded the curve in the lane. Jenny was thrilled and anxious that Todd was going on the picnic with them tomorrow.

Oh my, she had to decide what to wear. How would she wear her hair? Jenny raced up the stairs to her room and started planning her wardrobe for the picnic. After trying on several outfits, she laid out her favorite on the rocking chair. Jenny crawled into bed and lay there for nearly an hour thinking about what tomorrow would bring.

Chapter Three

  Jenny woke up early and fixed her hair and put on her short black skirt and pink sleeveless sweater for church. She worked for quite a while to get her hair to look just right. She finally had hair, make-up and clothes just right. She posed in the mirror and was very happy with what she saw.
  The adults were sitting at the kitchen table drinking coffee when Jenny came in. They all looked up at her. Poppy just shook his head. For once, Grammy was speechless. Barbara didn't know why the sudden silence surrounded the table. Then Bob spoke up.
  "Jenny, I think you will feel out of place dressed like that for church here."
  "What's wrong with what I am wearing?" Jenny asked anxiously.
  "Well, honey, you aren't in the city now. People do things a little differently here. That would be all right for a picnic, but not for church. Didn't you bring something a little more conservative?" Bob asked.
  "I like the way I look," Jenny cried. "Mom, don't you think I look good?"
  "Jen, I don't know how things are done here. Maybe you had better listen to your father about this one."
  "I don't have anything more conservative," Jenny said. "I just won't go."
  "Yes, you will, young lady," Grammy said. "Come upstairs with me and we'll find something for you. I know there is a skirt and blouse that will look good on you." Grammy headed up the stairs as Jenny turned to her mother. "Mom," she pleaded.
  Barbara just looked defeated. "Go on with Grammy," she said.

By the time Jenny got up to the landing, Grammy had a pleated dark green skirt and a pretty, but plain, yellow blouse for Jenny to try on.

"This will do just fine," Grammy said.

"You have got to be kidding?" Jenny said looking at the outfit lying in front of her.

"No. You will feel much more comfortable in this at church. I promise you that. Listen, Jen. I wouldn't make you look funny or out of place. But if you go dressed the way you are, people will snicker and stare at you." Grammy felt Jenny's pain. "I promise, honey. Trust me."

Jenny had no idea why they were making such a big deal about going to church anyway. They only went to church on special occasions at home ~ maybe three or four times a year at the most. She'd check it out to keep the peace with the old folks.

After Jenny changed clothes, she looked in the mirror and almost started to cry. The skirt came to the top of her knees and the blouse was buttoned to the neck. Then she noticed that a couple of tears had smudged her make-up. She started to wipe it all off.

"If they want me to look plain, then I will be as plain as ever," Jenny grumbled. After removing all of her make-up, Jenny brushed her hair as flat and plain as she could get it. She removed all of her jewelry and posed one last time in front of the mirror.

"Well, just call me plain Jane," she said aloud before turning to go back downstairs.

Barbara was shocked at the transformation. Poppy nodded his approval. Bob reinforced the importance of fitting in here.

"You look nice, Jenny," he said. "Just wait. You'll see this is best."

When the family walked into the small country church, Jenny looked around to see other girls her age and to check out what they were wearing. Every girl had on a nice dress or a simple skirt and blouse. None of them were wearing make-up and they all had very simple hairstyles. Many had their hair pulled back in a ponytail.

Jenny looked around to see if Todd was there. She had just about given up when she spotted George, Mrs. Kramer and a boy about John's age walk in the front door of the church. They walked past the Madison family and sat in the pew in front of them. Then Todd came in with a very pretty girl about his same age.

"Oh no," Jenny thought. "He's got a girlfriend." Jenny was so disappointed. She didn't even want to look at Todd or at the girl, but they slipped in the pew next to George.

The service was so boring to Jenny. She fidgeted in the hardwood upright pew.

"At least the pews at home had cushions. Who expects us to sit on these monsters for two hours?" she thought to herself as she would cross and uncross her legs.

There was no air conditioning and it was getting very hot in the crowded country church. Most everyone was fanning themselves with the Sunday bulletin and the swishing sound was becoming hypnotizing. Along with the heat, the mingling of cologne smells, the ho hum of the sermon and the sound of the fanning bulletins John was nodding off. Barbara had to nudge him to keep him awake. She then noticed that he was not the only one with drooping eyes. She tapped Grammy on the knee and pointed to Poppy. Instead of a gentle nudge, Grammy gave him a hard elbow to the ribs. He let out a "harrumph" and covered it with a cough. It seems several of the men had a slight cough in church that morning.

After the service, Grammy was introducing Barbara to George's wife, Margie and their younger son, Terry. The pretty girl was standing next to Margie.

"This is my daughter, Tamara," Margie said.

"I am really glad to meet you," Jenny said with a big smile on her face. "Maybe you can tell me what you do for fun around here."

"I can tell you anything you want to know," Todd said behind Jenny. "I see you met Tam."

"I thought she was your girlfriend," Jenny said. Todd and Tamara both chuckled.

"That's a first," Todd said. "Tam and I are twins."

Jenny started to giggle, but it was more out of embarrassment than humor.

"Are you going to the picnic this afternoon?" Tamara asked Jenny.

"Yes, I guess we are all going later this afternoon," Jenny replied.

"You'll enjoy it," Tamara said. "There's usually a ball game going on. Anybody can play. They don't usually keep score and it's just a lot of fun. Others just sit and watch all of the other people. There is a volleyball net set up. Ummm...what else is there, Todd?"

"Well, besides all of the food stands, there are several game booths, too. I think the community band is going to play this evening." Todd paused to think of other things that would be happening at the picnic.

Terry tugged at Todd's shirt.

"What is it, Terry?" Todd asked his little brother.

"Are they going to have croquet and Bouche ball again this year?" Terry asked Todd with great anticipation.

"I don't know, Terror. We'll probably find out later. We call him Terror because he was a terror at that Bouche ball, weren't you, buddy," Todd said putting a huge grin on the face of the youngster.

"Have you ever made ice cream?" Terry asked Jenny.

"I've eaten it, but never made it," Jenny replied.

"Well, everybody who wants to eat homemade ice cream has to help make it," Todd said. "It's the best ice cream you'll ever eat."

"I can't wait," Jenny said. She then took Tamara by the arm and pulled her away from Todd and the others.

"What are you wearing to the picnic?" she asked.

"What do you mean?" Tamara asked. "I'm just wearing a T-shirt and shorts."

"The reason I asked is that my grandmother made me change my clothes for church. I just wanted to make sure I wouldn't have to go through that hassle again."

"You look fine," Tamara said. "Just change into shorts and a T-shirt."

"Thanks, Tamara," Jenny said, as the two girls walked back to join the others. Todd told Jenny that he would see her later at the picnic and then left with his family.

The Madison kitchen was bustling with Grammy and Barbara preparing dishes to take to the picnic. Bob, Poppy and John were all sitting out in the yard relaxing under the huge oak trees. Bob was reading the Sunday newspaper. Duke, Poppy's Border Collie, was curled up next to John's chair. John was unconsciously petting the dog's sleeping head. Shortly, the silence of the countryside was broken by the sound of Poppy's soft snoring.

Jenny decided that her long jeans and a Chicago Cubs T-shirt would look fine for the picnic. She left her hair simple and only added a slight touch of eye shadow and mascara. She liked how she looked although she still felt very plain. She knew her friends back home would tease her merciless. But, after all, she wasn't back home now; and she did want the approval of the adults in the house. Since it was still early, Jenny went out on the balcony and relaxed in one of the whicker chairs. The breeze felt good against her face. Soon, she was dozing, too.

Around 3 o'clock, the family loaded picnic baskets, lawn chairs and blankets into the back of the truck. Grammy decided they would have to take two vehicles since they were taking so much stuff with them. Poppy had pulled the truck up close to the house and John slid in the seat next to him and Grammy sat near the window.

"Just follow us," Grammy yelled as they pulled down the lane.

Along the riverfront in Hamilton, the park was full of people enjoying the day. Poppy found a couple of parking spots close to each other and motioned for Bob to follow him. They unloaded the truck and carried baskets, chairs, blankets and even the croquet game to a flat grassy area with a clear view of the Ol' Muddy, as Poppy called it.

Grammy and John set up the chairs while Poppy and Bob moved a few picnic tables over. Jenny kept looking for the Kramer family to show up. Barbara nudged her a few times to bring her back to the task at hand.

About half an hour later, the Kramers were walking toward their picnic spot. Todd set two picnic baskets on one of the tables while Tamara helped her mother lay out the dishes. The older men decided to walk around the park to check things out. John and Terry, of course, had to tag along with them.

Todd, Tamara and Jenny wanted to check out some of the games that were going on. They couldn't agree on which one they wanted to play. Tamara saw a few of her friends playing volleyball and decided to join them. Todd and Jenny decided to walk down by the river.

Several beautiful pleasure boats were out on the river below the dam. Todd found a large tree that had fallen into the river. It was a great place to sit and dangle their feet in the water. It was the first time that Jenny had been this close to the Mississippi River. She had seen it several times from the car window, but this was great! A barge passed slowly by them after it had gone through the locks and the wake rocked the tree they were sitting on. The water splashed up on their legs. Now Jenny wished that she would have worn shorts.

"Look, Todd," Jenny cried as she pointed to a sailboat coming from behind a stand of trees. "Isn't it beautiful?"

"Yeah, it really is," Todd said surprisingly. "We don't see too many of them on this part of the river. She's a beauty."

After the sailboat disappeared Todd told Jenny all about his school and the basketball team that he played on. The team did pretty well last season and hoped to do better this year. He told her that he also played baseball in the spring.

"Our school doesn't have basketball, or any sports for that matter," Jenny said.

"You're kidding!" Todd exclaimed. "What do you do for fun?"

"Not a lot," Jenny said. "We had all extra curricular activities cut out a couple of years ago because the gangs would bring guns and knives to the games. They couldn't get referees to come to call a game after a while. And a lot of teams wouldn't come to our school to play. We would always have to play away. Dad wanted to send me to a private school but they are so expensive and I would have to go so far away from home."

"Hmm," Todd said, but he was thinking about something. "So what do you do up there?"

"Well, I have my friends," Tamara said. "We don't go out a lot. We usually just hang at each other's houses, listen to music mostly or rent movies. I really wish that I could go to a good school like Hamilton High School," Jenny said. "You make it sound nice here."

"It's not so bad for the most part. Why don't you ask your grandparents if you can live here during the school year?" Todd suggested.

"Oh my gosh, Todd, that is a great idea," Jenny exclaimed. "Help me think of how I can ask my parents and grandparents if they will let me stay here. I would help Grammy out with the housework. Is there a school bus or could I ride to school with you?" Jenny continued to fire questions at Todd. The two of them continued to make plans to try to keep Jenny in Hamilton for the school year.

After a delicious meal of fried chicken, Margie's potato salad, Grammy's Cole slaw, carrot and celery sticks, baked beans and lemonade, there was hardly room for Barbara's German chocolate cake. But, everyone except Grammy made room for a piece.

Todd and Jenny walked over to the main stage area of the park. There were several older men and women making ice cream on several picnic tables. They stopped by one table near a larger man cranking the handle of an ice cream machine.

"Jenny, all you have to do is crank the handle," Todd said. Mr. Davis stepped back from the crank and let Jenny take over. She started to turn the crank, but it got slower and slower. Finally she stopped and stepped back rubbing her upper arm. Mr. Davis and Todd began to chortle as Mr. Davis grabbed the crank again.

"That's hard work," Jenny moaned still rubbing her arm.

"That means the ice cream is getting hard," said Mr. Davis. "Todd, give me a hand here and you can taste test this batch for me."

Todd reached down and lifted the ice cream machine from the seat on to table. When Mr. Davis took the lid off the container, the sweet smell of vanilla filled the air.

"Mmmm", Jenny said. "It sure does smell good."

Mr. Davis took a plastic spoon and dipped a small bit out and handed the spoon to Todd. Instead of tasting the ice cream, he handed it to Jenny. She took the bite. She closed her eyes when the sweet cold mixture hit her tongue.

"Mmmm, That's delicious," she exclaimed licking the spoon.

Mr. Davis let out a hearty guffaw. The old man dipped two cones and handed one to each teen. Todd and Jenny headed back to their families after thanking Mr. Davis.

"I told you it was the greatest ice cream you'll ever have," Todd reminded Jenny who simply nodded as she took another bite.

When they got back to the group everyone was either relaxing in a lawn chair or lying on a blanket on the soft grass. The community band had started playing patriotic songs about 8:30. Poppy's foot was tapping to the beat and Grammy was humming softly. As soon as it was dark, a voice came over the public address system announcing that the fireworks would be starting within five minutes.

The "Star Spangled Banner" was blaring over the P.A. system as the first blast of fireworks lit up the sky. Greens, reds, and gold scattered across the night sky while reflecting off the water. With each explosion of color, people would oohhh and ahhhh with delight. Butterflies, rocket ships, and stars exploded across the sky. Jenny had never seen such fireworks, except on television. This was so much more thrilling. Jenny had chills from the excitement of it all. Each time the sky exploded the boats on the river changed colors and looked like toys on a plate of glass. At one time Jenny thought she saw the sailboat against the western shore line. The grand finale started with "America the Beautiful" playing. Explosions of red, white and blue were followed by green and gold. When the sky turned dark and the music stopped, applause rumbled all along the riverfront.

The families loaded up their baskets, coolers, chairs and other picnic necessities and carried them back to their cars and trucks. Jenny said she hoped to see Todd and Tamara again real soon, as the adults and the two younger boys said their good-byes, too. It had been a very long, but memorable day. John fell asleep as soon as Poppy pulled the truck onto the highway. Jenny sat alone in the back seat remembering when she and Todd sat on the log. It had been the best day of her life. Little did she know that the best was yet to come.

Poppy was carrying John upstairs as Bob pulled his car into the yard. Jenny helped Bob, Barbara and Grammy carry everything into the kitchen and Grammy said she would put everything away in the morning. Jenny walked up to her room and sat on the bed. She was thinking about how she was going to ask her parents about staying here as she got ready for bed. She played the scene over and over in her mind. Shortly she drifted off to a dreamless sleep.

Barbara and Bob decided that they would talk to the children in the morning about their plans. Barbara was worried about how Jenny would handle the news since she had so many friends back home. She knew that John would be thrilled to live close to his Poppy. Bob kissed Barbara and reassured her that everything would be all right. Soon Barbara and Bob fell off to sleep.

On the way up to her room, Grammy peeked in on Bob and Barbara; pulled the sheet up over John, and smiled remembering when Bob used to sleep in that bed. She was happy to see Jenny sleeping soundly. She patted Duke on the head before crawling into bed next to a sleeping Poppy. She kissed him on the forehead and rolled over, falling asleep serenaded by the night sounds on the farm.

Chapter Four

Early Monday morning, John had gotten up, dressed and downstairs before anyone else. He saw the coffee dripping through the filter so he knew that Poppy would be down very soon. John helped himself to a bowl of Corn Flakes and milk and was just putting the milk back into the refrigerator when Poppy walked into the kitchen.

"Morning, Poppy," John said with a mouthful of cereal.

"Uh huh," Poppy mumbled in response while pouring himself a cup of coffee.

When they had finished, John grabbed the egg basket and headed for the hen house. He gently lifted the sleeping hens off freshly laid eggs, and reached into empty nests to pick up a few more eggs. When he was done, he made sure that the chickens had fresh water and put chicken feed out for them. John made sure the gate was closed to the pen when he headed toward the barn where the young lambs were kept. John set the basket of eggs right outside the door of the barn and went in to water and feed the lambs.

When he came back out of the barn, not five minutes later, a big raccoon was sitting by the basket sucking on an egg. There were three broken eggshells next to the raccoon too.

"Scat! Get out of here!" screamed John as he flailed his hands in the air at the coon. The little thief dropped the egg it was sucking and scampered behind the barn.

"Dang coon," John moaned as he picked up his basket of eggs. He counted them as he walked toward the house. Well, he still had over a dozen eggs. At the house, he told Grammy about the coon. Instead of scolding the boy, she just smiled.

Grammy was kneading a big hunk of dough. She'd flip it and pound it as if she were mad at someone. John watched her with intensity, thinking that he sure didn't want Grammy beating on him that hard. Pretty soon Grammy took out a big knife and started cutting the dough into small pieces, rolling each piece in her hand and setting it on a cookie sheet. So that's how she made those great biscuits. John couldn't wait to bite into one dripping with jelly and butter.

Grammy pulled out her big griddle and cracked almost all of the eggs that John had brought in to her. She whipped them together and sprinkled a little salt, garlic, and pepper over them. She opened a container of left over ham and diced it on top of the eggs and added some shredded cheddar cheese. The eggs were sizzling when Poppy walked through the door. Grammy flipped the eggs over a couple of times before separating them into squares; one for each member of the family. John grabbed his fork and was ready to dig into the omelet as soon as Grammy put it in front of him.

John and Poppy were almost finished with breakfast when Bob, Barbara and Jenny came into the kitchen. Jenny was still in her nightclothes and looked as if she were still sleeping. Barbara had wakened her so they could tell about their upcoming plans.

"Kids," Bob started. "We have been talking to your grandparents about a big move. I want our family to move back here to Hamilton."

"Yahoo!" shrieked John as he ran over and gave his Dad a big hug. "That's great Dad!"

Looking over at Jenny, Bob and Barbara held their breath waiting for her response. Jenny's mouth dropped open. She could not believe what she was hearing. She had lost good sleep last night worrying about how to break the same news to them!

"You're serious," she said, half questioning.

"Yes, we are Jen," Bob replied. "How do you feel about that?"

"I think it is great, Dad. I was trying to think of a way to ask you to let me stay here for school next fall. Thanks, Dad, Mom, Grammy, Poppy" Jenny said with a true sincerity and choking back tears of happiness. She couldn't wait to tell Todd the good news.

Bob went on to explain to the children that he would be going back to Chicago to try and sell the house and get everything organized for the big move. As soon as the house was sold, they would start looking for a new house in town.

"Why can't we live here?" John asked looking from one adult to another.

"This is Grammy and Poppy's house, son," Bob explained. "They have already raised a family and want to relax without rug rats like you running around." John poked his father in the arm and they all started laughing.

That afternoon while Bob was putting his clothes into a suitcase, John walked into the bedroom. He sat down on the edge of the bed and stared at his father.

"What's up?" Bob asked the boy.

"Dad, I have a list of things for you to remember to bring back with you next time. It's not too much, but I sure could use them." John handed the list to his Dad. Bob read them off silently; my bike, baseball glove, bat and ball, basketball, roller blades, plus a few more necessities for John.

"I will try to get most of these things in the car when I come back the next time," Bob promised. "But, I am sure your mother and sister will also have a list for me. I'll see what I can do."

"Thanks, Dad," John said. As he headed for the door, John continued, "I have to get back to the barn. Poppy is waiting for me. I'll see you before you leave."

"OK," Bob responded, smiling at how mature his son seemed at that moment.

After bringing down his suitcase to the kitchen, Bob sat down and had a cup of coffee with his wife. Barbara had a small piece of paper in her hand. "A list, no doubt," Bob said.

As she handed the paper to Bob, she said "Can you try and bring back these things when you return? I definitely need my hot rollers here or else I am going to have to wear a hat all of the time."

"You look fine, honey," Bob said as he reached over and kissed Barbara.

"Dad," Jenny called from the stairway. "Dad, are you down there?"

"In the kitchen, Jen," he responded as she walked around the corner.

"Dad, could you bring a few things back for me when you come back?" Jenny asked.

"Sure Jenny," he said with a smile. "Just write down what you want and I'll see what I can do."

Jenny bounced down the stairs and handed him a rather long list of her necessities. Bob promised he would try to bring back what he could for her. She thanked him with a hug and went back upstairs.

"I'll need a U-Haul truck for all this stuff," Bob said. "And that would be just for Jenny's stuff."

The adults started snickering as Bob read off a few of the things from Jenny's list. At the top of her list was her CD player followed by her CDs. Bob wondered if she wanted all 200 of them. The list included her stuffed dog, her Cody Linley poster, the cordless telephone, not to mention a couple of her Teen Magazines.

"I just know she's having trouble sleeping without Cody watching over her," Bob said with a valley girl accent. Then women both giggled at that comment.

Bob would definitely try to bring back most of the requested items for all of the family. After all, he wanted them to be comfortable during this transition period. It was not going to be easy on any of them.

When Poppy and John came up to the house for supper, they noticed that Bob's car was still in the yard. John was glad that he had not missed saying goodbye to his father. When they walked into the kitchen, Bob had told them that he changed his mind and planned on leaving early on Tuesday morning. He figured the traffic would not be quite as heavy then.

That evening after supper, the family was sitting out in the yard. John was chasing after fireflies and Jenny was daydreaming in the old tire swing that hung from the biggest oak tree in the yard. Grammy was talking about the day's events and Poppy was dozing off occasionally, and then waking up with a snort. Barbara was still amazed at the clear sky and millions of stars twinkling above. The city lights never allowed for star gazing in Chicago. Bob pointed up towards the northern sky.

"Make a wish, honey," he told Barbara as they watched a falling star.

"I wish for a safe and easy move for all of us," she said smiling at Bob.

They all turned toward the lane when they saw headlights turn in.

"I wonder who that could be at this hour," Grammy said.

When the truck came around the curve, they all recognized it as the Kramer's truck. George and Todd got out of the pickup and walked into the yard. Todd went over to talk to Jenny as George sat in the empty chair near Poppy.

"Going to start cutting wheat in the morning," George started. "You want to start in your back field or down at Martin's place?"

Grammy popped up immediately, "Have you checked the fields, Hank? Are they ready to combine?"

"Either way," Poppy mumbled.

"OK Hank," George said. "I'll check with Sam in the morning and we can start wherever he wants to." George paused and looked over at the kids. Then he said to Bob, "I could have just called, but Todd wanted to come see the girl. This is all right with you, ain't it?"

"We'll just keep an eye on them," Bob said, and Barbara nodded in agreement.

The adults watched while Todd was pointing toward the stars. Apparently he was giving Jenny an astronomy lesson in which she showed a deep interest. Occasionally they heard Jenny giggle, probably at one of Todd's jokes about the stars.

After George and Todd left, Bob stood up and angled his watch to see the time. It was close to 10:00.

"I'd better turn in folks," he said. "I want to get an early start in the morning."

"Yes," Grammy agreed. "I want to make you a nice breakfast before you leave and pack you a couple sandwiches for your trip back. I'll put a couple of sodas on ice for you, too."

"Thanks, Mom," Bob said. "That will make the trip seem shorter and I won't have to stop to eat. Well, goodnight everyone."

As Bob turned to go into the house, he heard everyone say goodnight to him. Barbara stood and announced that she was going to go on up to bed, too. John was starting to doze off and Grammy said that it was time for him to hit the sack, too. John got up and whistled for Duke to follow him into the house. The dog perked up his ears and quickly pranced behind him. Jenny and Poppy also decided it was time to head inside.

Up in her room, Jenny was changing for bed, thinking about Todd, going to school in Hamilton and how wonderful her life would be now. She couldn't wait for her Dad to get back, although he had not even left yet. Climbing into bed, Jenny was asleep almost before her head hit the pillow. She pulled the sheet up over her shoulders as the breeze coming in through the windows had cooled off.

In the morning Grammy was shuffling around in the kitchen when Bob walked over to pour himself a cup of coffee. He informed her that everyone was still sleeping and he wanted to get started early.

"I don't want to wait too long to get started, Mom. If they come down, fine, but I am not going to wake them up to say goodbye."

At that moment, Poppy and John rounded the corner into the kitchen. John was still rubbing the sleep from his eyes as he poured a glass of milk for himself and got the box of Corn Flakes out of the pantry. Bob had to smile at him. He knew how hard it was to get him up for school back in Chicago, and to see him volunteer to get up at dawn seemed so unlike John. Bob had just finished his coffee when Barbara walked into the kitchen. She walked Bob out to the car to say goodbye to him. Jenny had just woke up and walked out onto the balcony and yelled at her father to get his attention. She waved to him and blew him a kiss goodbye. Bob kissed Barbara and then climbed into the car to head back to Chicago.

Chapter Five

Bob drove around the Quad Cities about noon and stopped just long enough to get gas and use the restroom. He pulled the car into his garage just a little before supper time. The sandwiches that Grammy had sent along with him filled him up at noon time, but now he was pretty hungry. He hoped that there was something good to pop into the microwave.

As Bob opened the door, Marble, the kid's calico cat greeted him. She scolded him for leaving her alone for so long as he walked across the kitchen into the bedroom. After putting his suitcase on the bed, Bob sat down and picked up Marble. She continued to scold him.

"Sorry, gal," he said to the cat. "Are you hungry?"

As if she understood, Marble jumped down off his lap and ran into the kitchen. There were still a few pieces of cat food in the bottom of her bowl and her water dish was not empty either. Bob filled both bowls and walked over to check the freezer for himself. He found a pizza and decided that would hold him over for tonight. After Bob put the pizza in the oven he looked down and Marble was rubbing against his legs continuing her cries. Bob recognized that cry. He walked into the utility room and cleaned her litter box. Now she was happy.

While the pizza was baking, Bob took a quick shower. After he ate his supper he decided to call the family to let them know that he had arrived safely. Before the call, Bob checked the mail. There were a couple of things for Barbara, a magazine for Jenny and, of course, a few bills that needed to be paid. Bob sat on the side of his bed with Marble curled up next to him. He picked up the phone to call Barbara when he noticed the answering machine flashing announcing new messages. He listened to Kelly asking Barbara to call her back. There was a message from Ted for John. Several of Jenny's friends had called. None of the messages were for Bob. Barbara's Aunt Milly had called and left the message that she just disapproved of what they were planning to do.

"How can he take you and the children away from your family?" the voice said. "You are just breaking your mother's heart."

Bob fast-forwarded through the rest of the message. Aunt Milly would find fault with anything that he planned for the family. Nothing he did met with her approval. He remembered when he and Barbara bought the house in Chicago. Aunt Milly had a fit that he moved her so far away. Actually they were less than a half an hour away from Barbara's family.

"Hello?" Grammy said answering the phone.

"Hi, Mom", Bob replied.

"How was your trip, Bob? Did you eat your sandwiches? How was the traffic?" Grammy was firing questions so fast. Poor Bob didn't have a chance to answer.

"Everything went fine, Mom. Can I talk to Barbara?" Grammy handed the phone to Barbara. She listened as Bob relayed the phone messages and told her about the mail. He informed her that Marble was fine and the house was still standing. Barbara, in turn, told Bob that everything was going well on the farm. She told him not to worry about Aunt Milly. Both of the kids wanted to say hello to their father and remind him about the things on their lists. After John said goodbye to his father, Barbara took the phone from him to tell him that they were going into town to just look around for available houses. They wanted to be moved in before school started in late August. Bob reminded her to *just look* because they had to sell the house in Chicago first. Bob said he would call again in a few days to keep the family posted on the house selling progress. Barbara said she would let him know of any fantastic bargains she comes across, too. They said their good-byes with "I love yous" before hanging up the phone. John just thought that was so mushy for old people to be doing that kind of stuff.

Grammy was reading the ads in the real estate section and commented there were several nice houses available in town.

"Are they in a good part of town?" Barbara asked Grammy after she mentioned some of the houses for sale.

"Barbara, there are no bad parts of town in Hamilton. Most of the people here still leave their doors unlocked. Neighbors know everyone on their block as well as everything that goes on."

"Do you recommend any particular realtor?"

"Not really," Grammy said. "We have never had dealings with any of them."

"Well, we will just have to choose one from the signs in front of the houses."

Grammy nodded as she put the paper down.

"Do you want to go with us tomorrow?" Barbara asked Grammy.

"No, I don't think so. The men will be cutting wheat in the backfield tomorrow. I'll have to make lunch for them. I had better stay home. Maybe another time," Grammy thanked Barbara and went up to bed.

Barbara felt that Grammy was disappointed that she would not be able to go with them. She would try to make it up to her somehow.

Grammy was bustling about the kitchen when Barbara came down in the morning. Poppy and John had already eaten and left to meet the other men in the wheat field. Jenny bounced down the steps and greeted her mother and grandmother as if she was singing the praises of the morning.

"What's got into her?" Grammy asked.

"Oh Grammy," Jenny sang as she gave her grandmother a hug around the waist. "It's just a beautiful day, the first of many days to come."

Barbara and Jenny planned to go into town right after breakfast and Grammy gave Barbara the keys to their car. It was an old, but reliable Buick and was much bigger than what Barbara was used to driving. But she just had to drive a little slower until she got the feel of it. By the time they reached the highway, Barbara was very comfortable driving the old car which really rode quite comfortably.

Barbara and Jenny wanted to find the school before looking for houses. It was located at the East end of town situated on a grassy knoll. The school looked relatively new compared to the old building Jenny had been going to. As they drove into the driveway of the school, they could see the football field behind the building. At the North end of the school was a shed which housed ten yellow school buses. Beyond the bus barn was a soccer field and tennis courts.

"It looks nice," Jenny remarked. "There are no fences, no bars on the windows or graffiti on the walls. I think I'll like it here."

Leaving the school, Barbara turned the car onto a shady street. They were looking for "For Sale" signs in front of houses. After driving down the street for six blocks, Barbara turned the car onto the next street. There was a ranch-style home for sale in the middle of the block. She stopped the car across the street and she and Jenny looked at the house from the car. It looked nice. There was a big yard and a two-car garage. Jenny had brought a notebook and jotted down the address and everything they liked about the house as well as any flaws they noticed. She also wrote down the name of the real estate company listing the house.

They continued down to the end of the street and turned the corner. There were stately old homes on this block. Barbara and Jenny both gasped in awe at some of them. On the corner of the third block there was a sign in the yard from Stone Mansion Realty Company. Barbara pulled the car over to the curb and they just stared at this home. It was a three and a half story brick house with a porch wrapping around three sides. On the West side of the house was a large, oval, stained-glass window. They could see that the front door had an etching in the glass window. Barbara pulled the car down the block to check out the back of the home. They couldn't see much of the back because of a privacy fence from the house to a large garage.

Jenny and Barbara both loved the old home. It was close to the school and the street was shady and beautiful. All the lawns were well kept with sculpted shrubs and flowers. Jenny wrote down the phone number on the sign because she just knew that her mother would be calling this realtor.

Barbara then drove to the downtown area of town. They planned to eat lunch in town and Grammy had recommended the Cardinal Inn Cafe. As Barbara pulled the car into a parking spot, Jenny noticed that the Stone Mansion Realty Company was just two doors down the block from the restaurant. Jenny and Barbara looked at each other, knowing exactly what the other was thinking. They got out of the car and headed straight for the realtor's office.

The office was sparsely decorated with plastic hanging plants and smelled of stale cigars. The front desk was empty although it appeared as if someone used it daily. The other two desks on either side of the office behind the front desk were also empty but one of the computers was turned on flashing its screen saver.

"Hello?" Barbara called from the front desk.

"I'll be with you in a moment," came a man's voice from the room behind the office. In a matter of seconds, a burly man dressed in a rust-colored leisure suit stepped out of the 1980's into the office. His hair was unkempt and a half chewed cigar dangled from his mouth.

"What can I do for you ladies?" he asked as he walked toward the front of the office. "The name is Brown; Jack Brown."

"We are interested in one of the houses you have listed for sale," Barbara said. "I'm Mrs. Barbara Madison and this is my daughter Jenny."

"Well ladies, have a seat," Mr. Brown said as he pulled a second chair closer to his desk. "You have definitely got my undivided attention."

Jenny told Mr. Brown the address of the house. He punched up the information regarding the house by pounding on the keyboard of his computer with his thick stained fingers. He put on a pair of glasses to read the screen, and then turned toward Barbara.

"Ahh yes. This is the Mayfield mansion," he said. "A very stately estate, I must say. Let's see, there are nine bedrooms, five baths, a formal living room, dining room, family room, and a parlor. The kitchen is quite large, too. Now for you, young miss, there is an in ground pool in the backyard."

Jenny was happy to hear that. She and John loved to swim; and what a place it would be to entertain her new friends.

"At the present time, there is no one living in the carriage house. The Mayfields rented the apartment upstairs until they decided to sell the place."

"There is an apartment above the garage?" Jenny asked.

"Young one that is not a garage. It is a Victorian carriage house. Upstairs is a quaint one bedroom apartment. It would be ideal for a single person or a couple with no children. It makes for a nice extra little income for the owners."

Mr. Brown continued to detail all of the amenities of the home such as two central air units, gas heat, stainless appliances in the kitchen, new roof just two years ago to name a few. Barbara and Jenny were both quite impressed. He printed a copy of the listing and handed it to Barbara. When she looked at the asking price of the home, she asked Mr. Brown if that price was firm and he informed her that anything is negotiable. Before Jenny and Barbara left the office, they made an appointment to inspect the house later that afternoon. Mr. Brown assured them that he would meet them at the house.

"Mom, do you think Dad will like that house?" Jenny asked.

"I am sure he would like anything we picked out – especially at this price. Jen, we paid almost twice as much for our home in Chicago as they are asking for this house. I just hope there is not a lot of work to do inside."

The girls went to the Cardinal Inn and ordered lunch. They chatted endlessly about the things they could do with that house. Jenny dreamed of parties she would have around the pool; while Barbara imagined large dinner parties in the formal dining room. After they finished eating, they had about an hour to wait before their appointment. They walked through a few of the shops downtown, taking in the country charm of the area.

Mr. Brown was waiting for them on the front porch of the house when Barbara pulled the car up in front. Once they reached the porch, Barbara and Jenny noticed that a huge "M" was etched in the heavy glass on the door. Perhaps this was a good omen for them. When he unlocked the door, a grand foyer welcomed them into the house. An open staircase curved up to the second floor passing under the stained-glass window that they had seen from the outside. It was directly in front of them now. The oak banister was polished and the hardwood floors gleamed as the sunlight shone in. To the left of the staircase were large pocket doors open to reveal a sitting room which Mr. Brown called the parlor. There was a large fireplace opposite the doors and floor-to-ceiling bay windows facing the street. The room was quite large; however, there was a warm cozy feeling to it.

Walking through a small doorway to the right, they entered a grand dining room. There were plate racks along one wall and a bay window looking out on to the lawn. Behind the dining room was a small room that Mr. Brown referred to as the butler's pantry. Next to this was the first floor powder room. There were built-in cabinets along the wall adjacent to the dining room. A door led them into a huge kitchen. The stove and sink were situated on an island in the middle of the room. Cabinets filled two of the walls while a confectioner's oven and double door refrigerator was on the other wall. A large area draped by windows on three sides was at the far end of the kitchen with a door leading to a small laundry room and then to the outside.

Barbara was so impressed with what she had seen thus far. She just had to convince Bob that this was the house. Jenny could not wait to go upstairs and see the bedrooms. But, before heading back to the foyer, Mr. Brown showed them a back stairway and the formal living room, which was also garnished with a marble fireplace and bay windows.

Once they had reached the second floor of the house, Mr. Brown showed them the first bathroom. It was quite large with an old claw-foot bathtub, a pedestal sink and toilet. On the short wall of the bathroom were built-in cabinets above cedar-lined drawers. Everything in the house was done with the magnificent taste of the builder.

Jenny and Barbara both gasped when they entered the master bedroom. It was actually a suite of rooms consisting of sleeping quarters, a dressing room with cedar-lined closets and a private bathroom and sitting room. Next to the master suite was a smaller bedroom that Mr. Brown said had been used for a nursery and a library at different times. Barbara thought this would make a perfect office for Bob. There were also two other bedrooms on the second floor across from the master suite which would be perfect for John and Jenny. Another smaller open staircase led to the third floor of the house. There were two bathrooms on this floor and both had been modernized with a shower, tub and double-sink vanity. There were five bedrooms on this floor. Mr. Brown informed them that this floor had been used for the servants of the house. Two of the rooms were large for the butler and nanny; and the other three were smaller but still good size for the other help. Jenny thought the smaller rooms were even bigger than her room in Chicago. A door in the middle of the hall opened to a small stairway leading to the attic which was just an open area that would be good for storage.

The group came back to the main floor by way of the back stairway and Mr. Brown took them down to the lower level to show Barbara the heating system and other mechanics of the home. There was a very large family room finished in a modern design next to the furnace room of the house. Jenny thought that their entire house in Chicago would fit into this one room. She loved this old house.

Barbara seemed so cool as she thanked Mr. Brown and said that she would discuss it with her husband and also explained that they would have to sell their existing house first. He handed her one of his business cards and told her he would wait to hear from her. Barbara thanked him again as she started the car to head back to the farm. Once they rounded the corner and were out of sight of Mr. Brown, Barbara let out a little scream.

"Oh, Jenny, I love that house," she said. "I was thinking about what it would look like with our things in it and with us living in it."

"Me, too, Mom," Jenny exclaimed. "I hope Dad likes it."

"Oh, he'll like it," Barbara said giggling. "He'll love it."

Once they were back at the farm house, Jenny jabbered continuously about the house. Grammy listened with an intent interest but dreaded the day when they would move into town. That evening Barbara called Bob and told him all about the place. He reminded her that they still had to sell their house. When Barbara told him the price of the mansion and that the house was in move in condition, Bob told her to make an offer on the house contingent to them selling their present home first. Barbara could not wait to tell Jenny that Bob had given his approval to move forward.

After Jenny told John all about the house, he asked his mom if he could stay with Poppy and Grammy instead of moving into town with the family. Barbara assured him that he would be able to come out to the farm on weekends and on days when there was no school. John seemed disappointed but satisfied with the arrangement.

Barbara's call to Mr. Brown went off without a hitch and she made the offer that she and Bob had agreed upon the night before. Mr. Brown said that he would present the offer to the owners and get back to them within the next few days. Barbara thanked him and reminded him that they had to sell their house in Chicago first. He said that he would pass that information on and told her good-bye.

Chapter Six

Barbara walked into the kitchen as Grammy had just walked into the house with a basket full of clean laundry.

"Let me help you with that, Ruth," she said.

"Oh there's another empty basket on the porch and you can get the rest off the line if you are looking for something to do," Grammy responded as the small woman continued to carry her load to the table. Then, yelling quite loudly, "Jenny!!! Come downstairs, girl! We need your help!"

Jenny came bounding down the stairs in a flash.

"What's wrong?" she said breathlessly.

"Nothing is wrong. Here, you can fold these clothes and carry them upstairs."

"Good grief, Grammy, the way you yelled I thought somebody was hurt." Jenny said, her heart still pounding. "You scared me!"

"I'm sorry. I didn't mean to scare you, honey. I just wanted to get your attention." Grammy said chuckling heading for the back door to retrieve another load of laundry.

"Well, you did do that," Jenny snipped back at her.

While Jenny was putting her clothes away up in her room she was playing with the radio dial. She was so upset that there were not many good stations in this area to choose from other than country and ancient rock & roll. She had already been to the top of the dial and was just about to give up when she hit 88.5 and a signal came in with some pretty good music. She sat back and listened for a while.

"What station is this?" She said aloud with a wrinkled forehead.

The music was kind of a rock station but the songs were about Jesus and God and doing the right thing. This was really a change for this big city girl.

"I guess it is better than the hillbilly stuff on most of the other stations," Jenny said with a heavy twang mocking the accent.

Jenny went about putting her clothes in the closet and drawers and listening to the radio. But she soon got into the music big time. It didn't take long before she caught herself tapping her toe and trying to sing along even though she didn't know the words. She'd pick up a shirt, flip out the wrinkles, spin around in a little dance and hang it up in between lyrics. She'd hum along and sing the words she kind of remembered and really blast the parts she really knew.

"I think …hmmm …… Beale Street ……. hmmm ……. He can hear …… hmmm …… cry out loud" And then at the top of her lungs, "I want to be like my Jesus ..…. hmmm ……. I want to be like my Jesus ….."

Jenny would learn parts of the songs and sing along until she became hoarse. She decided that this Jesus guy they were singing about was someone important to think about. The songs she listened to about this Jesus were so different than the Jesus who she heard about in church on Sunday. She liked this music "religion". But she sure didn't like going to church and she knew Poppy and Grammy would have a fit if she ever tried to get out of going with them. But the music felt so much better….so much happier. It brought Jesus so much closer to her.

Jenny needed to share her new feelings with someone. She knew that Grammy and Poppy wouldn't understand since they were the old time religion sort of Christians. And Mom, well, since they never were real regular church goers back home Jenny wasn't sure if her mother would even know that much about Jesus and God herself to understand how she felt. Todd, she would call Todd. He seems pretty cool and he goes to church all the time ~ and he is cute, too.

"Hello Todd?" Jenny called Todd on the phone to talk about her feelings about the music she had found. "Can I talk to you about something kind of personal and heavy? Can you come over?"

"What's up?" Todd asked.

"I'll tell you when you get here. Can you bring your personal stereo?"

"Sure, I'll be over in a little while. I have a few things to finish up here for Dad first."

"That's fine," Jenny replied. "So, I'll see you in about an hour or so?"

"No, it'll be less than that," Todd answered. "It's not much. See you in about 45 minutes."

"That's great," Jenny exclaimed as she said her good-bye.

Jenny grabbed a small cooler, a blanket, a couple of drinks and some snacks out of the kitchen pantry and met Todd when he was getting out of the truck when he pulled in almost forty-five minutes exactly after they ended their phone call. She suggested they go on a picnic so they could talk. On the way down to the creek by the spring Jenny was pretty quiet. She felt kind of stupid because she didn't know quite how to bring up the subject of the Christian music.

"What's the matter, Jenny? What's bothering you?" Todd asked. So many ideas were going through his mind.

Jenny was quiet until they reached the spring and then she put down the blanket and picnic basket. Todd set down the stereo and pressed the button to play the CD that was in it.

"Todd, put on the radio," Jenny requested.

"Oh, I doubt you would like my station," he said. But he turned on the radio and immediately went to change station.

"Wait, let me choose stations, please," Jenny said.

When she reached to change the station she noticed that Todd had the radio tuned to 88.5, the same station that she found the other night. She left the dial alone and looked at Todd. His face blushed a bit and Jenny's blushed a little then, too. Jenny reached over and gave Todd a quick hug.

"Oh Todd you made this so much easier for me." She squealed with delight.

"Huh?" Todd said in total confusion.

Jenny reached down to the radio and turned the volume up almost full blast. She stood up and twirled with the music and singing with the song.

"Oh no, You never let go
Through the calm and through the storm"

Then she pulled Todd up and spun him around.
"Oh no, You never let go
In every high and every low
Oh no, You never let go
Lord, You never let go of me"

They continued to dance and sing until the song was finished and fell onto the blanket and Jenny was laughing as though she were drunk.

"What are you on, girl?" Todd said breathlessly and totally confused.

"I'm on Jesus! Todd I was so scared to even talk to you about this. I was so bored the other night and found this radio station and started listening to it. At first I was kind of ~ *HUH?* ~ but the more I listened to it the more I realized what it was about. These songs are so great! They have a story to tell and the music is so," she paused catching her breath, "so, I don't know, they are just so *right!*" Jenny sat back on her haunches and just beamed. "Todd I was so afraid you would think I was a freak when I wanted to bring up Christian music and Jesus."

"That's so funny, Jen, because I wanted to change the station on the radio so you wouldn't think I was weird listening to Christian music," Todd told her. "I have been listening to 88.5 *The Mix* for a couple years now. I don't listen to anything else."

Jenny sat back and asked Todd, "Do your friends listen to it, too?"

"Some of them do. Some of them still listen to the country station."

"Do any of the other kids make fun of you for listening to it?"

"A few of them used to, but since SHOUTfest was here last year, most of them have changed their minds and are listening to it now, too. We're all 'Mixites' now," Todd said with a little chuckle.

"What's SHOUTfest?" Jenny asked as she sprawled out on the blanket and leaned on one elbow looking up at Todd.

"Have you ever gone to a concert in Chicago?" he asked. When Jenny nodded, Todd continued by asking her which group.

"A friend of mine got tickets to see the Beyonce in Chicago and some of us went. It was pretty cool," Jenny said.

"I imagine there was a lead band and the whole concert was a couple of hours, right?" Todd said. Jenny nodded. Todd stood up and stretched his arms out and continued to passionately describe the concert.

"Close your eyes Jen. Imagine you are along the river front. There are thousands of people dancing and singing to 12 bands playing this kind of music." Todd swept his arms through the air and pointed to the radio. "The Message is being sent! God is right here next to all of us! There are kids of all ages! There are city kids, country kids, junior high kids, and college kids. There are farm kids, rich kids, kids from St. Louis, black kids, white kids, Hispanic kids, Catholic kids, and Mormon kids. And I even saw some Menonite kids. There are grandmas and grandpas with their little preschool kids and just older couples. It didn't matter. Everyone is there. And everyone is getting along and there is no trouble. Oh Jen the electricity is right there and everyone is hugging everyone." Tears are falling down Todd's cheeks now as he pulls Jenny up to him. "You will never know how much God is among us every day until you feel him in the music and with the people there at the river with the music and the stories." Todd's voice became very quiet. "When Joseph Rojas spoke every single person was quiet. He didn't even need a mic. I dream for the day when Jesus touches me like He did Joseph."

"Who is Joseph Rogus? Or whatever his name is?" Jenny asked.

"Joseph Rojas," Todd corrected her.

Todd and Jenny sat back down on the blanket before Todd told the story of the lead singer of the band <u>Seventh Day Slumber</u>. "Oh my goodness, Jenny, his story will break your heart."

"His dad left when he was 3 years old. He was overweight, and other kids picked on him all the time making him feel worthless ~ a nothing. When he was 14 he tried cocaine and it helped him forget about those that teased him and he started to hang out with pot heads and coke addicts ~ guys just like him who were hurting like him. He turned to a $400-a-day cocaine habit and was in and out of jail. He said that he hated himself and continued the coke to forget. He said that he did not know God and was an atheist. He finally decided to end it all on a cocaine overdose. His mother walked in and she screamed out to God to save his life. He said his mother is an amazing woman ~ a Christian woman who prayed everyday for him. But in the ambulance on the way to the hospital he said that he was going in and out of consciousness. He said he felt this overwhelming power. He knew in a split second that Jesus Christ was real and alive. He said, 'Jesus would you save me?' That was the first time He felt the love of a father. He said it was a long hard road to kick the cocaine habit and he fell several times but with the love of his mother and God he did it. He says he is still the overweight Mexican who is called rude names but he says God loves him and has provided for him and has given him an amazing wife, son and career. He told us that he still cannot believe that God gave him, a plain looking Mexican, the most beautiful woman in the world. He said that she could have been a beauty queen but instead, she chose him and it amazes him everyday and he thanks God everyday for her. He also thanks God that he has the type of career that he has where he can tell his story to let others perhaps change their lives by letting them know that God loves them, too. He said that God is real but sometimes we have to wait for Him and trust Him."

With tears in her own eyes Jenny reached up and wiped a tear from Todd's cheek. "I am sorry I missed that. He really touched you. I wish I could have been there to hear him."

"But Jen," Todd yelled, as he jumped up, picked her up and spun her around. "You don't have to miss it. There is another SHOUTfest coming up very soon! We can go together. I can't wait to go again. Actually it is just a week from this coming Sunday. Last year we went with a church group but they left so late that we missed a couple of bands. Dad said that we can drive down ourselves."

"What time does it start?" Jenny asked.

"Well, the gates open at 12:00 but I am going to go early to help set up so I get a free ticket. I was planning to leave around 6:00. You and Tam could hang out and maybe help out, too. Tam said she wants to go and sleep until the gates open, but I bet she'll change her mind if you go."

Jenny's expression suddenly went from excitement to disappointment. "I bet I won't be able to go if it is on a Sunday morning. I can't miss church."

"But Jen this is better than going to church. Talk to your mom about it. I am sure she will let you go."

"It's not mom, or even dad for that matter that I'm worried about," Jenny said. "We have been going to church with Poppy and Grammy since we've been here and Poppy is so strict…Grammy, too. I just know they will have a fit about me missing church."

"You better start talking to your mom and dad about it now and try to figure out something early," Todd said. "Maybe you can come up with a plan about being away for the weekend."

"I sure hope so. I'd like to go. From what you said about last year it sounds like it is so cool. Do you know who is coming this year?" Jenny asked.

"There's a list at the WGCA.org web page. It doesn't matter who is coming, they are all great because they are sending the same message. I just wish you could have heard Joseph Rojas last year. Girl, I never cried so much and didn't care who saw me." Todd was so sincere as tears swelled in his eyes again. "I'll show you his story on the net."

"I'd like to read it," Jenny said with sincerity. "But first let's think of a plan to get me to this concert."

After Todd went home Jenny thought about different scenarios to put before the "Court of Poppy" this afternoon. Then she decided she would just bring it up at supper and talk about the music and perhaps the concert. No, that would be too bold. She decided she would just sing around the house and maybe that would win him over. Yeah, that'll do it.

Jenny was singing a <u>Third Day</u> song, *Cry Out To Jesus* while she was helping Grammy. She loved this song and thought that maybe it would be a good one that would help get her on the good side of her grandparents.

"There is hope for the helpless
Rest for the weary
Love for the broken heart
There is grace and forgiveness
Mercy and healing
He'll meet you wherever you are
Cry out to Jesus, Cry out to Jesus"

"What are you singing, child," Grammy asked.

"Oh, it's a song I heard on the radio," Jenny replied as she continued humming.

"I didn't realize they play songs like that on the radio. What station do you listen to?" Grammy asked with sincerely interest.

"It's a station in Quincy called WGCA. They play Christian music all the time. It is a Christian rock station," Jenny explained.

"I'd like to listen to it sometime with you," Grammy said.

"Grammy, it is really good music. So much better than the country music about drinking, divorcing and running off with the next door neighbor's wife. This is about Jesus and loving each other and hope." Jenny was so passionate about the music. She took Grammy's hands and continued. "Each song is like a prayer. It's like you are praying all the time."

Grammy pulled her hands away, "I'll listen with you sometime."

"What's wrong with now?" Jenny reached up to the old radio on top of the refrigerator and tuned it in to 88.5. The first song they heard was "You are loved" by Rebecca St. James. "See Grammy, isn't that a great song?

"That is nice," Grammy agreed as she continued her work.

The two of them continued to get supper ready while the music played and Grammy agreed she liked most of the songs. Some were a little too upbeat for her and some a little *hard rock* she called them.

But for the most part, she did enjoy this Christian music more than the country lyrics.

"That music is the devil's work," Poppy barked as he reached up and turned off the radio. "You can't understand half the words and the rest are blasphemous. I won't have it in my house"

"Hank!" Grammy exclaimed.

"I won't have it," Poppy yelled as he walked through the kitchen towards the bathroom.

Jenny knew she had her work cut out for her now and the concert looked almost impossible. When she looked back at Grammy, she had turned back to her work at the stove as if nothing had happened. Jenny felt so let down that Grammy would not even stick up for her and the music. It is good music! It is the message of Jesus!

Nothing more was brought up about the concert or the music during supper. But afterwards Jenny went to talk to her mom in her parents' bedroom. Barbara was reading a book and Jenny sprawled out across the bed and laid her head on her mom's lap.

"Mommy I have a problem," Jenny started.

Barbara put her book down and pushed the bangs off Jenny's forehead.

"You know the music I have been listening to lately?" Jenny said and Barbara nodded. "There is going to be a huge concert in a week and a half and Todd and Tam are going to it. I really want to go with them"

"That sounds great!" Barbara jumped in. "I sure don't see a problem there."

Jenny sat up and looked at her mom with moist eyes. "Poppy hates that music. He came in tonight and turned the radio off and yelled at Grammy and me for playing blasphemous music in his house. And the concert is on a Sunday. He'll never let me skip church to go."

"Where is this concert and what time of the day is it?" Barbara asked.

"Well, it is just less than an hour away in Quincy, but the concert starts at 2 and lasts until almost 10:00 at night. It is a *huge* event. I can show you stuff about last year's concert on the net. Todd can tell you about it. It is like a revival. Oh mom, please, please let me go." Jenny took her mom's hands and held them to her chest and begged with all her might. "I will do anything you want for a year if you let me go to this concert."

"It sounds OK to me." Barbara said. At that point Jenny tackled her mother and with hugs and kisses and squeals of thanks. "Wait! Wait! Stop! I still have to talk to your father and I do want to talk to Todd about last year's concert. But I think we can let you go. As far as missing church for a revival of sorts, I think we can allow that, too.

Jenny called Todd and asked him to come over to talk to her mom about SHOUTFest from last year. He was so glad that they were considering the idea of letting her go to the concert that he grabbed Tamara and came over right away. He knew that Poppy was going to be a hard sell so he even asked his dad to come along for back up. When they walked in Poppy was sitting at the dining room table sipping on a cup of coffee. Although Todd grew up next to Poppy and worked by his side, tonight Todd felt very intimidated by the old man.

George walked over and helped himself to a cup of coffee and sat down next to Poppy and started talking to him about the county fair coming up next week. Todd thought that he could talk to Barbara first while his dad kept Poppy busy. Jenny, Tamara, and Todd talked it over quickly and ushered Barbara out to the side yard where they could talk without the grandparents.

"So tell me about this concert," Barbara said as she got comfortable in one of the Adirondack chairs.

"It is so hard to put into words, Mrs. Madison. You really had to have been there," Todd started. Again he stood up and using his arms and entire body tried to tell Barbara how he felt about last year's event. He turned on the radio while he talked.

"You've been to the riverfront in Quincy. Imagine 7,000 people of all ages, all colors, and all ethnic groups standing together enjoying this kind of music." He pointed to the radio. "The sea of people was swaying back and forth, everybody was singing. We were all singing for Jesus." Very passionately Todd continued. "There were 7,000 people there with NO drugs, NO alcohol and NO fighting and no body got arrested. Can you believe that?" Todd threw his arms in the air and said, "Teenagers are good; and people can be good when they come together for Christ. We don't need dope or booze." He got very close to Barbara and took her hands in both of his and very quietly said, "7,000 people and no one was hurt or arrested....all in the name of Jesus."

Todd stood up then and tears filled his eyes as he told about Joseph Rojas telling of his cocaine addiction and how he witnessed to the 7,000 people there.

"While Joseph talked the entire riverfront was quiet. We could hear the water lapping against the sea wall and his voice. When he was finished he asked those who wanted to give themselves to Jesus to go to the counselors' tent. There were several who gave their lives to Jesus that night. I don't know how many, but I know there were a lot who went over to that tent because I was one of them. Last year, SHOUTfest saved a lot of kids and this year more will be saved….and next year," Todd shouted. "AND THE YEAR AFTER THAT!" he shouted louder.

"If you aren't sure you want Jenny to go with me and Tam, come and go with her. Maybe I can't explain it right, but you have to experience it to really understand how great it really is." Todd dropped his arms to his side. "You just have to experience it."

Barbara looked at Jenny and said, "If it is that great, maybe we should all go."

Jenny jumped up and hugged her mom. "Oh thank you, mommy."

When they went inside to tell Grammy, Poppy and John, the mood definitely changed.

"I saw how it was on the news last year at that thing. Those people hugging and jumping. It's a cult. Not right, just not right," Poppy said as he took a sip of coffee. "It's the devil's work."

Jenny looked at her mom with pleading eyes. No one dared argue with Poppy, especially at his table. Barbara looked back at Jenny as if to say they would talk about it later.

Later that evening Barbara was talking to Bob and told him about the concert. Bob suggested that she take John and Jenny to Quincy on Saturday and just spend the night there…sort of a mini vacation. After all, they had been doing an awfully lot of work on the farm and needed a break. That way they could go to the concert with no problem from the older couple. When Jenny heard that idea she was excited, but John decided he wanted to stay home on the farm. So it was decided that Barbara and Jenny, along with Tamara, would have a girls' weekend. Jenny quickly called Todd and Tamara with the news. Jenny was so excited about the concert. She hoped that the time would go by fast. Next week was the county fair so that should help speed things along. She was so happy and excited she had a hard time falling to sleep.

Chapter Seven

When Barbara came down to the kitchen the next morning, she could smell the coffee and cinnamon rolls that Grammy had left. Barbara knew where Poppy and John were, but she had no idea what Grammy could be doing so early in the morning. She poured herself a cup of coffee and placed one of the rolls on a napkin. As she walked out into the morning sun, she saw Grammy bent over in the garden.

"What are you doing out here so early, Ruth?" Barbara asked as she walked toward the older woman.

"Got to get my work done before the heat of the day," Grammy said rising up for just a moment to answer Barbara. "I want to get these beans picked and canned before it gets too hot in the kitchen."

Barbara looked at the long straight rows in the garden. The green bean patch was five rows deep with each row stretching over 75 feet. She finished her roll and set her coffee cup on one of the fence posts. With a heavy sigh she picked up a bucket and started at the opposite end of the row where Grammy was working and began picking beans. Barbara wasn't used to bending over and her back began to ache within a few short minutes. When she looked over at Grammy, the old woman's hands were pulling beans off the vine faster than the eye could see. There were already two 5-gallon buckets full of green beans sitting at various points along the bean rows. This was going to be a big job and Barbara knew that she and Jenny were going to have to help with the canning.

When the beans were almost all picked and in buckets, John came into the garden pulling an old Radio Flyer wagon. He lifted three buckets into the wagon and pulled it over to the back door of the house.

He repeated this trip several times before all of the buckets were out of the garden. Grammy and Barbara carried the last two buckets as they came toward the house. John quietly turned the wagon around and headed back toward the barn.

"What in the world is this?" Jenny asked as she stepped out of the back door about 10:30 in the morning.

"Green beans, sleepy head," Grammy said as she walked through the door while Jenny held it open. "What do they look like to you?"

"A lot of work," Jenny mumbled under her breath.

Yesterday Poppy and John had retrieved baskets of canning jars from the basement of the old house. Grammy gave Jenny the option of cutting the beans or washing and sterilizing the jars. Jenny chose to sit outside and prepare the beans for canning. Grammy took the first bucket of beans and dumped them out on the old picnic table. She explained to Jenny that both ends of the beans had to have the tips cut off and then demonstrated how to cut the beans into bite sized pieces. Jenny figured she could handle this easy job.

After the second bucket of beans had been cut, Jenny's hands began to hurt. She wanted so bad to go into the house and watch television or just relax. But, she knew that her mother and grandmother needed her help with this chore. She stood up and stretched with her hands way over her head before picking up the next bucket. At least she was getting some sun on her arms and legs.

Once the beans were cut, Barbara took a bucket into the house. She poured the beans into a strainer in the kitchen sink and sprayed and washed the beans. Then Grammy took the clean beans and stuffed them into a quart canning jar. She had prepared a juice of hot water and canning salt and poured some over the beans in each jar. After placing a lid on a jar and screwing the ring down tight, Grammy placed ten jars at a time into a huge canning pot. She cooked the beans before taking them out of the canner and placing each jar on the kitchen table. Before long, they heard the popping of the lids signifying that the jars were now sealed and safe for storage.

Between batches of jars, Grammy put a huge pot of beans on the stove in an open kettle. Then she peeled and cut up potatoes, added onion and sliced up some ham to throw in with the beans. Before long, Jenny could smell the aroma of lunch floating out into the yard.

The women had finished sixty jars of beans before John and Poppy came up for lunch. Jenny didn't think that the concoction that Grammy prepared for them looked very inviting. But, after that first bite, she felt that she had gone to Heaven. This was great! John ate two big helpings and wiped his plate clean with a couple pieces of buttered bread. Grammy shooed the men out of the house as soon as they finished eating. Barbara and Jenny quickly cleaned off the table and did the dishes so they could get back to work.

By supper time, they had carried over 150 quarts and 80 pints of green beans down to the basement for storage. Grammy told them that she enjoyed opening a jar of home canned green beans in the dead of winter because it reminded her of the good ole' summer time. All three women were tired from a very long and hard day of canning. When Poppy and John came up to the house for supper, Grammy told them that they would have to find something to eat on their own.

"Poppy is going to take us to town for pizza," John said. "We talked about it after lunch and he figured you all deserve a break tonight."

What a wonderful idea it was! After everyone cleaned up and changed clothes, they piled into the old Buick. They went in to the only Pizza Hut in town and ordered two family-sized pizzas. Grammy really didn't like pizza all that much but she enjoyed getting out of the house and having a night free from cooking and cleaning up afterwards.

Grammy said that she was going to keep two of the nicer jars of green beans out to enter at the County Fair. Every year she entered canned goods, baked goods and a quilt. Well, this year, she had not finished the quilt, but she would enter the others. She asked Jenny if she would like to take part in the fair.

"What could I do?" Jenny asked as she picked a piece of ham off of her pizza and popped it into her mouth.

"Well, there are all sorts of categories available…gardening, canning, baking, sewing, drawing or painting, handicrafts, quilting….the list goes on and on," Grammy said. "Or you could take care of one of the animals and get it ready for the show."

"Poppy said I could take a lamb this year," John beamed. "I have to brush him everyday to keep his wool pretty and white. I have already got it trained to walk with a lead and Poppy has taught me how to walk and show the lamb's best traits to the judges. I can't wait for the fair."

Jenny thought about the fair quite a bit over the next couple of days. What could she do for it? She didn't know much about cooking or baking and she couldn't sew a stitch. Then, one evening Grammy got the bright idea that Jenny should enter flower arranging. At least every other day since she had been there, Jenny walked along the lane or down in the woods and picked wild flowers. She brought them home and arranged them in one of Grammy's old vases and graced the dining room table. Grammy thought that Jenny would have a good chance to win one of the prizes in that category. Jenny agreed that she would enter a wild flower arrangement in the fair.

Sunday evening Bob called to tell the family that they had received an offer on their house. Bob said that it was very close to their asking price and that he would accept it if Barbara agreed. Barbara remembered that their offer on the mansion had been accepted but could only be held for 30 days. She immediately told Bob to accept whatever the offer was, and as soon as it was settled she would call Mr. Brown.

When Barbara shared the news with Jenny and John, the kids were glad. Jenny was happy that they would probably be moved in before school started but John was happy just because his Dad would be coming back sooner than expected. Grammy knew the time was coming close to an end to be with the family, but she was happy for them, too.

By the following Tuesday, the papers for both houses had been signed and all of the paperwork would be done within 30 days. Bob knew he would have to secure a mover, get everything packed and ready to go. Barbara wanted to go back to Chicago to supervise the packing and moving, but Bob assured her that he could handle it himself. He then promised the kids that he would be home very soon.

Chapter Eight

That afternoon Todd came over to the farm to see Jenny. They had become good friends over the summer and Jenny still blushed when Todd paid extra attention to her in front of the family. Jenny poured two glasses of lemonade and they sat outside under the trees. Jenny rattled on and on about the new house. Todd was so happy that Jenny was going to school with him, but he said he would miss her being so close here on the farm.

Jenny told Todd that she was going to enter a flower arrangement in the County Fair so they decided to take a walk and pick some flowers so that she could practice. They started down the long lane, stopping occasionally to pick some Day Lilies. Along the edge of the woods were wild Cone Flowers and Black-eyed Susans. Todd helped Jenny over the fence and they began walking deeper into the woods. Jenny found some wild fern, Queen Anne's Lace and wild Larkspur. She had enough flowers now to make six centerpieces.

When they reached the spring under the big oak, Todd suggested that they sit and talk for a while. Jenny laid the flowers down on a flat rock near the spring. Todd walked over and reached under some overhanging tree roots and pulled out a small tin cup. He held the cup at the mouth of the spring and filled it with cool, clear water. He drank all that was in there and then refilled it, offering it to Jenny.

"How can you drink that dirty water?" Jenny asked him twisting her mouth into a funny scowl.

"What do you mean? This is the purest and cleanest water you will ever find." Todd explained how the water came from deep within the earth and was filtered by the rock of the earth's core. Accepting his explanations, Jenny took a sip of the water. It was good and it was so cold on this hot summer day. Todd put the cup back in the hidden spot until the next thirsty person came along.

"You want to go wading?" Todd asked Jenny.

After leaning down and feeling the water with her fingers, Jenny replied "No, it's too cold."

"Oh, come on you sissy," Todd teased her as he pulled off his shoes and socks and rolled up his pant legs. "It's great! It feels cool and refreshing. Besides you just said that you were hot."

Jenny didn't answer, but instead slipped off her shoes and stepped into the creek. It was cold at first, but then it felt so good against her feet. She was so glad that she had worn shorts today. Todd warned her to watch her step because some of the rocks were a little slick.

After walking down the creek a little way, Todd stepped up onto the bank. He grabbed Jenny's hand and helped her out of the water. Jenny thought she heard rushing water. But, the creek looked so calm here.

"Shhh," Todd said. "Hear that? That is the waterfall right around the bend. You want to see it?"

"Yeah," Jenny responded with much enthusiasm.

As they rounded the bend of the creek, Jenny saw the most beautiful sight. A small waterfall was splashing into a pool of clear water. Todd told her that the pool was their swimming hole. They would play under the falls and slide down one of the rocks and splash into the water.

"How deep is it?" Jenny asked.

"Well, it is over my head in the middle. The rumor is that it is over 20 feet deep. But nobody has ever measured it." Then, as if it were a spur of the moment thought, Todd asked "You want to go for a swim?"

"Now?" Jenny asked him in complete shock.

"Yeah, why not?"

"We don't have our swimsuits with us," Jenny said with a blush coloring her cheeks.

"Do we really need them?" Todd joked as he started to unbuckle his belt.

"Yes, we do!" cried Jenny. "Todd, stop!"

Todd was laughing and buckled his belt again. He had no intentions of skinny dipping with her. But he promised to bring her back someday when they had their suits with them.

On the way back to the house Jenny picked up her flowers and picked a few more lilies on the way. It was almost suppertime and

Todd had to get home. He told Jenny that he would see her tomorrow at the fair and then left.

In the morning John came bouncing into the kitchen talking a blue streak. "Hurry up you guys", he said. "I have to get my lamb ready for the fair. When are we leaving? Mom, when will you be ready to go?"

"Settle down, son," Grammy said. "Your lamb is ready to go. Poppy already has him in the back of the truck. Sit down and eat a decent breakfast."

John looked up at the clock. It was just a little past 8 o'clock. Well, he had to wait for every one else to get ready anyway, so he decided to have breakfast with the family.

The Madison clan reached the fairgrounds just before 11 o'clock. Jenny met Tamara at the judge's table to enter her flower arrangement and then the two girls walked through the exhibits and both decided that Jenny's was the nicest arrangement there.

John and Poppy went down to the livestock barn to unload John's lamb. John quickly took the lead from Poppy and led his lamb into the stall with a sign reading "Madison Farm". He immediately got a bucket of fresh water and put it in the stall with the lamb. Then, he pulled out the brush and began to groom the young lamb until every piece of wool was in its proper place. The lamb looked perfect.

John helped Poppy unload one of the steers he entered as well as two older ewes. John promised to help Poppy show the ewes, but his lamb was more important to him. After the animals were taken care of, Poppy took the truck out of the barn area to a waiting parking place.

John and Poppy walked around surveying the other animals in the long barn. Poppy told John that the Kramer Farm raised fine sheep and they would be one of their biggest competitors. John had seen their sheep and he agreed that they had a nice looking herd.

John and Poppy had to walk over to the judge's stand and register their animals. John would be in the junior category while Poppy would enter into the adult program. The judge handed them a schedule of shows and Poppy and John found the times they had to show. Both shows were on the same day but at different times. The women would have to come for the showing of the animals as well as the judging of Jenny's flower arrangement. Grammy would bring her entries on the morning of the judging for baked goods and canned goods. She was also going to enter some doilies that she had crocheted last fall.

The big day finally came. Barbara, Jenny and Grammy met John and Poppy at the fairgrounds for breakfast. They were walking toward the food tent as John and Poppy were coming from the other direction of the tent.

"Perfect timing," Grammy remarked.

The family quickly ate a big country style breakfast of biscuits and gravy, sausage, eggs and hash browns. John had two cartons of milk with his meal before he felt full. Barbara wondered where that boy put it all.

After breakfast the ladies went over to the craft barn while the men went back to the barn to check on the livestock. Grammy had entered her things before meeting the others for breakfast. All that was left now was to wait for the judging. An announcement was then made that the cake judging would start in five minutes. Grammy knew the judging for the pies, cookies and other baked goods immediately followed the cake judging. She had entered some cinnamon rolls which Barbara and Jenny knew were the best they had ever tasted.

Mrs. Taylor won for her wedding cake. It was her fifth year running winning the cake contest. Grammy thought that she should change her entry to something else and give others a chance to win. Mary Robinson won for her Oatmeal Raisin Cookies. It was her first year winning after entering the same cookies for the past three years. Alice Moore won for her Strawberry Rhubarb Pie. Alice not only made the pie, but she also grew the strawberries and rhubarb in her garden.

The judges moved toward the other baked goods. Grammy held her breath as the judges took bites of her rolls. The judges were so good that no one could tell what they were thinking about the entries until they were announcing the winners. They moved away from Grammy's rolls and tasted muffins, sweet rolls and corn bread before going back and placing a blue ribbon next to Grammy's rolls. Grammy let out a little holler and Barbara and Jenny congratulated her on the victory.

Tamara was standing next to Jenny while the judges walked through the area where the flower arrangements were displayed. They looked at all sides of the arrangements and even smelled the flowers. Jenny was so nervous although she felt that her arrangement outshined all the others. The judges walked out of the area and over to the sewing area.

"Aren't they going to choose a winner?" Jenny asked.

"They will be back in a little while," Grammy said. "They might have to discuss their choices before naming a winner. Just be patient, Jenny."

"You'll win, Jen," Tamara promised. "I know your arrangement will win."

A few minutes later, one of the judges walked back into the barn with a handful of blue, white and red ribbons. He stopped in front of the crocheted items and placed a second place white ribbon on Grammy's doilies. She was satisfied with second for them. The judge placed the ribbons in front of various entries before he came back to the flowers. He had a blue ribbon in his hand and started to put it next to an arrangement of roses and baby's breath. When he noticed the color of the ribbon, he quickly switched it for a white ribbon. He then placed the red ribbon next to an arrangement of garden flowers submitted by a Mrs. Kelly. Finally, the judge placed the first place blue ribbon in front of Melody Scranton's arrangement of wild flowers mixed with garden flowers in an old tin bucket.

"You're arrangement was prettier than hers," Tamara said.

"Oh, I don't know," Jenny said. "It is very pretty. And putting it in the bucket was very creative."

"She enters every year but this is the first time she has ever won," Tamara said. "I still liked yours better, Jen."

By that time, the girls had to run to the livestock show ring to see Poppy show his steer. It was a prize winner for sure. Poppy had to lead the steer around the arena, pause in front of the judges and then walk back to his spot amongst the entries. After lengthy deliberation, the judges announced that the steer from Madison Farm was the winner. Jenny, Tamara, Grammy, and Barbara broke into cheers for the winner. There was a splattering of applause from the other onlookers, too. Poppy led the steer back to the barn and told John that he would be the next winner in the family.

John had practiced for so long for this day that he was not nervous at all when his name was announced to show his lamb. The lamb behaved perfectly as John led him to the judge's stand, paused and returned to this place. The other lambs in the group all looked as good as John's. Terry Kramer led his lamb with confidence and authority. John knew that Terry would win. Finally the judges came down among the contestants. They awarded Terry second place. Mike Graves received the red ribbon and the judge came over and pinned the blue ribbon onto John's lamb. Again, the Madison clan burst into applause. They sure had something to celebrate this evening!

At supper that evening Poppy explained that he and John had to show the steer and lamb again tomorrow. They could potentially win grand champions. John was excited to hear that. If they won grand champions, they would automatically be entered into the State Fair. That would be quite an honor. John and Poppy decided to spend the night on the fairgrounds with the animals. They had brought sleeping bags and air mattresses to put in the back of the pick-up but John wanted sleep in the hay next to his lamb. The women left and promised to be back before the main judging took place tomorrow afternoon.

The next morning John was up bright and early grooming his lamb. Poppy was taking care of his steer. John had already brought fresh water and feed for all of the Madison Farm animals. Todd walked over to the food tent and brought breakfast back for Poppy and John as well as his Dad and little brother. Poppy had said that it wasn't a good idea to leave the animals unattended before the main judging.

"You just never know what someone might do to win," he had told John.

John had to show his lamb first and he had him looking perfect. He walked proudly out into the arena with his lamb and when his name was called he presented him to the judges. The lamb behaved perfectly, but so did all the other lambs in the competition. It seemed it took the judges forever to make up their minds to choose a winner and when the ribbons and trophy were awarded John was left empty handed. When the group was excused, John walked out of the arena a bit disappointed but still as proud as when he walked in.

A few minutes before the main judging for the steers was to start, John joined the women in the bleachers of the arena. John saw Poppy and the steer waiting by the door. At the judge's signal, the contestants began entering the arena. All of the steers looked very good. Any of them could win the grand championship.

Once again, Poppy led his steer in front of the judges, paused, and then returned to his designated spot. After seeing all of the entries, the judges asked to see Poppy's steer as well as two others one more time. John figured that must have meant that Poppy was in the final three. The judges were talking amongst themselves and furiously writing figures on a pad.

The crowd became very quiet when the head judge stood up. He walked down to the arena followed by the Fair Queen carrying the ribbons and the other two judges carrying the trophies. The judges stopped in front of the steer owned by the Carson family. They were presented with the third place trophy, red ribbon and $100. The judge then walked over to Poppy. He was presented with the second place trophy, the white ribbon and $250.

Although they were somewhat disappointed, everyone in the Madison family cheered for Poppy and his steer. The judge finally walked over to Todd Kramer. Todd's dimples flanked the biggest smile when the judge awarded him the first place trophy, the blue ribbon and $500. Again, the Madison family cheered for their neighbor. Jenny felt a little jealous when the Fair Queen leaned over and kissed Todd. Barbara could see the green-eyed-monster and poked her in the ribs.

Both families gathered at the livestock barn to congratulate Poppy, John and Todd for their fine showings. While they were patting Poppy on the back, a man in a slick cowboy shirt, brand new blue jeans and cowboy hat walked over to them.

"My name is Doug Rathburn," the cowboy introduced himself. "I represent McDonald's restaurants and I would like to talk to you about buying that fine Angus steer."

When Poppy told Mr. Rathburn that he was interested in hearing what he had to say, John was amazed that Poppy would even think about selling his prize-winning steer. Mr. Rathburn and Poppy walked away from the others and they could see Poppy nodding occasionally at whatever it was that Mr. Rathburn was saying. Finally, Poppy shook hands with the man and turned back to the family. The McDonald's representative walked out toward the parking lot.

"I knew you wouldn't sell him," John said with a huge grin.

"Oh, but I did," Poppy said as John's smile immediately turned upside down. "Mr. Rathburn just left to get his truck to load him up. He'll be right back with a check."

"How can you sell him, Poppy?" John said, almost in tears.

"John, this is what we work so hard for. It is an honor to have a major company offer to buy your animal. There'll be another next year."

John still didn't understand. It was only when Poppy showed him the check with golden arches on the end that John finally understood the glory of being in the final three for the grand championship. Later on, the family learned that Todd had sold his grand champion steer at the State Fair Auction for over $13,000. That money would go straight into Todd's college education fund.

On the way home, John was sad that the fair was over, but he promised that he would get another animal ready for next year's fair. Maybe he would train a grand champion for McDonald's. He had all year to think and plan. They had not driven very far before John leaned over and fell asleep against Jenny's shoulder.

Barbara took Grammy to see the new house the afternoon after the fair. They wanted to do some cleaning before all of their furniture arrived. When Barbara pulled up in front of the house, Grammy could not believe her eyes.

"What on earth are you going to do with such a big place? How will you ever keep it clean? How can you afford to heat it?" Grammy asked before she even got out of the car.

"Ruth, don't worry about that. Bob has a great job and the kids will help keep it clean. Besides, it was a real bargain as far as we are concerned," Barbara tried to console her.

"It is so beautiful," Grammy gasped once she stepped inside. "Just look at the detail of this woodwork and crown molding. Hank will be very impressed. I can't wait to see the kitchen."

"Oh Ruth, you won't believe it. You'll be so jealous," Barbara grinned. "The kitchen is big and open. You'll have to come in sometime and do your canning here. We sure won't be running into one another."

Grammy was very impressed with the kitchen, as well as with the entire house. She volunteered to come in only once a year to help with the spring cleaning. Barbara put her arm around Ruth's shoulders and gave her a little squeeze. They started dusting, cleaning the fireplaces, washing counters and wiping out cabinets. Jenny cleaned out the refrigerator and Barbara cleaned up the stove and ovens. Around noon they were satisfied with their results and decided to grab a bite of lunch at the Cardinal Inn before going back to the farm.

Jenny made a beautiful centerpiece for the evening table. She had so many flowers left over that she put some in a vase for her room. The family was just sitting down to supper when Duke started barking outside and they heard a car door slam.

Poppy walked to the window to see who it was. Bob was home. Jenny, John and Barbara forgot their supper and ran out to greet him. Behind the family car was a U-Haul trailer. Everything they had asked Bob to bring, plus a lot of other things were in the trailer. He told them that he had seen the moving van pull out a few minutes before he left to come home and the movers had told Bob that they would arrive in about two or three days. Bob gave them Grammy's phone number and told them to call when they reached Carthage. That way, he could leave and meet the van at the new house. In just a few days, they could be living in their new home.

Bob reached into the back seat of the car and handed John Marble's litter box and bag of litter giving him orders to take care of her box. He then handed Jenny her water and food bowls, bag of food and gave her orders to take care of her food and water. Then he picked up the pet taxi and carried her in. Duke was not too thrilled with a new member of the family coming in to his house and Marble hissed right back at him. Inside, Barbara took Marble out of her carrier, hugged her and showed her where her litter box was going to be. She gave her a drink of water and let her loose in the downstairs bathroom for the time being.

Grammy herded the family back to the table and set another plate in front of Bob. Poppy started the meal as usual, with a long prayer. The topic of conversation revolved around the move, and whether Bob remembered everything. He assured Barbara that everything had been taken care of right down to having transcripts sent from the children's schools. It was real now and Chicago was only a distant memory to the family.

Chapter Nine

Jenny was a little tired from being at the fair most of the week and working at the new house but she was truly looking forward to going to Quincy and SHOUTfest. She figured she could rest in the hotel room this evening and be ready for the day long event tomorrow. The weatherman was predicting rain but she was praying so hard that it would stay away. By 2:00 Barbara was ready to go and Jenny called Tamara to say they were on their way to pick her up.

"You are sure you want to stay here?" Barbara asked John one more time.

"Sure Mom, I'd rather stay on the farm with Poppy. Maybe next year," he assured her as he gave her a hug good-bye.

Barbara said good-bye to Poppy, Grammy and Bob, and said that they would be back on Monday morning. Once the car was rocking down the lane with the radio tuned to 88.5 ~ *The Mix*, Jenny's excitement level tripled. When Tamara got in the car, the volume was turned up and the girls sang along all the way to Quincy.

When Barbara exited the highway at Quincy and Jenny saw TJ Maxx, Old Navy and Kohl's she immediately wanted to go shopping.

"There is life close to Hamilton," she giggled putting her hands against her heart.

"Quincy is a nice size city." Tamara said. "They have a nice mall with some cool stores. Will we have time to stop at the Mall, Mrs. Madison?"

"I suppose we could take time to go there since it is on the way to the hotel," Barbara said as she noticed both a Lowe's and Home Depot stores at their exit.

After a quick shopping spree the girls decided they were hungry. Tamara said that she heard that you could get really good meals at the HyVee grocery store. She said that a friend of hers had their wedding catered by a guy named Nolan from there. They said he did a great job. They said that there is a great cook named Curtis there and a real sweet lady named Linda that works in the Deli, too. They decided to stop there since it was right on Broadway which was the main road to the hotel. Their home style meals were delicious and very filling. Barbara decided to pick up some breakfast food and milk for in the morning while they were at the grocery store, too.

"This sure beats the Wilson store back home," Jenny whispered to Tamara.

Tamara agreed and both girls giggled.

Barbara checked in at the Days Inn and after the girls checked out the room they ran over to the pool area. But instead of going swimming they ran to the back fence. Tamara stretched out her arm and pointed down toward a small park with several fountains and a gazebo along the Mississippi riverfront.

"That is where the concert will be tomorrow," Tamara said. "There will be tents sent up for vendors in front of the gazebo all the way to that building with the blue roof way back there. That is where the bands will sell their stuff."

"Wow! That's a pretty big area," Jenny said. "It is so pretty here with the bridges over the river." Then wiping her forehead Jenny muttered, "I sure hope it cools off some."

"Me, too," Tamara responded as the two girls started walking back to their room.

Barbara met them at the gate and Tamara showed her the area where the concert was going to be held.

"How beautiful!" Barbara exclaimed. "What a lovely place for an outdoor wedding."

"My friend's cousin got married here," Tamara said. "They had the reception here, too. It was so pretty."

"I can only imagine with the bridges in the background, all the flowers and the fountains. It is a lovely park," Barbara just went on and on about the area.

The girls decided to try to call it an early night and ended up falling asleep around 11:00. All three were wide awake at 8:30 and had no idea what they were going to do until 1:00. After breakfast, Jenny and Tamara walked back over to the pool area to see if anything was happening at the concert area. When they got there they were both shocked.

"Holy cow, Jen, look how much they have done already," Tamara squealed, pointing toward the park.

"Wow, they have the stages and all the tents up already," Jenny said. They must have started working last night."

"There are a couple of buses here already. I wonder if they are for some of the bands," Tamara said questionably.

"Probably so, I wonder which one. I heard that <u>Building 429</u> was going to play early and leave right away. Maybe it could be them," Jenny said. "Let's go see." The two girls giggled with excitement.

Around noon people were starting to go into the SHOUTfest venue so Barbara decided that they would go on down, too. Jenny and Tamara grabbed their tickets and their chairs-in-a-bag and went to the front desk where Barbara had summoned the hotel van. The van would take them right to the front gate.

As they walked along the merchandising tables Jenny was so disappointed that the table was empty for the band <u>By The Tree</u>.

"The band is here and they'll be set up very soon. So be sure to check back," the lady at the table said. "They don't play until 6:30."

"Thank you," Jenny said. "We'll be back. I really want to meet them."

"Didn't they do *Beautiful One*?" Tamara asked Jenny.

"Yeah, they also did *Hold You High*," Jenny responded.

"Oh, I love that one," Tamara said. "We definitely have to get up close when they play."

The girls watched the local bands and truly enjoyed them. Jenny liked <u>Goat</u>, but Tamara liked <u>Damascus Road</u> the best and Barbara said she preferred <u>Release Restraint</u>. But they all agreed that <u>Building 429</u> was totally awesome. Barbara found a spot some ways back from the stage that had a bit of shade and set up her chair. It was so hot and humid and she needed to sit down and get some water. The girls put their chairs on the ground next to Barbara still closed in their bags.

"Look, Jen, <u>By The Tree</u> is here now. You want to go over? There's not anyone at their tent right now," Tamara said as she pointed over toward their tent.

"Sure, let's go. Mom, we won't be long," Jenny said as she skipped to catch up with Tamara.

The girls talked to Aaron, Ben and Garrett for several minutes learning about the new album, *World On Fire* coming out. The girls were definitely star struck although they were both trying to act cool.

"How did you get your name?" Jenny asked Aaron.

"Well," he said. "It was by the tree of Adam and Eve that we became sinners but it was by the tree of the cross of Jesus Christ that we were saved."

"That is so cool," Tamara said as chills ran down her spine. "I never thought of it like that."

The girls talked a little longer, bought the group photo and had it signed by all the band members including their manager, Scott. They went back to Barbara and told her every detail about their encounter with By The Tree. You would have thought they had met someone much better known.

"I have been looking everywhere for you guys," Todd said with some disgust as he walked toward Jenny, Barbara and Tamara.

"We've been here since 12:30," Tamara said. "What time did you get here?"

"I've been here since 7:00 this morning. I helped put up all those canopies," Todd said motioning to the canopies along the wall where the bands were set up with their merchandise.

"We just came from talking to By The Tree. They are so nice," Tamara said almost gushing their praises.

"Yeah, they're pretty cool," Todd said kind of matter of fact. "I was talking to Josh from Day of Fire for a long time this morning. He's really cool."

"I thought the people in the bands would be more....what's the word I want?" Jenny searched for the word she wanted looking in the air.

"Arrogant?" Todd finished her sentence.

"Yeah, or maybe not quite that bad. But you know what I mean," Jenny said.

"Well, you know they are Christian bands," Todd reminded her.

"That's true," Jenny said.

"But they are award winners and they know they are good," Tamara interrupted.

"Tam, they are playing their music for Jesus Christ," Todd snapped.

"And they are making a very good living at it," Tamara snapped back.

"And they are away from their families for months at a time," Todd recounted.

"Enough, you two!" Jenny cried. "Let's have fun. We could argue this all day. Yes, it is a job for them, but so is being a preacher. I bet they aren't making millions like main stream bands. But I bet they aren't on drugs either. At least I hope they aren't." Jenny looked over to the guys under the canopy to whom they had just spoken and under her breath she said, "No, they aren't. They're high on Jesus."

Barbara, Jenny, Todd and Tamara enjoyed all the bands until it started to rain during the last act. It was cut short and all the fans were disappointment but were totally satisfied with a wonderful day of music, togetherness and fellowship. It was decided earlier that the group would just walk the few blocks back to the hotel and slipped out behind the stage instead of walking back to the entrance. By the time they reached their room they were all wet and tired. Todd and two of his friends got a room at the same hotel to stay Sunday night; so he went off with them and said he would meet the girls for breakfast.

Jenny slipped into the bathroom and pulled off her wet clothes and changed into her "Tree Hugger" shirt that she bought from <u>By The Tree</u> and then fell across her and Barbara's bed.

"What a fabulous day! I loved everything about it," Jenny said as she held up her autographed photo of <u>By The Tree</u>.

"All the bands were very good," Barbara said. "I am surprised I liked them, but I did. I didn't even mind the rap band either…I could understand them for a change."

The girls laughed at her.

"Mrs. Madison, you're a hoot," Tamara said. "I can just see you trying to keep up with <u>Manifest</u>." Tamara stood up and did a little hip hop dance and they all started giggling.

"Don't be so quick to write me off," Barbara said as she stood up and did a little wiggle herself. "I used to keep up with <u>MC Hammer</u> when I was pregnant with you, Jen."

"MC who?" the girls said in unison teasing the older woman. Barbara threw a pillow at them and fell back onto the bed. They just laughed at Barbara and at each other.

Barbara was awaken early in the morning by her cell phone.

"Hello?" She said half asleep.

"Barbara," Bob said back to her. "Did I wake you, honey?"

"Well, yeah you did." Barbara said regaining her consciousness. "Is something wrong?"

"No. I just wanted to let you know that the POD is sitting in front of the house."

"What?" Barbara shrieked in a whisper, so as not to wake up the girls. She leaned up on one elbow. "It's there already? That sure didn't take long. We can be home in a couple of hours."

"Take your time. It's not going anywhere and we still have it for a few days," Bob replied.

Bob asked how they liked the concert and Barbara asked how everything was on the farm. After they talked a few minutes and got their answers they said they would see each other soon; that they loved each other and then they said good-bye. Barbara woke up the girls and told them about Bob's call and told them to get dressed. She called Todd and asked him to meet the girls for breakfast before they had to leave to go home.

On their way back out to the farm they decided to take a detour past the new house. And, sure enough, right in font of the house there was a white moving POD that held all of their belongs. It looked so small dwarfed by the big house. Barbara wondered if they had enough furniture to fill the house. She would have to worry about that later and drove on out to the farm. She was anxious to see Bob.

Chapter Ten

Tuesday morning the POD was still sitting there just as Bob had said. He had hired a couple of professional movers and one of them opened the back of the van revealing all of the family's belongings neatly stacked in the POD.

"Ma'am, all you have to do is tell us where you want things and we'll take it from there," the bigger of the two movers said.

They pulled out a platform that dropped to the ground like a gangplank for them to carry things from the truck to the house. They started with some lamps and Barbara directed them to the living room. Jenny and John sat on the front porch watching as the two men walked back and forth carrying boxes and furniture into the house. Barbara was giving directions and Bob was following them through the rooms.

A few long hours later, Bob handed the driver an envelope containing a tip. They thanked him, climbed into their truck, hooked up the POD and took off down the street.

Barbara was in the kitchen fixing a light supper for the family. When she walked through the house to let them know that supper was ready, she realized that the house looked so empty. Later she asked Bob if she could have some money to buy new furniture for the parlor, living room and third floor bed rooms. He felt that they could afford to buy some things as they had nearly $60,000 left from the sale of the house in Chicago. They decided to put all of their existing living room furniture in the family room and to furnish the main floor in a Victorian style. Barbara said she would start on that project after the kids went back to school.

Barbara looked in on Jenny before going to bed. Jenny had arranged her room so nice.

"It reminds me of the bedroom at Grammy's house," Jenny said.

"It sure does," Barbara agreed. "But where's Cody Linley?" She asked jokingly.

"Mom, I'm past posters on my wall," Jenny said as she sat the small, autographed picture of <u>By the Tree</u>, now framed, on her dresser.

Then Barbara told Jenny that they would go shopping and buy her new sheets and bedding. Jenny had to decide what she would like before they went. She had a tough decision on how she wanted the final design of her room. Oh well, she would have to sleep on it.

Barbara walked down the hall and peeked in on John. He and Bob had set up his room and it, too, looked very nice. John was already sleeping soundly so she closed the door quietly and walked across the hall to the master suite.

"We sure could have fun running around here", Bob said as he grabbed Barbara from behind and kissed the back of her neck. Barbara turned around and agreed with Bob, kissed him, and suggested that they try out the master bathroom. Bob read her mind as they walked through the dressing room and into the bathroom.

"We could get lost in here, too," Barbara said with a giggle. Bob gave her a little smirk as he closed the door behind him.

The next morning Jenny woke early and went downstairs to the kitchen. She was sitting at the table looking out at the swimming pool when Barbara and Bob walked into the kitchen. Barbara quickly filled the coffee pot with water and turned it on. Bob reached for a box of cereal and a couple of bowls. He sat down next to Jenny and poured a bowl for himself before sliding the box and a bowl toward her.

"Dad, can we fill the pool?" Jenny asked still staring out the window.

"Not this year, Jen," he said. "School will be starting in a couple of weeks and I need to learn how to maintain a pool before we fill it. You will have a lot of opportunity to use the pool next year. We are staying here for a very long time."

Jenny nodded and took the cereal box from her Dad and filled the bowl half way. Barbara said the phone company was coming to install the phones today. They decided to put a phone in each bedroom on the second floor, the family room, the parlor and the kitchen. Bob suggested that they put a phone in the hall of the third floor. Barbara agreed with that idea. In the meantime, they both had their cell phones to use.

Jenny and Barbara looked through the classified ads from the Hamilton and Keokuk newspapers for furniture ads and upcoming auctions. Barbara circled the auction ads and made a note on the calendar regarding the ones she was interested in. She walked through the parlor and living room and decided what might look good in each room. This was a job that Barbara was truly going to enjoy.

The Madison family had gotten all of their belongings settled into their new home. The family room in the basement was the only room that was truly finished where the entire family could relax together. The furniture from their old living room and family room filled the space nicely and made two areas down there. One area was for watching television and another area for playing games around the table.

Jenny and Barbara had gone shopping and Jenny chose curtains, a bedspread, and shams in a dainty rose pattern. It looked very nice in her room and the pink tint in the roses brought out the color in the wallpaper. Standing back and surveying their handiwork, Jenny and her mother both felt they had done a marvelous job choosing the right fabrics and furniture.

This morning at breakfast Barbara announced to the family that she was going to an auction this afternoon. After explaining that there should be a lot of antiques at this auction, Bob decided to go along, too. Jenny had never been to an auction before and she wanted to go as well. John begged his parents to take him to the farm. Bob said they would drop him off on the way and pick him up on their way back.

"That's a deal," John said giving his dad a high five.

When they pulled into the yard of the homestead, Jenny noticed that Todd's truck was there. Todd came over to the truck and asked how she was doing. Jenny started talking to Todd until her dad yelled that it was time to go. Jenny would have liked to stay and chat with Todd some more, but he had chores to do and he would not have the time to spend with her. Jenny said she hoped that she would see him when they returned to get John.

The auction was at a farm about three miles from Poppy and Grammy's farm. Cars were parked all along the gravel road; some halfway in the ditch. Bob drove by the driveway to the farm when he saw someone just ahead of him pull out and head down the road. What Luck! Bob pulled into the empty space and they only had a short walk back to the auction. People were milling around and looking at all of the items for sale. There were tables and hay wagons stacked with boxes of books, pots and pans, Christmas decorations and so much more. There was an old saxophone lying in an open case next to a guitar with no strings. They walked around the back of the house and saw all kinds of garden tools, lawn mowers and hoses. There was a washing machine sitting next to a dryer. Two refrigerators that looked as though they had cooled their last glass of milk were sitting with the doors propped open. Turning the corner to go along the side of the house was all of the furniture. There were new bed frames as well as antiques. Some of the furniture looked as though it was brought from a California home in the 1950's. Other stuff looked like it had just come off the showroom floor. Then Barbara saw it.

"This would look wonderful in the parlor," she exclaimed.

She walked over to a Victorian style couch. The wood trim looked to be either maple or cherry. The legs curved down to huge claw feet. The material on the couch was well worn and torn in a few places. Bob thought that Barbara had totally lost her mind.

"I could get this recovered and it will be perfect," Barbara said, surveying the piece.

"And this could look great sitting next to it," Jenny said as she pointed to a wobbly end table with a cracked marble top.

"Don't tease you two," Barbara scolded. "This will look marvelous next to the couch. All it needs is a little polishing. You just wait."

Barbara looked around and found a few other pieces that she had picked out for the house. There was a large cabinet with beveled glass in the double doors. Barbara had big plans for this cabinet. It would look great in the foyer of the house. Before she was married, she had started a collection of figurines. She had Hummel and Precious Moments figurines as well as some from the Hamilton Collection and the Bradford Mint. They had been in boxes in Aunt Milly's attic since she and Bob moved to Chicago. Now she could display them in the wonderful old cabinet.

They could hear the rambling of the auctioneer. He was selling things off the long tables and wagons. It would be quite some time before he got around to the furniture. Bob and Jenny had walked away from Barbara and looked at some of the other items for sale. Bob saw a flyer on a car sitting in the front yard.

"To be Sold at 1 o'clock Sharp"

The car looked to be in decent shape. It was a 1996 Ford Taurus. Bob knew that they were good cars. He looked under the hood and noticed that the engine was clean and had apparently been taken care of by the owner. He looked inside the car and was surprised at how neat it was, as if it had just come off of the assembly line. What surprised Bob the most was the car only had 32,000 miles on it.

"Go ahead and start 'er up," a voice from behind Bob said.

The voice startled Bob and he jumped back from the car for a second.

"My wife drove this car for almost seven years," the man said. "She treated it like her baby. Them's the actual miles on 'er, too. Been sitting around for a few years now, but she started right up this mornin' when we brought 'er out here."

Bob opened the door to the car, slid in behind the wheel and turned the key. The car started right up and the engine purred like a kitten. He pressed down on the accelerator and revved the engine. It sounded great. There was no whine, knocks or squeal at all. Bob liked this car. He figured Barbara could use it as a second car or perhaps Jenny could use it when she got her license. Bob decided that he would bid on it.

Jenny wasn't paying any attention to what her father was doing. She had found some old quilts that she liked. There were so many of them! A couple of ladies walked over to the quilts, picked up a few of them and walked over to where a rope had been tied between two trees. They draped the quilts over the rope to better display them. It would take them quite a while to hang up all those quilts, so Jenny asked if she could help. The ladies welcomed her help and Jenny took a few of the quilts over to the line. Each one was more beautiful than the one before. Jenny had to talk her Mom into getting one.

Bob and Jenny walked back over by the furniture. Barbara was still looking at all of the pieces. She had a notebook where she was writing down the items that interested her and approximately how much she wanted to pay for them. The page showing was almost full of items.

"We shouldn't have let that moving van go," Bob teased her.

"Oh, I won't get everything," Barbara said seriously. "I may not get anything. It just depends on how things go."

"Mom, you have to come over and see these quilts. I sure would like to have one for my room," Jenny said. "There are probably 30 or 40 of them. They are all hanging on clotheslines in the front yard."

"I didn't see them when we came in," Barbara said.

"No, they just put them up," Jenny informed her. "Come on and look at them."

The three of them walked over toward the quilts. Barbara gasped at the color and beauty of the work that was done on each of them. She knew that they were old, but they were all in such good shape.

"Oh, Jenny," Barbara said. "These quilts will go high. I bet you couldn't get one of these for less than $300."

"Wow," Jenny said. "That much?" she was so disappointed.

"We will watch and see; if they are not too bad…well, we'll have to just wait and see," Barbara said. "I'm not making any promises, you hear."

Bob looked at his watch. It was only 11:45, but he was already getting hungry. He suggested that they go over to the food tent. The local Christian Church was selling maid rites, chips, hot dogs, pies, and cakes. They also had coffee, soda, tea and lemonade. They chose what they wanted for lunch and Bob paid the bill. Barbara found three empty chairs at one of the long cafeteria tables set up right outside of the tent. As they were eating, she kept looking to see how close the auctioneer was getting to the furniture. It would be at least another hour or so.

After they finished eating lunch, Barbara and Jenny walked around for a while. Bob went to listen to the auctioneer to see if he could figure out if things were selling high or low. It had been years since he had been to an auction and he doubted if Barbara had ever been to one. He wanted to be sure she knew how to bid and still get the best deal. He really wanted that car. He figured he would go as high as $3000 or even $4000 on it. He looked at his watch again. It was just about 12:30. It wouldn't be long now, so Bob headed over to where the car was parked. There were two guys looking under the hood. Bob hoped that they wouldn't bid it up too high.

A number! Bob needed to get a number. He had totally forgotten. He rushed over to the auctioneer's truck, signed his name and took a number. He was 182. Then he hurried back to the car.

Jenny and Barbara were standing next to the table where the auctioneer was selling the last few pieces of crystal glassware. When he had finished, the auctioneer announced that they would move to the front of the house to sell the car and then move on to the quilts. Barbara realized that the furniture would be sold last. It was a good thing they had no other plans for the day.

The auctioneer came around the corner of the house carrying his stool, while two assistants carried the speakers for the PA system. Once in place, the auctioneer tested his microphone and announced that the car would be sold in 5 minutes. He gave the terms of the sale and said that the owner of the car would sign over the pink slip upon full payment. Bob was getting anxious.

"All right folks, what do I hear for this beauty? Do I hear $3000 for this fine car, do I hear $3000?"

Bob about flipped. That is what he was intending to pay for the car.

The auctioneer did not receive any offers and immediately dropped down to $2000. Again he received no offers.

"Come on folks, you know you're getting a bargain here at $1000 on this sweet set of wheels. Somebody out there start it off."

A voice in the back of the crowd yelled out, "I'll give you $100."

Bob waited.

"Thank you, sir, "said the auctioneer, and he was off. "I have $100, do I hear two? I have one, do I hear two? Two, two, two, do I hear two?"

A man standing a short distance from Bob hollered out "Two!"

Immediately the man in the back yelled out "Three!"

Bob was about to make his bid when a third man yelled "Four!"

The bidding went on like this for what seemed like a long time. The auctioneer was keeping up with several bidders just fine. Finally, three of the bidders had quit. There were only two men bidding on the car and the bid was up to $1800.

"I have 18, do I hear 19? 19, 19, 19, do I hear 19? I have 18, do I hear 19?"

The second bidder said, "I'll give you $1850."

"OK, I have $1850, do I hear 19? I have 1850, 1850, 1850. Do I hear 19?"

The man in front said, "19."

Bob turned around and looked at the man in back. He was shaking his head.

"I have 19, 19, 19, do I hear 1950?"

Bob made his move. "I'll give you 1950," he said.

The man in front countered immediately with 20. Bob counter attacked with 2050.

The other man said, "2100 dollars."

"2150" Bob retorted.

"22" said the first bidder.

Bob bid fifty dollars more and the man immediately increased his bid by fifty dollars. This went on for a few minutes. The auctioneer tried to keep up and then just watched the two bidders go at it. The bid was up to $2950 when Bob had made the last bid. The man shook his head and waved his hand in the air in disgust.

"I have $2950, do I hear three?" The auctioneer finally spoke up. "I have 2950, do I hear 3000?" He said as he scanned the audience of onlookers. "I have 2950 once, 2950 twice, sold! Sold for $2,950 to number 182. Whew, that was a tough one. Congratulations, sir. You have yourself a nice little car here."

Bob felt as though he had just won the biggest prize in the whole world. He could not wait to tell Jenny and Barbara. But, he didn't have to.

"What did you just do, Robert?" Barbara asked.

"I got us a second car," Bob grinned. "For that price, you can use it and Jenny will be driving soon enough. What do you think, Jen? Nice car, huh?"

"Yeah, I guess so," Jenny stammered. "I never gave a car a thought."

"We're going over to see about those quilts," Barbara said. "Do you want to come?"

"I'll be right over," Bob said. "I want to go and take care of the paperwork for the car now."

Jenny and Barbara walked away from Bob and watched as the quilts were being sold. The auctioneer started at the far end of the line and the two quilts that Jenny liked were right in front of them. There were at least twenty quilts to be sold before these. The first quilt sold for $620. Barbara cringed. The second quilt, which wasn't nearly as nice as the first one, sold for $575. The quilts were selling very high. Barbara was afraid that Jenny would be terribly disappointed. By the time the tenth quilt had sold, Barbara noticed that the crowd was thinning out a bit. That quilt sold for $480. She thought that the prices were going down a little, when all of a sudden a log cabin pattern quilt sold for $750.

"What's so special about that quilt?" Jenny asked her mother.

"I don't know, Jenny," Barbara replied. "Maybe it has sentimental value for someone."

Three quilts away from the ones Jenny liked, Barbara saw that the crowd was getting very thin now. The last quilt sold for only $200; and the auctioneer had to beg to get that price. Finally it was the first of the two quilts.

The auctioneer was getting tired of quilts by this time. He said, "OK ladies; give me an offer on this next quilt. We have several more to go now, so, let's just get it over with."

Barbara piped in and said "I'll give you fifty dollars for it."

"Thank you, ma'am," said the auctioneer. "That's what I like. Instead of starting out at five or ten dollars, this is a lady who knows what she wants to pay. I have 50. Do I hear 60?" An elderly lady across from Barbara offered 60. Barbara countered with 70 and the elderly lady said 80.

"OK ladies, who wants it bad enough?"

"100 dollars," Barbara said.

The auctioneer smiled as the old lady just shook her head and walked away. Barbara had gotten the first quilt for less than half of what she planned on spending for it. The auctioneer started the bidding in the same manner with the next quilt. Again, Barbara started the bidding with 50 dollars. No one else counter offered. Barbara got the second one, too. Jenny was thrilled.

"OK ladies; are there any more quilts that you are interested in? If not, I am going to sell them in groups of three or four. We need to move on to the other things."

Jenny pointed to a double wedding ring pattern and Barbara offered the auctioneer 25 dollars for it. The auctioneer asked if there were any others interested in this particular quilt and when no one responded, Barbara got that one, too. As they were walking away with their treasures they heard the auctioneer begging for bids on the remaining quilts.

The girls almost ran into Bob with their huge bundles blocking their view. He offered to take the quilts to the car and said he would meet them back near the furniture. Jenny and Barbara quickly accepted his offer and unloaded their bundles and then headed over to the couch.

An old dresser with missing handles sold first. It went for 20 dollars. Then, a walnut coffee table with matching end tables sold for 45 dollars. Things were moving at reasonable prices. There were not many people standing around to bid. That was good news for Barbara. After watching several items sell at reasonable prices, a roll top desk sold for 200 dollars. It was quite beautiful. Barbara's couch was next to be sold.

The auctioneer started the bidding very low. He knew that the couch needed a lot of work. The bidding went fast before he said it was sold for 15 dollars, to Barbara. She was so happy. The next item that

Barbara wanted was the marble top table. She bid on it and got if for 22 dollars and 50 cents. By the time she was finished, Barbara had bought two Louis XIV chairs, another end table, a cedar chest, a fainting couch, a desk, desk chair and the cabinet with glass doors. When she went to pay her bill, she was so surprised at how low the total was. She even double checked the tickets to be sure. She was very proud of herself.

Bob figured they could not get all of the furniture in the two cars so he called his dad on his cell phone. Poppy knew exactly where they were and came right over with the truck. John just shook his head when he saw all the 'junk' his mother had bought. Poppy followed Bob driving the Taurus and Barbara driving the family car. Once they arrived home, Poppy backed the truck up to the carriage house and he and Bob unloaded the furniture and stacked it against the wall. Bob pulled the Taurus in with plenty of room to spare.

Poppy waved goodbye as he pulled out of the driveway. Bob pulled the family car into the garage and closed the door. He walked into the kitchen where Barbara was waiting for him with a hot cup of coffee. He sat down, sipped his coffee and sighed.

"We did very well today, honey," he said. "But, I sure am bushed."

"Me, too," Barbara said. "I can't wait to start working on those pieces we got today. I wonder who is a good upholsterer here in town. Maybe Ruth will know of someone."

"You don't think you and Mom can do it yourselves?" Bob asked teasingly.

"Well, maybe we could," Barbara replied with some confidence. "I'll call her tomorrow."

"You've got to come up and see the quilt in my room," Jenny said as she walked in to the kitchen to say good night to her parents.

"I'll peek in on my way to bed," Barbara promised.

Jenny walked over and hugged her Mom. "Thanks, Mommy. I love them. And, I love you, too."

"What about me?" Bob teased. "I just bought you a car. No big deal, huh?"

"Oh, Daddy, don't tease. I love you, too. Now when are you going to take me out driving?"

"Not until you get your white slip," Barbara interjected. Then the three of them started laughing.

Barbara and Bob stopped at Jenny's room on the way to their suite. She had laid the double wedding ring quilt on her bed. The pastel star quilt she folded and hung over the back of a chair. They looked very nice in her room. Barbara said that the cedar chest they bought today would look nice at the foot of Jenny's bed. She would work on that first thing.

Jenny said goodnight to her parents, thanked them again and crawled into bed. Her parents both tucked her in just like they used to when she was a small child. Barbara kissed her on the forehead and Bob ruffled her hair. They said goodnight for a third time and closed the door as they left her room. Jenny rolled over, pulled the quilt up over her shoulders and quickly fell to sleep.

Chapter Eleven

The Sunday paper had a big article on the back page announcing that school registration would be on Wednesday of this week. All new students were required to register before being accepted into classes on the following Monday. Jenny would register at Hamilton High School and John would be in the seventh grade at Hamilton Junior High School. John would have to ride the bus since the junior high was clear across town. One of the boys that lived on their street in John's grade had told John all about the school; and John said that it sounded petty neat.

Jenny called Tamara on Monday afternoon. She needed to know what the girls wore to school.

"Oh Jenny," cried Tamara. "Let me come in and stay over with you and we can go shopping for school clothes. I'll show you the best places to shop in Hamilton."

"I can't afford to spend a lot on school clothes," Jenny said. "My Mom just bought me some quilts at an auction and my Dad just bought a car for me. I can't drive it for a while, though." Jenny started pouting.

"Lucky you," Tamara said. "Well, listen, girlfriend, you don't need much money where I am taking you. If you can get about twenty or thirty dollars for school clothes, we can get you an entire wardrobe."

"Where are you taking me?" Jenny inquired.

"We have three great little thrift stores in town. A lot of the girls shop there. You can get some really great outfits for under a dollar."

"I can't believe that," Jenny said.

"Just wait," Tamara said. "You'll see what I mean when you see the places. You'll like them as much as I do."

Jenny told Tamara to hold on while she checked with her Mom about spending the night and if they could go shopping tomorrow. Barbara agreed and welcomed the chance for someone else to take Jenny shopping for school clothes. Tamara said that her mom would bring her in after supper.

A couple hours later, Jenny met Tamara at the door and they headed up to Jenny's room.

"I love it!" Tamara exclaimed. "This is so cool. These quilts are beautiful. I just love your room!"

"Mom bought a cedar chest at the auction, too. She wants to put it at the end of my bed. It's real nice, with a needlepoint lid. She said she would work on it first. I think all she has to do is clean it up a little."

"Did you go to that auction out by our place?"

"Yeah, it wasn't far from your farm."

"You know," Tamara said almost in a whisper. "Rumor has it that the old lady that lived in that house hid all of her money over the years in secret hiding places. They figure there is more than a million dollars around that house somewhere."

"Oh Tam," Jenny grinned. "I'm sure that she hid that much money somewhere. Maybe she sewed it in her quilts."

"I'm serious," Tamara squealed rubbing her hand across the quilt on Jenny's bed. "She never went anywhere and never spent any money. She made all her clothes. They never had any children to spend money on either. Look how nice that car is that your Dad bought. And she didn't like banks."

The girls then started making up stories as to where the old lady had hidden all of her money. They had some buried in the backyard in cigar boxes, some was sewn in the lining of the drapes, and some was even stuck in the gas tank of the car. The girls giggled and carried on until they were exhausted from laughing.

Barbara stuck her head in Jenny's room about 11 o'clock. She told them it was time to get to sleep if they planned on shopping by 9 o'clock in the morning. When Barbara shut the door behind her, the girls decided she was right and crawled into bed. They talked a while longer, but soon fell to sleep.

Barbara had fixed a fruit bowl for breakfast and the girls ate their share of it. John didn't care for fruit that much so he just ate cereal.

Barbara asked the girls if they wanted a ride to wherever they were heading to shop.

"No, thanks, Mrs. Madison," Tamara said. "It's really not that far. We can walk."

"If we buy too much stuff, we might have to call you to come get us though," Jenny said with a chuckle.

"Well, I will be here all day. Your dad will be working upstairs, so he will hear the phone."

Jenny and Tamara were all ready to leave when Barbara handed Jenny her credit card.

"Mrs. Madison, where we are going to shop, they don't accept credit cards," Tamara informed her. "They only take cash or personal checks."

Barbara went upstairs then to get some cash from Bob. All he had was a fifty dollar bill. Barbara reminded Jenny to spend it wisely and Jenny promised to bring home some change for her mom. Tamara said that there would be a lot left over.

The girls then left the house and began walking toward the center of town. They had gone about six blocks when Tamara pointed to an out of the way shop. The girls went into the quaint little shop. Here they found racks of skirts, slacks, sweaters, blouses, dresses, jeans suits, and even swimsuits. Jenny could not believe all of the clothes in this little store; and the prices were so cheap. Tamara pulled her over to a rack in the corner. There were blue jean skirts on the rack. Tamara held one of the skirts up to her waist. They both agreed that it looked good. Jenny could not believe the price tag read only fifty cents. Tamara explained that the two racks in the corner were clothes that had been here for over a month so they were discounted 50% - 75%.

Jenny found two sweaters, a couple of vests, and two skirts that she really liked. Then she spotted a cute jacket that would be perfect for fall. She carried all of the clothes to the counter to pay for them. She just smiled when the clerk asked her for $4.25. Tamara also had several items. She even bought some shoes. Her total came to $3.75. The girls were thrilled with their bargains.

When they left the store, Jenny told Tamara that this was the best way to shop. Tamara reminded her that she had to look carefully to be sure nothing was stained or torn. Sometimes there are some junk clothes that get mixed in and so they have to be careful.

The next shop was a little further than Tamara had remembered. They finally reached the shop and walked in. This store was probably three times the size of the previous one. Tamara led Jenny over to the discount section again. Jenny found a lot of things in this store that she was interested in. Tamara found an ankle length brown skirt. It looked like it would have been a very expensive skirt if bought new. Jenny looked at the tag and it was a Calvin Klein designer skirt. Tamara told Jenny that brand names did not mean much to any of the girls here. They just liked to look hot and not spend a lot of money to look that way.

Tamara decided to buy the skirt plus two pairs of jeans and three sweaters. Jenny got several items as well, including a dress, two polo shirts, a pair of shorts and two business suits. After paying their bills, the girls realized they had not even spent ten dollars each on their purchases.

When they left the shop, they walked downtown to the Cardinal Inn. They had a light lunch and Jenny decided that they should call Barbara to take them and their bargains home. But Tamara wanted to take Jenny to one more place. They quickly ate their lunch, paid the bill, gathered up their packages and walked out onto Main Street. At the end of the block, they turned left and walked to the middle of the block where the biggest thrift store was. They had to check their packages at the counter upon entering this store.

Tamara led Jenny to the back of the store and up a creaky stairway. The second floor was stocked with all sorts of clothes. Many of the articles looked like things from an attic of the 1960s. There were tie-dyed shirts, hip-hugger jeans, platform shoes and bell-bottom pants plus so much more. Tamara and Jenny had so much fun trying on a lot of the clothes. They couldn't decide what they wanted to take home with them. Most of the items cost less than a dollar.

Jenny stepped out of the dressing room wearing a pair of hip-hugger, bell-bottom pants with a cropped T-shirt and a vest with leather fringe. She had on a puffy red beret and a huge peace sign on a leather string around her neck. When Tamara saw her, she began to whoop and holler.

"You look awesome!" Tamara said. "That is just so cool!"

"Yeah, right," Jenny said. "I was just joking around with this outfit."

"No, really Jen, you look good."

"You really think so?" Jen asked. She turned to see herself in the mirror. "I do look pretty hot, don't I?"

"You sure do," Tamara agreed.

"I'll get this if you find something similar."

"OK," Tamara said. "Come help me look."

Within a few minutes they had found the perfect outfit for Tamara. It was almost identical to what Jenny had on, except that Tamara was wearing a hat with flowers sewn across the brim and her vest was a loosely knitted black fuzzy yarn. They stood next to each other and looked in the mirror. They then turned to each other and gave a high five.

They quickly changed back into their own clothes and loaded up all of their choices to buy. They were chatting and giggling as they went to the counter to pay for their purchases. Jenny decided then she should call her Mom for that ride.

Bob answered the phone and said that he would come pick them up in front of the Cardinal Inn. He would leave right away. The girls took all of their bags and walked over to the restaurant. A girl that Tamara knew from school spotted her and came over to talk to her.

"Hi Tam," the girl said. "I see you've been shopping."

"Carol, this is Jenny," Tamara said as she introduced the two girls. "She just moved here from Chicago. She'll be in our class this year."

"Nice to meet you," Carol said. Jenny responded the same.

Tamara was showing Carol some of their bargain clothes they had bought. Carol was impressed with some of their things. She told the girls she was going over to Keokuk this weekend with her Mom to go shopping and Tamara told her to check out the shops they had been to first. After hearing how little they spent on their clothes, she said she would definitely tell her Mom about it.

About that time, Bob pulled up. The girls said good-bye to Carol and that they would see her on Monday in school. Bob could not believe all of the packages the girls had.

"Did you leave anything for anyone else to buy?" He asked as the girls piled their packages in the car.

"Here's your change, Dad," Jenny said as she handed him $32.50. I spent 4 dollars for lunch."

"Well, I am quite impressed, Jen. You do have things in those bags, don't you?"

"Wait til we get home and I show you what we bought. I can't wait to show Mom."

When they arrived home, Barbara was out in the garage working on the sofa that she bought at the auction. She had already stripped the old material and was fighting with some crushed velvet that she got for it. Barbara looked so funny. The girls roared when they saw her.

"Don't laugh at me, give me a hand." Barbara pleaded as she was half wrapped in the material.

Jenny and Tamara looked at each other and began applauding.

"Very funny," Barbara grumbled.

"Mom, take a break and come in and see what bargains we found," Jenny said, as she held up her packages.

"I need a break," Barbara said as she placed the material on the sofa and put the tape measure and tacks in a plate nearby.

Once inside the house Jenny laid the bags on the kitchen table. Barbara sat at the far end of the table and Jenny opened the first bag. She pulled out the outfit that she tried on at the last shop. Barbara chuckled when she saw the same clothes that she had worn when she was Jenny's age. Jenny showed her the rest of the clothes that she had bought and Barbara was quite impressed. When Bob told Barbara how much change he had gotten back, Barbara was doubly impressed. Jenny told her mom that she should check out some of the shops. She said that there were a lot of name brand clothes for very little money. Barbara promised she would go when she had more time.

Tamara's mom came to pick her up about an hour after their shopping spree and Jenny thanked Tamara for helping her pick out some cool clothes. Jenny said that she would call her after she registered for her classes tomorrow so they could compare their schedules.

Barbara and Jenny walked through the double doors of the high school promptly at 9:00 and the student advisor directed them to the registrar's office since she was a new student. The rest of the students were being ushered toward the gymnasium to pick up their schedules and get their books and supplies. Jenny was assigned to a faculty advisor, Mrs. Dieker, who would check over her transcript before assigning any classes for this year. After checking the transcript she indeed agreed that Jenny was a junior and asked what classes she would like to take. Jenny didn't know she would even have a choice in the matter and admitted she hadn't thought about it. Mrs. Dieker told Jenny that she had to take English, Math and History as well as pass Driver's Education sometime before she graduates. Other than that she had a lot to choose from. When her schedule was finally set, she was taking Physics, Art, Spanish, P.E. and Computers along with the three required classes. It seemed like an awful big load for her compared to what she had in Chicago but Mrs. Dieker assured her that she would do fine. She also signed up for early morning Driver's Ed so she could get her license as soon as possible. It only took a couple of minutes for Jenny to get her schedule once the classes were chosen and Mrs. Dieker handed her a book list, a supply list and a student handbook of rules and regulations of the school. Now they walked over to the gymnasium to where all the books and supplies where displayed for students to purchase.

"This is really a nice school," Jenny said to her mom as they walked down the wide hall with beautiful clean walls and lockers, the bright sunshine coming through windows without bars and pictures of past classes smiling down at them. In the gym they were impressed with the bleachers with no graffiti painted or scratched on them, the IHSA Championship banners floating from the rafters and the huge Cardinal head painted on the north wall above the basketball rim.

"It is a very nice school," Barbara agreed choking back tears knowing what her children left behind.

Once Jenny got home she immediately called Tamara to compared schedules and figured out that they would be in Physics and English together. Tamara got Todd's schedule and said that he and Jenny would be in Spanish, History and Computers together; and all three of them had the same lunch period. Jenny was happy with her schedule and was anxious for school to start. She flipped through the pages of some of her books. They looked pretty standard to her and the history book had a lot of information that she had already studied in her old school. This would be an easy year for sure. Jenny carefully stacked her books and supplies on the dresser, decided what she was going to wear for the first day on Monday, and crawled in bed.

Chapter Twelve

Before they knew it the last free weekend was gone and the school buses were rolling. John had to meet the bus at the other end of the block at 7:45 and he only had to ride about 15 minutes before getting to school. He had talked to a couple of the neighbor boys about the school and found out that Chad, who lives three houses down, would also be in his same grade. John met him at the bus stop, and after they were settled on the bus, Chad started to tell John about their teacher.

"I heard she is kind of nice," Chad said. "My brother had her two years ago and he did all right."

John felt pretty good about that and this school had to be better than his old school. The bus ride was already a thousand times better. The kids on the bus were talking and excited about the first day of school, but there was no smoking or drug dealing in the back of the bus. The bus was clean and there were no rips in the seats or scratches on the backs of the seats. Yes, sir, John was going to like it here just fine.

Jenny had already left for school by the time John was on the bus and had slipped into the Driver's Ed room but noticed that no one was there yet. She saw a small sign taped on the chalkboard and read it:

Classes start on Tuesday after Labor Day

"Why didn't somebody tell us this," a voice over Jenny's shoulder said. "Hi, I'm Heather."

Jenny had met her first new friend at Hamilton High School. They walked back up to the main floor and found that their lockers were right next to each other. Jenny studied her combination and tried it. Let's see, 32 right ~ 14 left ~ she had to make sure that she passed 32 again ~ then 21 right. She pulled on the lock and it came open. Jenny was pleased with herself that she got it open on the first try. She neatly stacked her books and a couple of notebooks in the locker and then checked her schedule. She asked Heather where her classes were and decided she had better take her books for most of the morning with her.

Her first class was pretty interesting and then she had to go to English. Tamara practically knocked her over flying into the room. They quickly found two seats next to each other and sat down. Jenny wanted details on their English teacher, but Tamara said that he was new this year and she didn't know anything about him. Just then the bell ran and a very masculine voice ordered them to be quiet.

His name was Mr. Hill and he looked to be fresh out of college; both Jenny and Tamara thought he was a hunk. How were they were going to concentrate with this guy for a teacher? Jenny reached over and poked Tamara in the ribs to bring her back to reality. Mr. Hill told them that they would be studying British and American literature which brought about some groans from the students and then he said they would do some creative writing during the second semester. He said they would be writing their own poetry, essays and stories which brought a lot of smiles back to the faces of some of the students. Mr. Hill had barely given an assignment before the bell rang ending the class emptying the room. Tamara yelled at Jenny that she would see her at lunch while fleeing down the stairs. Jenny saw Todd heading up the stairs as she walked into the Spanish room. There were no two seats next to each other for them which disappointed Jenny. Todd sat a couple of seats behind her and they talked for just a couple of minutes before class.

"Me llamo Señora Del Castillo. Soy las maestra de la clase de español." The small woman in front of the classroom spoke totally in Spanish. "Bienvenidos estudiantes. En ese cuarto solamente hablamos el español. ¿Sí?"

"Oh Brother! This is going to be tough," thought Jenny. She wasn't that good in oral Spanish. At her last school they did a lot of vocabulary work and written assignments. It would take some time getting used to listening and understanding everything. Still speaking in Spanish, Mrs. Del Castillo said that she had a specific seating arrangement for the students and she wanted to place them in the assigned seats at this time. Jenny understood most of what she said and figured out the rest. When all of the students were in their assigned seats "Juanita" was directly across the row from "Teodoro". Jenny and

Todd giggled at their Spanish names but were thrilled at their seating assignments.

When the bell finally ended La Clase de Español Jenny had to rush down two flights of stairs to go to her Art class in the basement. The art room was bright with windows all along the north wall. Apparently the school had been built on a hill with a walkout basement. The tables were arranged in a large square with a smaller table in the middle for displays. Mrs. Schneider, the art instructor, announced that today they would begin a sketch as she had set up a still life on the table and asked the students to draw what they see. Jenny began to sketch the flowers, fruit and bottles that had been arranged on the table. She figured this was going to be a fun and easy class, too. When she thought she was done with her sketch, Mrs. Schneider asked if she could see any shadows or contrasts. Jenny went back to work on her drawing and had second thoughts about how easy the class was going to be.

When the bell rang Jenny quickly put her art supplies away and walked around the corner to the room next door for Computer class. She slipped into a chair in front of one of the computers and shortly Todd sat down next to her.

"How's it going?" he asked her.

"Not too bad," Jenny replied. "I've already got homework for tonight in two classes."

"Me, too," Todd said as the bell rang for the start of class.

Mr. James handed out flash drives and told the students to be sure to identify them in some way and try not to lose them. They were given their first assignment which was basic keyboarding and Jenny flew through that. Several of the students were having a hard time since many of them could not even type. Jenny checked her email and played a couple games before class ended.

Todd and Jenny walked to the cafeteria for lunch but Todd left her when Jenny got in line to get her meal. Tamara slipped in line in front of Jenny and started talking about the morning classes. They walked over to a table and sat down. Shortly Jenny saw Todd carry his tray past them and sit down at a table next to a girl with long blonde hair.

"Who's Todd sitting with?" Jenny asked Tamara.

"Oh, that's Lori Simms. She and Todd have been dating for over a year now," Tamara said as she took a bite from her sandwich, then realizing Jenny looked hurt.

"I didn't realize Todd had a girlfriend," Jenny said laying her sandwich back on her tray. All of a sudden her appetite had disappeared.

"Oh, Jen, I didn't realize that you really liked Todd. He never mentioned anything to me," Tamara said feeling a little sorry for Jenny.

"It's OK. He never gave me any reason to think that I could even have a chance with him," Jenny said, looking as if she were ready to cry.

About that time a tall boy came over and sat down next to Tamara. Jenny figured he must be Tam's boyfriend and she started to get up to leave.

"Hey, where are you going? Tammy hasn't introduced us yet and I sure do want to get to know you," the young man said.

Tamara introduced the boy as Larry Masterson. He played forward on the basketball team and Jenny figured he was a real jock. She also thought he was a little arrogant. Before she had a chance to decide whether she liked him or not, he had asked her to go out with him this coming Friday night and Jenny declined his offer saying that her parents didn't allow her to date yet.

"Give me a call when they do, pretty girl," Larry said as he picked up his tray and walked away. Jenny blushed.

The afternoon classes were only a blur to Jenny since she had found out that Todd had a girlfriend. She had written down teachers' names and assignments, but nothing else mattered at the moment. She walked home slowly, kicking rocks along the way and wondered if she would ever have a nice boyfriend here in Hamilton. Barbara noticed her mood when she walked in the house and asked about her day. Jenny simply said that she had a lot of homework already and went up to her room and Barbara accepted the explanation and went about her business. Although Jenny opened her books to read her assignments, she couldn't concentrate. She walked over and fell across her bed and took a nap until Barbara called her for supper. Jenny ate just a small supper, picking at her food. She was depressed. When Barbara and Bob asked her what was wrong, she just shook her head and said that she was all right. When supper was finished, Jenny helped Barbara clear the table and do dishes.

Jenny was on her way up to her room when she heard the phone ring.

"Jenny, it's for you," John screamed from the parlor.

"I'll get it my room," Jenny yelled back from the stairs.

After she said hello, she realized that it was Todd on the other end of the line.

"Jenny I just had a long talk with Tam. I don't know what to say to you," Todd sounded very sincere.

"It's all right Todd," Jenny started. "I know you just want to be friends. I can handle that."

"You sure, Jen? Gosh I am so sorry. I never even thought… I mean I would never want to hurt you, Jen." Then Todd asked, "Still friends?"

Jenny paused for a moment and choked back a couple tears and composing herself she answered him.

"Sure, Todd. I hope we will always be friends. It was just a little misunderstanding. I'll see you at school tomorrow."

"Good night, Jenny," Todd said as he hung up the phone.

After putting the phone down, Jenny lay across her bed and started to cry. She was hoping that she and Todd would be a couple once school started. She was so upset that she cried herself to sleep.

Chapter Thirteen

The first week of school flew by and both Jenny and John were very happy in their new surroundings. The homework was more than they were used to, but neither of them complained.

While the family was eating supper the phone rang. Bob went to answer it and handed the phone to Jenny.

"It's a boy," he teased. "Are you keeping something from us?"

"Oh dad," she said as she took the phone from him. Then into the phone she said, "Hello."

"Hi Jenny, this is Randy Akers. I am in your Art Class," said the shaky voice on the other end. "I sit over by the windows."

"I remember you," Jenny said. "What can I do for you?"

Randy was a junior. He was a tall quiet guy and wasn't bad looking. Jenny thought he might be shy since he never talked to anyone in class.

"This Friday is our first football game and I was hoping maybe you would want to go with me," Randy had talked so fast that Jenny had to stop and think of what he had just said.

"Friday? Football?" She repeated while looking over to her parents.

"Will you go with me?" Randy asked again still somewhat out of breath from asking the first question.

"Sure, I'd like that," Jenny said as Bob nodded his approval.

They made plans that Randy's mom would drive and they would pick Jenny up around 7:00. Randy liked to get there early to get a good seat and visit with his friends before the game. He also wanted to show off a little with Jenny as his date, but he didn't tell her that.

When Jenny got to school on Thursday morning, Randy was waiting at her locker.

"Hi," he said as he stood watching her every move.

"Hi," Jenny replied.

Jenny was fumbling with her lock and couldn't get it open. This was the first time that it didn't open on the first try. She tried again and it still didn't open. She was getting frustrated and couldn't figure it out. Heather walked up next to Jenny and seeing Randy standing there, whispered in her ear, "It always helps if you start with the right locker."

Jenny looked up and noticed the number on the locker. She had been trying to get into Heather's locker. Jenny moved over in front of her own locker, blushed and smiled as she opened it with no problems. Heather just smiled back at Jenny knowing how stupid she must feel at this moment. Randy was cool about the ordeal and never said anything about it. Jenny was hoping that everyone would just forget it. Randy said he would see Jenny in Art Class as the two of them parted to go to their classes.

In Art Class Randy had made arrangements with Mrs. Schneider and moved his seat and supplies over next to Jenny. He didn't talk to her with the exception of a hello and got right down to the business at hand. Jenny looked over at his pad and he was pretty good. The shading and texture of the still life on his paper made the bottle and fruit look as if they were standing on his tablet. Jenny looked at hers and wanted to hide it.

After school Randy hurried over to Jenny's locker to walk her out to the buses. When Jenny told him that she always walked home, he was disappointed. He was hoping to talk to her while they rode the bus, but he promised he would see her tomorrow at school and couldn't wait for their date.

After school on Friday Jenny rushed home and picked out what she wanted to wear to the football game. She opted for a pair of nice jeans and a school sweatshirt. The doorbell rang promptly at 7:00 and Bob went to answer. Randy stood there like a nervous cat in a room full of rocking chairs. Bob invited him in and said that Jenny would be right down. After one more quick glance in the mirror, Jenny came bouncing down the stairs.

Randy turned to Bob and said, "I'll have her home early, Mr. Madison."

"You do that son," Bob said with a grin. He couldn't believe how different things were here compared to Chicago. He remembered fathers telling him that boys came for their daughters and simply honked the horn. Bob was glad that they had moved here where the boys still had some respect for the girls. He peeked out the front window with Barbara and saw Randy open the back door of the car for Jenny. Once she was in he slid in next to her.

"How sweet," Barbara said.

"How polite," Bob replied as they walked away from the window.

Randy's mom parked the car and they all walked into the stadium together. But once inside Mrs. Akers went off on her own while Randy and Jenny walked over to the cheering section reserved for students. Jenny felt like everyone was looking at her and checking out the guy she was with. Randy motioned to a section of the stands and started climbing the stairs. He turned around and took Jenny's hand as if to help her up the stairs which Jenny felt was more out of respect than being nice. Randy moved into the middle of the row and sat down and Jenny sat next to him. Randy waved to some of his friends and they waved back and Jenny waved to Tamara and Heather and they waved back to her, too. Oh how she wished they would come up and sit with them. When Todd waved to Jenny, she did not return the gesture and Randy figured the Todd must have been waving at him so he waved back at Todd.

Jenny stood as they played the National Anthem and the school song. They sat down right after the first kick off and Jenny thought maybe Randy might say something to her about the game or something ~ anything! After the first quarter Jenny excused herself when she saw Tamara. She almost fell out of the stands trying to catch up to her.

"How's it going?" Tamara asked when Jenny caught up with her.

"Tam, he doesn't talk! I have no idea what's on his mind," Jenny cried.

"Surely you've talked about something?"

"Nope, not a word. He told my dad that he would have me home early. I am so ready to go now. I am so bored," Jenny acted as though she was going to faint.

Tamara grinned at her. "I'll get Heather and we'll come sit by you."

"Oh would you?" Jenny asked grabbing Tamara by the arm. "Thank you so much. I really mean that, too. I'll owe you a big one."

The two girls took their time walking back to the stands and they were about back to where Tamara and Heather were sitting when the buzzer sounded ending the first half. Almost immediately waves of people moved out of the bleachers and headed toward the restrooms and snack bar. Randy stopped where Jenny and Tamara were standing waiting to get back to their seats.

"You want a Pepsi?" Randy asked Jenny.

"Sure, thanks," Jenny said. "I'll wait for you back at our seats."

Randy left without saying a word and went to the snack bar while Jenny, Tamara and Heather went back to where Randy and Jenny had been sitting. Randy didn't get back until after the second half had started. When he handed Jenny the Pepsi he bought for her he also offered her some popcorn. Jenny thanked him for the soda, shook her head at the offer of the popcorn, and took a sip of her Pepsi.

Randy seemed more interested in the game than he did in Jenny, so she talked to the two girls beside her. Heather giggled a couple of times at remarks Tamara made about how talkative Randy was and Jenny poked Tamara in the ribs a couple times and all three girls cracked up. It seems Randy hadn't noticed their laughter or occasional glances over at him.

Finally the game was over and the Titans won by a field goal. Randy was happy about that and Jenny said she was happy, too, even though she really didn't care. Walking toward the gate Randy was a couple steps ahead of Jenny so she just walked out with Heather and Tamara. When she saw Mrs. Akers at the gate, she said good-bye to her friends and walked over to Randy and his mom.

Randy opened the car door again for Jenny like a perfect gentleman and his mom was taking about how great the game was and wanted to know if they had a good time. She also wanted to know if they wanted to go for sodas at the Cardinal Inn. Jenny lied when she said that she enjoyed herself, but declined the offer of the soda. When they pulled up in front of the Madison's house, Randy got out and walked her to the front door and Jenny thanked him and ran into the house before he could do or say anything.

When Barbara and Bob asked how she enjoyed her date, Jenny simply laughed and told them how terrible it was. She said she had doubts whether Randy ever asks her out again. Bob teased her and said it is the quiet ones that she should watch out for. Jenny threw a magazine at her dad and ran upstairs laughing.

Chapter Fourteen

Saturday morning the Madison family loaded into the car and headed out to the farm. Grammy and Poppy had called and said that they missed seeing them. Grammy was going to can tomatoes and wanted some help, too. Jenny and Barbara said they would come out and help her, and John always jumped at the chance to go out to be with Poppy. Bob knew there was always something that needed to be done on the farm.

Duke barked and wagged his tail when he saw the car round the curve in the lane. John ran straight down to the barn with the dog trailing behind him. The rest of the family went into the house and saw Grammy sitting at the table peeling tomatoes. There were baskets of jars to be washed so Barbara started working on them. When Jenny asked what she could do, Grammy said that she and her father needed to go to the cellar and get more jars. She figured she would need about 50 quarts and 40 pints since she had lots of tomatoes going to waste if she didn't get them processed today.

"Dad! Mom! Grammy!" It was John screaming as he was running toward the house. He got to the back door, huffing and puffing barely able to speak.

"What is it?" Bob asked.

"Poppy," John said breathlessly. "Poppy's hurt!"

Bob burst out the back door and ran toward the barn. Jenny and Barbara were at his heels but Grammy was quite a ways behind them. John finally caught his breath and called 911 and told the operator that they needed an ambulance and gave directions to the farm. The operator told John to stay on the line with her so he stayed in the house.

Bob rounded the corner of the barn and saw Poppy lying under an overturned tractor. He quickly bent down to check his father's condition. Poppy was conscious.

"My legs are pinned," Poppy groaned.

Grammy came around the barn and started screaming when she saw the upturned tractor. Barbara ran over to her, held her up and tried to calm her telling her that he was conscious and talking to Bob. Bob handed Jenny his cell phone and told her to call 911 but when she did, she was informed that they had already dispatched an ambulance to the farm. Bob then told her to call the Kramers and ask George and Todd to come over right away.

It seemed just minutes when they heard George's truck pull around the barn and he, Todd and Terry jumped out of the truck. Margie stayed with Barbara and Grammy and tried to calm her.

"He'll be all right," Margie said. "The men will get him out. Let's go back to the house now and let them work."

Grammy protested but allowed Barbara and Margie to lead her back to the house. Barbara took the car to the end of the lane to signal the ambulance and the sheriff so they would not miss the turn into the lane. She was only there for a few minutes when the ambulance pulled up and turned up the lane.

Meanwhile back at the barn George had positioned a pipe under the tractor and propped something under the pipe for leverage. He and Todd tried to lift the tractor up enough for Bob to pull Poppy out but the two men couldn't do it. Jenny suggested that she and Terry could pull Poppy out if Bob wanted to help George and Todd. The three men pushed with all their weight on the pipe and the tractor moved just a little but it was enough that Jenny and Terry could slide Poppy out. They had to pull with all their might and as fast as they could. The three men were grunting and straining and Bob hollered that they couldn't hold it for much longer. Jenny yelled at them when Poppy was free and they released the pipe and the tractor fell back down.

Poppy was moaning and said his legs were hurting real bad. Bob looked at the legs but saw no blood. He hoped that was a good sign. Poppy's face was getting very pale and his flesh felt very cold and sweaty. Todd ran into the barn and grabbed an old horse blanket and laid it over Poppy.

"He's probably going into shock," Todd said. "Keep him warm."

When Jenny heard the wale of the sirens come up the lane, she comforted Poppy, telling him that help was there. The ambulance came all the way down to the barn and the paramedics rushed over to Poppy and immediately went to work on him, inserting an IV and immobilizing his legs. They laid him on a stretcher, put him into the ambulance and were off down the lane heading for the hospital in no time at all.

Grammy ran out of the house when she saw the ambulance flash by the house. She wanted to ride along with Poppy but Bob said he would take her to the hospital. Margie came out with Barbara and they climbed into the car with Grammy and Bob. John was standing next to Jenny with tears in his eyes holding on to her. He wanted to go to the hospital and be there for Poppy and so did Jenny. George told them to climb into the truck and he would take them. Jenny didn't even notice that she was sitting close to Todd at that time because she was just worried about Poppy.

When Todd, Terry, George, Jenny and John walked into the emergency room they saw Barbara and Margie and were told that Bob and Grammy were in with Poppy. Barbara said that Poppy wasn't doing very well and the doctor hadn't said much about his condition yet, but they knew that both legs were broken. John burst into tears and buried his face against his mother. Barbara hugged him and assured him that Poppy would be all right but John continued to cry uncontrollably.

The sheriff had also come to the hospital to find out how Poppy had gotten hurt and to see how he was doing.

Between sobs John said, "It's my fault. It's all my fault."

Barbara asked John what he meant by that statement and John told her and the sheriff that he and Duke had run down to the barn and didn't see Poppy on the tractor. They both ran out in front of him and Poppy had to slam on the brake to keep from hitting him or the dog and the tractor jerked and flipped over landing on Poppy. John was sobbing inconsolably now. Barbara didn't know what to say or do when she heard John's story.

George leaned down to talk to John. "It was an accident, John. It could have happened anytime, anywhere. Just be glad that you were there to get help right away. You are a hero to have saved your grandpa."

John shook his head and quieted down a little but he still leaned his head against his mom with tears streaming down his face. Todd walked over and patted John on his shoulder as Jenny sat down and put her arm around him, too. The sheriff told them that he would just rule this as a farm accident, hoped that Poppy would be all right and then he left. All they could do now was to wait until the doctor finished the examination and pray.

Bob and Grammy came into the waiting room and sat down next to the rest of the group. Bob said that they were going to take Poppy to surgery to set his legs. The doctor said that one of Poppy's legs was seriously injured, but the other one had a simple fracture of the femur. None of Poppy's major organs had been affected in the accident which was very good news to the family. Since the doctor said that the surgery would take a few hours, Bob suggested that they all go to their house to have supper and take a break. Again Grammy protested but was outnumbered and they all went to the Madison's house.

Once at the house Grammy said she would rather lie down than eat so Jenny took her up to her room and pulled a quilt over Grammy's shoulders. Grammy began to cry softly. It broke Jenny's heart. She asked Grammy if she could sit with her, but Grammy had already fallen asleep from exhaustion.

Jenny went back downstairs to help Margie set the table while Barbara and Bob set out plates of cold cuts, cheese and bread. John grabbed a bag of chips from the pantry and poured them into a bowl. After a prayer blessing the food and asking for blessings for Poppy, everyone ate in silence. When Barbara went up to check on Grammy she was still asleep. Jenny suggested that Grammy stay with them while Poppy is in the hospital and Barbara quickly agreed.

The women had just finished cleaning up the kitchen when the phone rang and Bob answered it. It was the hospital with a report on Poppy and the room was totally quiet until Bob thanked the person and said good-bye.

He turned to everyone and said, "Dad came through surgery just fine. He is in recovery and should wake up in about a half an hour. They set his one leg, but he will have to go back for more surgery again to fix the other leg."

Barbara immediately went upstairs to wake up Grammy. She was so relieved to hear the news and got up to leave for the hospital. Margie and Barbara decided that Barbara would ride to the farm with them and get some of Grammy's things together and drive the Buick back home. Grammy told her what she needed and where to find the keys to the car. She also reminded Barbara to bring her purse, too.

Jenny and John sat in the waiting room while Bob went in to see his father and talk to the doctor. The doctor explained more about Poppy's condition than he had said on the phone. The left leg had a simple fracture and a cast was put on the leg. The right leg, however, had severe damage and Poppy would need another operation to repair more of the damage. The doctor wants to wait and see how well Poppy gets over the trauma before doing any more major surgery. He explained that a rod would have to be inserted in Poppy's leg to replace the crushed bone but he felt that Poppy would be ready to get back in the fields for spring plowing.

Bob thanked the doctor and went in to sit with his dad and mom. Poppy was still sleeping but the nurse said that his vital signs were very good. Bob told Grammy what the doctor had said and Grammy nodded as she laid her head down on Poppy's arm. They would just have to wait until he wakes up now.

Chapter Fifteen

Two days after the accident Poppy had the second surgery to repair his leg. The entire family was sitting in the waiting room when the doctor came in to tell them the news.

"He's a trooper," the doctor reported. "He did just fine. We replaced the crushed bone with a stainless steel rod and secured it with pins. In a week or so, we will start his physical therapy. He will be transferred to long term care in a couple of days and I imagine he should be able to go home in a few weeks. It just depends on how well he does in physical therapy."

Bob and Grammy thanked the doctor and went in to sit with Poppy. He was just coming around when they walked in. Grammy walked over and kissed him on the forehead. He smiled. Bob told Poppy what the doctor had said and Poppy said that he would be home in a few days instead of a few weeks.

"Don't you rush things, old man," Grammy warned. "I want you around for a long time and I don't want to have to wait on you hand and foot. You just give it plenty of time to heal. Then I just might take you home with me."

Bob had to grin because he knew Grammy would take care of Poppy no matter what shape he was in. She worshipped that old man and would do anything for him.

The nurse came in and asked Bob and Grammy to leave because they were going to take Poppy back to his room. Grammy stepped back and waited right there until they guided the bed down the hall. She even slipped onto the elevator with Poppy and the orderlies. The rest of the family had to wait for the next elevator before they could go up to Poppy's room.

Grammy stayed in town while Poppy was in the hospital and spent most of each day with him. On the fourth day after surgery Grammy walked into Poppy's room and he wasn't there. Grammy quickly went to the nurse's station and was informed that Poppy was down in Physical Therapy and that he would be back in a couple of hours.

Grammy walked down to see how Poppy was doing and found him lying on a table with a therapist lifting his leg and then bending it at the knee. She was told that he would be trained to use a walker this afternoon. Poppy grumbled that he could walk without any help. The therapist smiled at him and told him that he should behave himself. Grammy snuck a quick kiss and told Poppy to mind the therapist and that she would be back later this evening after his therapy sessions.

Back at the house Grammy told Barbara that she wanted to go home and check on the house to see if everything was all right. She also said that Poppy wanted his own robe and pajamas and she wanted to get a few of her own things, too. When Barbara said that she would drive Grammy out to the farm, John and Jenny jumped at the chance to go, too.

Duke welcomed them when they pulled into the yard and John slowly walked down to the barn to check on the animals. Grammy, Jenny and Barbara walked into the house. When they walked into the kitchen all the jars and tomatoes were gone and the kitchen was spotless.

"What on earth!" Grammy exclaimed. "Did you do this?"

"Not me," Barbara said as Jenny just shook her head.

Grammy walked into the pantry and saw that there were new jars of canned tomatoes, tomato juice and home made ketchup on the shelves. She estimated that there were probably over 100 quarts of tomatoes and at least 50 pints and she couldn't even count all the jars of juices and ketchup. Granny stormed out of the pantry, through the kitchen and out the back door. Once at the garden, Grammy noticed that all the tomatoes were gone and there were few cucumbers left on the vines. Grammy had no idea who would have done such a thing. When she turned around, she noticed that the row of carrots was now just a row of loosened dirt. She stood there staring with her hands on her hips.

She quickly spun around and headed toward the house but instead of going into the house she lifted the cellar door and went down the stairs into the cellar. When she pulled on the light she noticed that her shelves were full. Someone had come in and canned all the carrots and there were new jars of dill pickles, sweet pickles, bread and butter pickles, and lime pickles. She even saw that there were about ten quarts of home made sauerkraut on the shelf.

As Grammy was climbing the cellar steps, she saw Margie walking in the back door with a basket full of jars.

"So it was you!" she exclaimed.

"I didn't do it all," Margie confessed. "Several of the ladies from church came over when they heard about Hank's accident. They all pitched in to help out their neighbors in a time of need. You've done it for us, Ruth."

Grammy choked back some tears and said, "Thank you, Margie. And please tell everyone who was involved in helping that this means so much to us. I will never be able to repay all of you. Thank you so much."

"As Margie set the basket of freshly canned sweet corn on the table, she asked, "Well, where do you want this?"

"I didn't plant any sweet corn this year," Grammy said. "That must belong to someone else."

"Sorry about that," Margie said with a grin. "This corn just happened to find its way into your canning jars. So I guess you are stuck with it."

Grammy was so overcome with gratitude that she couldn't speak so she motioned for Margie to put the corn into the pantry. There were 14 quarts and 6 pints of sweet corn that she and Hank would sure love this winter.

Grammy went up to her bedroom and packed a small suitcase of clothes for both her and Poppy. She straightened the wrinkles on the bed and came on down to the kitchen. When she took a quick tour of the house to see if anything needed to be done she noticed the entire house had been dusted and the vacuum cleaner had been run over the carpets. She felt so blessed to have such good neighbors. When John came up to the house he reported that the tractor had been turned upright and put in the shed. All the animals had been taken care of and the cows had been turned out to pasture down in the woods and the water tanks were all full of fresh clean water. The sheep were in their small pasture and their mangers were full of fresh hay. John said he checked the hen house but didn't find even one egg so someone must have been taking care of the chickens, too.

Margie said that the eggs had been collected every day and passed around to the neighbors that have been helping. Grammy agreed that was good so they wouldn't go to waste. Margie did say she put a couple dozen in Barbara's car and that Grammy could expect some home made noodles soon, too. Satisfied that everything was all right at the farm, Grammy was ready to go back to town. Jenny and John were amazed that people were so friendly and helpful here and were glad that they had moved here.

When Grammy and Bob walked into Poppy's room that evening he was sitting in the chair next to the bed. His legs were up on a stool and he was eating the last few bites of his supper. He said that he felt tired but other than that he felt pretty good. Physical therapy had been pretty rough on him but the therapist said that he was doing quite well and way ahead of schedule. Grammy told Bob and Poppy all about what the neighbors had done and were continuing to do out at the farm. She was so impressed with all the work that was being done for them,

"Why are you so surprised, Ruth?" Poppy asked. "You and I have helped others when they were down on their luck."

Grammy shook her head as she remembered when Luella Carson was in the hospital after having her last baby. Several of the women went over to help Don with the other six. Then there was the time when Joe Mast broke his leg and was laid up for a long while. Poppy reminded her about the time when Virgil died in the truck accident and everyone went over to his farm with combines and trucks to harvest his crops.

"There were over 100 people there," Grammy remembered. "Us women fixed lunch for the guys. We had everything imaginable to eat. I'll never forget seeing those combines side by side in the field. It was a magnificent sight that I'll never forget."

Poppy agreed and then added, "And to think that we got over 450 acres of crops out in one day. That's when folks pull together to help."

Bob had never heard that story but knew that farmers always helped each other when they could. But he never knew that over a hundred people from all over the county took the time and used their own equipment and gas to help Virgil's family. He was blown away by the story. Grammy promised to show him the pictures and the video from the TV news as well as the newspaper articles once they got back home.

"Yup," Poppy reminisced, "We were on television ~ all three stations, too."

A nurse came in then and helped Poppy into bed and he was putting weight on the leg that wasn't hurt too badly and said that it didn't hurt much. Once he was in bed and comfortable, the nurse left the room. Very shortly, a different nurse came in to take Poppy's vital signs. Bob and Grammy were real quiet while she checked his blood pressure and took his temperature.

"Well," Grammy said questioning for the results.

"Oh Hank is doing just fine," the nurse said. "He is in very good shape for a man of his age."

"What do you mean by that?" Poppy teased in a gruff voice.

"Well, Hank, you aren't a spring chicken anymore," the nurse teased back. She patted him on the arm and walked out of the room.

"According to the doctor you might get sprung in a week or so. How does that sound?" Bob said.

"I'm ready to go now," Poppy said and he was serious.

Bob suggested that Poppy and Grammy stay in town with them for a while since Poppy would still have to go to PT every day for quite a while. He said they could fix up the parlor for him and Grammy so Poppy wouldn't have to climb stairs. Poppy didn't think too much of the idea but as usual Grammy overruled him and he accepted the offer.

When Bob and Grammy got home and told Barbara about Bob's offer she said that she would have it no other way and expected them to stay as long as they needed and wanted. The next day Barbara called around to find a hospital bed to set up in the parlor for Poppy and they brought down another bed for Grammy. She and Jenny replaced the lace curtains on the front and side windows with heavier draperies so they would have a little more privacy. John brought in a television and radio so Poppy wouldn't get bored during his recovery. By the time Poppy was ready to be released, the room looked very welcoming and comfortable.

Exactly two weeks after the accident Poppy was released from the hospital. The doctor made him promise to behave himself and not try to do any work until he said it was all right. Grammy promised she would see to it that Poppy would be good and she wouldn't let him do anything he shouldn't. When Poppy walked into the parlor he was very impressed with everything the family did to make him comfortable during his recovery.

"If I can't be in my own bed in my own house," Poppy said, "I would choose to stay right here." The family all smiled at the best compliment Poppy could muster for them.

Chapter Sixteen

Jenny was so glad that Randy moved his seat back over under the window in Art Class since he was such a boring guy. Besides, she had her eye on another boy that was in her Art Class. She would have to find out his name and more about him very soon. Today they were doing another still life and each student had to choose some thing in the classroom to sketch. Jenny decided to sketch the books and backpack lying on the floor next to the guy that she was interested in. After asking permission, she moved over closer to him so she could see better. She began working but every now and then she would check him out. He looked up from his work and noticed Jenny staring a few times.

"What's your problem?" He asked noticing Jenny staring at him.

"Oh, sorry," Jenny said. "I'm just sketching your backpack and books here on the floor."

The boy got up and walked over to look at Jenny's drawing.

"Hey that's not too bad," he said. "I'm trying to draw this box of pencils in front of me."

Jenny looked at his sketch and it was pretty bad. It looked like an abstract and she had to choke back a giggle, but she told him it was nice.

"So what's your name? It says here JRM," the boy said.

"Jennifer Ruth Madison, but my friends call me Jenny," she said.

Extending his hand, he said, "Mark Gregory Wilson at your service. My friends call me Mark."

"Nice to meet you, Mark," Jenny said grinning from ear to ear.

They both went back to their work but continued chatting softly about their likes and dislikes. Jenny learned that Mark played football and ran track. He lived across town, had just gotten his driver's license this summer and his dad bought him a Mustang for passing the first time. Jenny was impressed. When the bell rang to end the class Jenny picked up her books and walked out into the hall. Mark caught up with her and asked what her next class was. When Jenny said that she had Computer Class, Mark was surprised because he also had that class and had never seen her in there before. Jenny had not seen Mark either, but then Todd was in there, too.

When they walked into the classroom, Mark sat in the seat next to Jenny. Todd had sat there a few times, but now Jenny was glad it was Mark. When Todd walked in Jenny leaned over to Mark and giggled loud enough for Todd to hear. She had told Mark that she really liked this class before she giggled, so Mark figured it was a sarcastic remark so he chuckled a little, too. Todd looked over at them and frowned.

After class Mark walked with Jenny as far as he could before going into his next class. Jenny met Tamara at lunch and told her she was interested in Mark. Tamara said she didn't know anything about him except that he was on the football team and he was very good looking. Although Todd was sitting across the cafeteria with his girlfriend, he kept looking over at Jenny and frowning.

"Who are you looking at, Todd?" Lori asked him.

"Oh just my sister and her friend," Todd said as he took a bite out of his sandwich.

"Oh you mean that Jenny girl?" Lori said with disgust.

"Yeah, Why? Do you know something about her?" Todd's interest was primed now.

"Well, yeah," Lori started as if Todd should already know what she was going to say. "I've heard from a lot of people that the big city girl is real easy."

"That's not true!" Todd roared at her.

"Well I heard that even that geek Randy scored with her. All the guys are after her. She'll sleep with anything in pants."

"Shut up, Lori! Don't talk about her like that. It's not true!" Todd was getting very angry now.

"Why do care, Todd?" Lori asked.

Thinking for a just second Todd replied, "Well, she hangs around with my sister. I don't want Tam to get a reputation. Besides, we're neighbors of her grandparents."

"I think it is more than that," Lori said. She was getting angry now, too. "I think you are sweet on her. Tell me, Todd Kramer. Is that it?" Lori was standing now.

"You're nuts, Lori," Todd said as he stood up, picked up his tray and walked out.

"Wow," Tamara said. "Looks like Todd and Lori just had a fight.

Jenny forgot about Mark for a moment. "Really?" She asked.

"I wonder what that was all about. I'll have to ask him tonight," Tamara said as she went back to her lunch.

Jenny really liked Todd and she hoped that she would have a chance at getting a real date with him if he and Lori would break up. Homecoming is just a couple of weeks away and she really wished he would ask her to go with him even if it were just as friends. Mark was nice but he would be playing in the game and she really would rather go with Todd. Was their fight bad enough that they were breaking up? So many thought were going through Jenny's mind right now.

On the way home Tamara could tell that Todd was in a bad mood but she slipped in the seat across from him on the bus.

"What's the matter, Todd?" She asked him.

"Not now, Tam." He snapped back.

Tamara knew that she had better back off as she had seen Todd angry and upset before and she knew that he was really hot. So she just let him alone on the bus. Once they got off the bus and were walking up the lane toward their house, Todd told Tamara what Lori had said about Jenny.

"That's not true at all!" Tamara exclaimed. "I know Jenny is still a virgin. As a matter of fact, Randy was the first guy she ever went out with."

"You sure, Tam?" Todd asked.

"Of course, I am, Todd. Jenny and I talk about every thing." Then Tamara repeated, "Every thing!"

"Why would Lori say things like that if they weren't true?" Todd asked shaking his head in disbelief.

"She's jealous," Tamara said manner of factly.

"Of what?" Todd yelled. "She's the only girl I am dating or have ever dated. What's her problem?"

"Wake up, Todd! She knows that you and Jen are friends," Tamara said. "Maybe she thinks there's more to your relationship than just friendship."

Tamara just shrugged her shoulders. Todd felt that Lori was getting too possessive and he should giver her something to be jealous about. But, he really didn't want to lose her. But, she lied to him. But, she is very pretty and sexy looking. But, she hurt the reputation of one of his friends. Todd was confusing himself. He decided that he would have to pray on this for a while and he never really thought about Jenny as a girlfriend but just as a good friend. He'd have to pray about that, too.

The next day at school Jenny and Tamara were walking to class when they saw Todd walking alone and Lori was no where to be seen. When Jenny asked Tamara if they had broken up, Tamara said that she thought so but wasn't sure if it was final. She then told Jenny what Lori had told Todd at lunch yesterday and Jenny was shocked. She stopped and leaned against a row of lockers. Tears swelled up in her eyes. Tamara tried to comfort her by telling her that Todd stood up for her.

"Listen, Jen. I told Todd that Lori just said that because she is jealous. She never heard any of that from anyone. She had to think of something to make Todd stop looking over at you. He likes you, Jen. You know that."

"Like a sister," Jenny said through her tears.

"Oh, I think it is more than that. He just doesn't know it yet. Just wait and see."

Jenny wiped her tears and went into class. She wasn't paying much attention to Mr. Hill but she looked busy. She wanted to talk to Todd, but wasn't sure what to say to him. She finally decided to wait and see if he comes to her first. She began to pay attention just in time to hear the homework assignment for the class.

Todd didn't pay much attention to her in Spanish class but Mrs. DelCastillo ran a pretty tight ship and there was never much chance for talking there. In Art class Mark took her mind off of Todd almost immediately.

"Hey, Jenny," Mark said. "Looking good today, girl."

"Thanks, Mark," Jenny said as she sat down next to him. She was wearing one of her thrift store jean skirts and a sleeveless pink sweater.

"Maybe, I'll sketch you today," Mark said.

Jenny just giggled not realizing Mark was flirting with her.

When Art class ended and they had to go to Computer class Mark put his arm around Jenny's waist and walked her over to class. Jenny didn't say anything one way or the other about that so Mark figured it was OK with her. When they were getting ready to sit down, he slid his hand down to feel her bottom. Again Jenny didn't say anything one way or the other.

During lunch Jenny set her tray down across from Tamara. She was still somewhat upset at the rumor Lori was trying to start and hoped she hadn't told anyone else. They saw Lori sitting at her regular spot but Todd was nowhere to be found. Tamara figured he must be outside with his friends just to avoid Lori. No sooner had she said that to Jenny when Todd set his tray down next to Tamara and sat down at their table.

"Hi girls," he said.

"Hi Todd," they both said in unison. Then Tamara added, "What's up? Did you decide to break it off with Lori?"

"Yeah," Todd said, somewhat distraught. "I told her I couldn't go with someone who would lie and slander another person. She called me a few choice names and gave me back my class ring." He showed them that he had his ring on his finger.

"Good for you brother," Tamara said as she patted him on the back.

"I'm just hoping she doesn't spread those lies around school. That would really make me mad." Todd pounded his fist on the table.

Jenny sat quietly hoping the same thing. How could she prove otherwise if Lori started telling lies? At least Todd and Tamara knew her well enough to know better than to believe anything like that. She knew that she would be all right.

The next day in Art Class Mark asked her if she wanted to go to a movie on Saturday night.

"I have a football game on Friday night, but I sure would like to take you to a movie on Saturday. I hear there is a good show playing in Keokuk. Robin Williams is in it," He said.

"Are you talking about the RV?" Jenny asked.

"Yeah that's it," Mark said. "I heard it is supposed to be really funny."

"So did I," Jenny said. "I'll have to check with my parents before I can accept. They haven't let me go out on car dates yet."

"Oh, OK," Mark said. "I'll call you tonight when I get home from football practice."

"I'll be home waiting," Jenny said. She was so excited that Mark had asked her out. He seemed like such a nice guy and he was smart, good looking and an athlete, too.

Barbara and Bob wanted all the information about Mark. Jenny told them that he seemed to be a very nice guy. His dad owned the chain of Wilson Grocery Stores in the area including the store in Hamilton; and his mom was a teacher at Hamilton Junior High. They lived out near the Country Club in a real nice house. Mark was a senior but was taking Junior Computer and Art Classes. He was a linebacker on the football team and was heading for Western Illinois University on a football scholarship next year. Bob finally agreed with the stipulation that they meet him before he takes Jenny out. Jenny agreed and when she told Mark, he also agreed to meet Bob and Barbara the night of the date.

Saturday night Mark rang the doorbell at the Madison home at 6:30. Bob answered and invited Mark in. Barbara had pulled the doors of the parlor closed as she stepped into the foyer and invited Mark to come into the living room. Mark seemed very confident and comfortable with the adults.

"I saw where you beat Lincoln last night," Bob said.

"Yes, sir," Mark replied. "It was a tough game, too. They just didn't want to give up."

"So I heard," Bob said. "Did it go into overtime?"

"No sir," Mark replied. "They tried a field goal at the end which would have tied the game but it went just right of the goal post."

"Too bad for them," Bob said as Jenny walked into the room.

Mark stood up when she walked over to him. He promised Bob and Barbara that he would have Jenny home early. The movie would be over around 9:30 and then he wanted to take her for pizza. Barbara shook her head in approval when Bob said that Jenny had to be home by 11:00. Mark agreed to the time as Jenny rolled her eyes.

Mark pulled away from the curb very carefully but once he rounded the corner, he sped up a little. This was the first time that Jenny had gone across the Mississippi River. She had never been to Keokuk before and it seemed such a big city when looking at it from the Illinois side.

They arrived at the cinema with enough time to buy popcorn and drinks. They found seats near the back and got comfortable. Jenny was really interested in the movie and didn't notice at first that Mark had put his arm around her and pulled her closer to him. She liked the feeling of a guy holding her and snuggled a little closer to him but didn't want to give him any ideas. When he put his hand on her leg she would reach down and grab the bucket of popcorn, offer him some and set the tub on her lap.

"That was a super movie," Jenny said once they were in the car. "Thank you so much for taking me. Did you like it?"

"It was OK," Mark replied. "Not quite what I expected, though."

Mark said he knew a quaint little pizza place on the outskirts of town that had really good hand tossed pizza that he wanted to take her to. They had driven all the way through town and were out in the country when Todd turned down a blacktop road. The road was dark and there were no businesses or houses anywhere near, but they were heading back toward the river so maybe they were going toward the pier. Jenny had heard about some restaurants along the river.

They had gone down the blacktop about two or three miles when Mark turned off onto a gravel road. He pulled off the road once they had gone about 500 feet from the blacktop. Now Jenny was real nervous. She didn't like this at all.

"What's up?" Jenny asked. She was really scared now.

"I am," Mark said as he placed Jenny's hand on his crotch.

Jenny quickly pulled her hand away and told Mark to leave her alone.

"Come on, Jen. I know you want it as much as I do," Mark said as he leaned over and started kissing Jenny.

"Stop it!" She screamed. He was so strong that she couldn't push him away from her. "Stop it, Mark!" She cried out again.

"I've heard all about you. Now don't play hard to get with me," Mark said.

He was trying to get under Jenny's shirt and bra. She kept squirming and trying to push him off of her. He was so strong. She started to cry. She was trying so hard to figure how to get out of this predicament.

"Come on slut; give me what I want so I can get you home to Daddy before your curfew." Mark was so rough. He ripped her shirt and popped the hooks on her bra. Mark had his hands inside her jeans and was pulling at her panties and she kept kicking and screaming at him. He had unbuckled his pants and started to pull them down. Jenny was petrified now. He was holding one of Jenny's wrists against the dashboard and the other hand was free and she kept hitting and scratching him. Mark finally got his pants down and was ready to get into position. Jenny wanted to get away from him, but she had no clue what to do but to pray.

Jenny knew no one would hear her scream this far off the main road. So she started to pray.

"Dear Lord, Forgive him for he knows not what he is doing," she said while struggling.

"Oh yes I do. And I know how to do it quite well," Mark said as he smirked at her. "Prayers aren't going to save you."

"Our father, who art in Heaven..," Jenny continued the Lord's Prayer. When she was finished she simply said, "Lord give me strength."

She kept kicking and swinging at him and then Jenny grabbed Mark's manhood and squeezed her fingernails deep into it.

Mark jumped back off of her screaming in pain and at her. He punched her so hard in the face that she hit her head on the windshield. When Jenny saw that she had drawn blood, she quickly opened the car door, pulled up her pants and ran as fast as she could across a field. Mark yelled at her and cursed her. He started the car and sped down the road kicking up rocks and dust.

Jenny lay down so Mark couldn't see her and watched as he turned the car around and came back toward her. She ducked down as low as she could in the newly harvested corn field. When the car stopped she stopped breathing.

Mark yelled from the car. "Try getting home to Daddy on time now." Mark sped away and Jenny could her him cursing.

When Jenny saw the tail lights disappear into the night she finally started breathing and stood up. Her shirt was torn and a button had fallen off. She had lost one of her shoes fighting Mark. How was she ever going to get home? She started walking down the gravel road and the rocks hurt her bare foot so she walked over in the grass. She paused when she got to the blacktop road. She could see lights down the road but they were so far away. Jenny knew what was in the other direction and knew that it was at least two or three miles before the highway. She pulled her shirt around her the best she could to protect her from the cool fall night air.

"Thank you God, Thank you God, Thank you God," Jenny kept saying over and over. Although it was the dark of the moon the sky above her twinkled like millions of diamonds on black satin and she had no trouble seeing where she needed to go. She headed toward the lights down the blacktop road.

She started humming to herself and then the words formed.

"Oh no, You never let go
Through the calm and through the storm
Oh no, You never let go

In every high and every low
Oh no, You never let go
Lord, You never let go of me"

She remembered singing this with Todd in her grandparents' woods. Where was Todd now? She really needed him now. All she could remember was the chorus to that song, but that was enough to get her to where she needed to be.

Jenny had been walking and singing for almost twenty minutes when she came to a short driveway in front of a large farm house. She turned into the driveway. There was a large dog that started barking from the side yard and she figured he couldn't hurt her any more than Mark had already. But, the dog just sat and watched her as she walked up to the house and knocked on the door.

A woman came to the door and opened it. When she saw Jenny, she yelled for her husband to come. Jenny stepped into the house and fainted into the arms of the woman.

When she came to, Jenny was lying on a sofa with a blanket draped over her and there were more people in the room. She recognized the lady that opened the door and figured the man next to her must be her husband. Behind them were two policemen, a couple of paramedics and another woman. She realized then that she must be in trouble.

"How do you feel?" asked the lady of the house.

"I'm not sure," Jenny said softly.

The woman in the back came forward and sat on the edge of the sofa next to Jenny.

"I'm Officer Graves," she said. "Can you tell us what happened to you tonight? Can you tell us your name?"

"Jenny," she said. "I'm Jenny Madison from Hamilton. I want my mom and daddy." Jenny started to cry.

Officer Graves took Jenny's phone number and had one of the other officers call Barbara and Bob. They said that they would meet Jenny at the hospital. The paramedics put Jenny on a stretcher and into a waiting ambulance then rushed her to Keokuk Hospital.

"Will my parents be there when I get there?" Jenny asked as she pulled the blanket up close to her neck?

"We'll probably beat them by a few minutes, but they're coming," one of the paramedics told her.

Jenny just closed her eyes during the ride and prayed that they would hurry because she was so scared.

Chapter Seventeen

    Officer Graves was standing next to Jenny while a doctor was examining her. She had a bruise coming on her cheek and around her left eye where Mark had hit her, and her eye was almost swollen shut. She had a small cut with some bruising above her right eye where she had hit the window. Her lip was cut and swollen; her wrist had finger mark bruises from him squeezing her against the dashboard. An X-ray showed that there were no fractures but she did have a sprain from the fighting. She also had several scratches and small bruises around her waist and breast from Mark ripping at her clothes. Jenny had told the doctor that Mark had not raped her but for the police record they had to examine her pelvic area. Jenny started to cry.
    "Can we please wait until my parents get here?" Jenny asked as she looked at Officer Graves pleadingly.
    "Wait for her parents," Officer Graves told the doctor sternly and without emotion and walked out of the room.
    "Thank you," Jenny called after the officer and then laid back on the gurney, pulling the sheet up high around her neck. She felt so dirty and alone. The nurse stayed with her and rubbed her shoulders as tears flowed freely down her cheeks.
    "It'll be all right, honey," she said. "The worse is over now and he won't hurt you anymore."
    Barbara and Bob rushed into the examination room and Jenny sat up and hugged her mother sobbing uncontrollably. Barbara was choking back tears, too, asking Jenny if she was all right. Bob asked Officer Graves what had happened and she told him that Jenny hadn't told them anything yet.

"I'm sorry, Daddy," Jenny said through her sobs.

"About what, baby," Bob asked as he walked over and hugged her.

Jenny just shook her head and grasped a hold of her mother tighter. Officer Graves asked Bob to step out into the hall with her. She needed to get more information about Jenny; and she hoped Jenny would tell her mom what had happened if they were alone. It worked.

After Jenny told Barbara every detail of the attack and how she had walked to the farmhouse, Barbara went to recount the events to the police. Bob went in to be with Jenny. He assured her that nothing was her fault and he was glad that she was all right.

When Barbara walked back into the examination room, the police photographer followed her. Barbara explained to Jenny why they needed the pictures and Bob slipped out. The photographer tried to make Jenny feel as comfortable as possible during the ordeal, but Jenny still felt so dirty. When the picture of her waist and breast were being taken, Jenny started to cry again. Barbara explained that in order to prosecute Mark for attacking Jenny, the police needed the pictures as evidence. She also told Jenny that she should not worry about anything because Mark was already in custody. Officer Graves said that they had already had police go to his house and arrest him for assault. She said that they found Jenny's shoe and ID in his car and that was enough evidence to arrest him. Jenny's statement and the pictures would be enough to put him away.

The doctor released Jenny and told her to rest for a few days and she would be fine. The nurse gave her some information regarding sexual assault and support groups available at the hospital. Jenny, Barbara and Bob thanked the doctors and nurses and then left the examination room. In the hall, Officer Graves explained to them that since the attack happened in Iowa, Mark would be prosecuted here. Jenny would probably be called to testify.

At the Keokuk police station Mark continually denied that he was with Jenny earlier in the evening. He said that he had gone to the movie with a friend and had gone right home afterward. One of the detectives recounted Jenny's story to Mark including the scratches on Mark's face. He still denied everything. The interrogating officer then mentioned the injuries that Jenny inflicted to Mark's privates.

"Man, you're crazy." Mark smirked. "I couldn't walk if something like that happened to me."

Mark's father was trying to get his son out of jail on bail, but the officer at the desk said that Mark would be arraigned on Monday morning. Mr. Wilson said that he would see to it that Mark would show up at court, but still the officer refused to release him. The medical officer called Mr. Wilson into the interrogation room while he examined Mark for any injuries on Mark's privates. Although Mark protested, the examiner had Mark drop his pants. There were blood stains on Mark's underwear and upon further examination they saw deep scratches and puncture wounds. The scratches were red and puffy. Mark told the examiner that it really hurt and asked if anything could be done for him.

"I think you've done quite enough already, young man," the examiner said. Then he handed Mark some salve and told him to put some on twice a day.

Mark knew he had been caught now. Mr. Wilson just shook his head as he started to walk out of the room.

"Dad," Mark pleaded. "You can't leave me here. Dad, please help me."

"There is nothing I can do, Mark. I'm sorry, son. Real sorry," Mr. Wilson said as he opened the door and walked out totally disappointed in his son.

The investigating officer took Mark through the booking process, finger printing him and taking his mug shot before leading him back to the cell block. Mark was locked in a cell by himself and was told that he would appear in court on Monday morning probably around 10:00 or 11:00. Mark would be in jail the rest of the weekend. He sat down on the hard cot and started to cry. He knew he would probably lose any chance for a football scholarship for this. Man, he would probably go to prison for this! He lay down on the cot and cried himself to sleep.

Once Jenny was back home and had taken a long hot shower she felt a little better. She read over some of the pamphlets that the nurse had given to her and learned that she was not to blame for the attack. Her attacker was trying to show his superiority over woman and the only way he could do that was through force. Jenny put the material down and went to brush her hair and noticed the bruising on her face was quite dark; and she definitely had a shiner. Her wrist was very sore but she had an ice pack that her mom made for her. With the pain pill that the doctor had given her, Jenny slept quite soundly that night.

Jenny didn't want to go to church with the family looking the way she did this morning and Barbara agreed that under the circumstances she could stay home. The family was going out to the country church because this was going to be Poppy's first time out in public since the accident. When they walked in to the church, everyone was so happy to see that Poppy was doing so well. He had graduated from using a walker to using crutches. He was getting around quite well. George and Todd stopped to talk to the family after church and when Todd asked about Jenny Barbara simply said that she didn't feel well today. When Bob gave Barbara a stern look, Todd felt that there was something more and he wanted to find out what was wrong with Jenny but decided to call her when he got home.

Poppy needed to know that everything was all right at the farm so he ordered Bob to take him home. Grammy kind of missed the place, too, so Bob turned the car toward the farm instead of the town. When they rounded the curve in the lane, the place sure looked good to Poppy and Grammy. After the women were out of the car, Poppy asked Bob to drive down around the barns. Everything looked great. All the animals were being taken care of and the last cutting of hay had been baled and put in the barn. Someone had even repaired the hole in the roof of the calf pen. Poppy was quite happy and wanted to go up to the house. John helped him into the back door and up the two steps into the kitchen.

Grammy had already made her inspection of the house and everything was spotless and in its place. She just couldn't believe how wonderful their neighbors had been. There were ten new bags of home made noodles; they had finished all the canning and they had kept the house spotlessly clean in their absence. She would have to have a party for everyone who helped. Bob and Barbara said they would be happy to help and John suggested they make it a Halloween Party. Poppy said that they would probably wait until Thanksgiving but Grammy said she wanted to wait until after the first of the year before Spring Planting Season. They decided they had plenty of time to plan something after Poppy got back on his feet.

Jenny rolled over in bed to answer the phone. On the third ring, she picked it up and said a sleepy, "Hello."

"Hi Jen, it's Todd. I saw your family at church but I missed you. How are you?"

"Oh Hi, Todd. I'm fine. How are you?" Jenny tried to sound chipper.

"You're mom said you weren't feeling well. What's wrong?" Todd asked with true sincerity.

"I think I might have the flu or something," Jenny lied.

"Is there anything I can do for you? Want me to bring over a magazine or some ice cream for you?" Todd asked as he really wanted to see Jenny. "Or I could just come over and baby sit." Todd started chuckling at his own joke.

"No, thanks, Todd, I think I might be contagious so you had better not come over today." Jenny felt so bad lying to Todd like this, but she would just die if he ever found out what had happened to her.

Todd accepted the explanation and told her to take care of herself and he would see her at school when she was better. Jenny thanked him for calling and said that she felt better just hearing his voice. After hanging up the phone Jenny decided to take a hot soaking bath in her parents' Jacuzzi.

The family returned home about 2:30 and they were all quite hungry. Bob said that he would run out and get something for lunch so Barbara and Grammy wouldn't have to cook. Instead they all decided that pizza sounded good so Bob called Pizza Hut and ordered a couple of family size Meat Lovers Pizzas to be delivered instead.

Barbara went upstairs to check on Jenny and was worried when she saw Jenny's empty bedroom. She was about to call Bob when she heard music coming from their bedroom. She opened the door to the master suite bathroom and smiled when she saw Jenny singing to the radio neck deep in bubbles.

"Feeling better?" Barbara asked.

"Well, this sure feels good, Mom," Jenny smiled and blew a handful of bubbles at her mother.

Barbara sat down next to Jenny on the edge of the tub and said they needed to talk. Jenny knew this was coming.

"Sure, Mom, what is it?"

"Jenny we are going to try to keep this out of the news. But, this is a small town and people may find out. We will be with you every step of the way." Barbara choked back a tear and continued. "Honey, you may be asked to testify against Mark. I hope that doesn't happen. But you know you have to see this through because he can't get away with hurting women like this."

"Mom, I read the pamphlets that I got from the hospital. I feel pretty good about everything now. I swear, Mom, I didn't come on to him. I tried to fight him off. I had to hurt him in order to get away."

"In a way it is a good thing that you did hurt him. That may be all the evidence that they need to prosecute him," Barbara got up to leave.

She turned back to Jenny and said, "I love you, baby girl. Just remember that."

"Love you, too, Mom," Jenny said as Barbara walked out and closed the door behind her.

Jenny got out of the tub, dried off and put on her pajamas and robe. She went downstairs to have pizza with the family. It was the first time that John had seen her injuries and he was quite surprised at the bruises and black eyes. Jenny could see the shock and pain in his eyes.

"You should see the other guy," she teased and let out a little giggle.

"I'm so sorry, Jenny," John said as he walked over and gave his big sister a gentle hug. He then pulled out a chair for Jenny to sit down and handed her a big piece of pizza. Barbara and Bob were very impressed at how John was treating his sister even though they always got along, but this was special.

Chapter Eighteen

On Monday Bob went over to Mark's arraignment. Naturally Mark pleaded not guilty to the charges and Bob was disappointed when the judge set bail for Mark at $100,000. Mark was released shortly after his lawyer posted bond for him and they walked out of the courthouse.

Jenny stayed home from school on Monday, too. When Bob arrived home and told her the news she was very upset. How was she going to face him at school? She was so upset, but she was not going to allow him to ruin her life. She would have to pray to God and ask him to give her strength and knowledge on how to handle the situation.

"You ought to listen to what the words are to that music you listen to, girl," Poppy said quietly as his sipped on a cup of coffee.

"What did you say, Poppy?" Jenny asked.

"Do you ever listen to the words of those songs? There're some good messages there. I been listening to those fellas in the morning on your radio station. That J.T. says that power verse every day. Kinda gives thought to get a guy going." Poppy took a sip of his coffee and said no more.

Jenny and Bob just looked at each other in total shock. Poppy had been listening to what he called "the devil's work" just a couple of months ago and now he had been totally converted to a 'Mixite'.

"You're right, Poppy. That gets me off on the right foot every morning," Jenny said. She gave him a quick hug as she went up to her room to pray about this.

Todd called her again Monday evening to see how she was feeling. He asked if he could bring her assignments over to her. She told him that she still didn't feel well enough to read very much or study. Todd was so sweet on the phone and he was truly concerned about her. Jenny hoped that he and Lori had not gotten back together again but she didn't want to ask. She really wanted Todd to ask her to homecoming in two weeks. She knew her bruises and cuts would be healed by then. She asked Todd if she could talk to Tamara for a couple of minutes. He said good night to her and said that if she needed anything, he would be there for her. Then he put Tamara on the phone.

"Hey girl, we miss you at school," Tamara said. "When do you think you will be coming back?"

"I'll probably be back in a few days, next week for sure," Jenny said. "Listen, Tam, I got a question to ask you but you have got to keep it a secret ~ deal."

"Sure Jen, what is it?"

"Well," Jenny stammered. "Well, what do you think my chances are of Todd asking me to homecoming?"

"Wow!" cried Tamara. "He hasn't said anything about asking anyone yet. You know he and Lori are history. They had another fight today. He said they are totally through. He found out that she went out with somebody else over the weekend."

"Well then can you kind of hint around to him about it and let me know, please?"

"I'll see what I can do," Tamara promised.

Jenny thanked Tamara, said good-bye and hung up the phone. She sat daydreaming of dancing with Todd. It would be so much fun going to homecoming with him. She knew that he would not try anything with her. She knew just the dress she would wear, too. It was the one that she got for her cousin's wedding last fall in Chicago. It would be just perfect for homecoming since no one here has seen her wear it. She fell across her bed, grabbed her pillow and hugged it. She closed her eyes tightly and prayed aloud.

"Dear Jesus, please let Todd ask me to the dance. He's so cute and such a nice guy. I know he wouldn't do anything to hurt me, Jesus. Thanks for listening, Amen."

On Tuesday afternoon Jenny and Poppy were playing cards at the kitchen table when the front doorbell rang. Barbara went to answer the door and was surprised to see Todd standing on the porch.

"Hi Mrs. Madison," Todd said. "I brought Jenny's homework and hoped I could see her for a little while. Maybe cheer her up, too."

Barbara glanced over her shoulder then back at Todd. She knew Jenny didn't want anyone to see her with the bruises, especially Todd.

"I'm sorry, Todd," Barbara said loud enough for Grammy to hear in the parlor. "Jenny is taking a nap."

She stepped back to let him into the foyer. Grammy quickly sneaked through the other door of the parlor to the kitchen to tell Jenny that Todd was here and Jenny slipped up the back stairs. Grammy sat down and continued the card game with Poppy just as Todd and Barbara walked into the kitchen.

"Todd is going to try to explain Jenny's assignments to me," Barbara told Grammy and Poppy. "We'll try not to bother your game."

"Nice to see you again, Mr. & Mrs. Madison," Todd said. "How are you coming along, Mr. Madison?"

"Ready to go home," Poppy grumbled.

"I'll bet you are," Todd said with a smile.

"Nice to see you, too, Todd. How are your folks? Did they get all their crops out this fall? Your mother do a lot of canning?" Grammy fired her usual barrage of questions to Todd as he nodded or waited for her to take a breath to slip in a quick answer.

Todd sat down at the end of the table and told Grammy and Poppy all about the farm and how he had been helping his dad and a couple of the other neighbors check out Poppy's animals. Everything had been taken care of at the Madison farm and they need not worry about a thing. Since they had been working so much lately his dad gave him the afternoon off so he could come in to see Jenny. His mom was going to pick him up around 4:30 and he hoped that Jenny would be awake before then.

Jenny had slipped quietly down the back stairs and was sitting close to the bottom listening to the conversation. She felt so bad that she couldn't go out and talk to him, but she didn't feel like explaining things to him.

Just then John came in the back door, greeted everyone in the kitchen and headed straight for the back stairway to go to change his school clothes. When he turned the corner he was surprised and startled to see Jenny sitting there.

"Jenny!" He cried as he jumped back in surprise dropping his books. "You scared the crap out of me. What are you doing sitting here?"

She had been caught. When she walked down the few steps and into the kitchen Todd's mouth dropped open and he jumped out of his chair toward her. He went over to her and offered her his arm and led her to a chair by the table.

"Jenny, my gosh, what on earth happened to you?" Todd asked showing true concern for her.

"I fell down the stairs," Jenny lied as she looked toward her mom and grandparents. "I hit the side of my face on the banister when I went down and then hit my forehead and wrist on the stairs." That sounds reasonable, yeah, that sounds good, she thought. Then continuing she said, "It looks worse than it feels."

"Why didn't you tell me that when I called on Sunday?" Todd asked.

"I didn't want you to see me all bruised like this or think that I am a real klutz," Jenny said.

"Does it hurt real bad?" Todd said as he reached out to touch her face.

"It's getting better," Jenny said. "It sure was ugly on Sunday. "It's a little better today."

Grammy and Poppy had gone back into the parlor and Barbara went up to Bob's office. The two teenagers were sitting in the kitchen alone and Todd was explaining the assignments to Jenny. He kept staring a Jenny's face wondering just how she could hurt her face the way she explained it when she fell.

"What are you staring at?" Jenny asked.

"You," he replied. "Your face is still so beautiful. I am so sorry that you felt that you had to hide from me."

"Todd I'm sorry. I was just so embarrassed that I didn't want anyone to see me. It was so much worse after it just happened." Jenny definitely wasn't lying about that.

Todd reached over and gently ran his fingers down the right side of Jenny's face and then he leaned over and just barely kissed her cheek. Jenny blushed.

"I hope that makes it feel better," Todd said.

She assured him that it did. Then Todd leaned over and gently kissed Jenny on the lips. It was a very sweet kiss. Jenny pulled away quickly though as she had flashes of Mark holding her down.

"Sorry, Jen, I shouldn't have done that." Todd apologized.

"It's OK Todd. It just took me by surprise," Jenny said.

Todd smiled at her and decided he had better get back to the school work. While he was explaining some of the assignments, Todd's arm was draped across the back of Jenny's chair. Every now and then he would rub her back and shoulder. Jenny didn't mind his touches. She had to remind herself that this is Todd and that Mark would never hurt her again.

The time went by so quickly and Todd's mother arrived exactly at 4:30. He sure didn't want to leave yet. Jenny walked him to the front door but before they got close enough for Todd's mom to see, Todd reached over and gave Jenny a gentle hug and a sweet kiss. This time Jenny did not pull away but instead she returned the kiss. Jenny felt like a million butterflies were let loose in her tummy. It was a strange feeling. As Todd walked down the steps he promised to call Jenny tomorrow after he finished his chores.

When he arrived home Todd told Tamara about Jenny's accident. Tamara told Todd that she heard a different story at school today.

"The story going around school is that Mark was arrested for sexually assaulting a girl on Saturday night. Todd," Tamara paused quickly debating whether to continue because she knew how Todd would react to the news. "Todd, Jenny went out with Mark Saturday night and I think she was the one he attacked."

Todd's face had gone ashen and then red. He was so angry he was looking for something or someone to hit or kick. He was mumbling and cursing under his breath. As he walked out the back door slamming it against the house with a loud bang he yelled, "I'll kill him."

"Todd, no," Tamara screamed running after him. "I knew I shouldn't have said anything. He has already been charged and is out on bail. He hasn't come back to school either. Someone said that he's off the football team and that his court date has been set for the 4th of October. He'll get what he deserves. Let him be."

"I'd like to give him what he deserves," Todd said as he walked in circles in the front yard like a caged lion.

"Let him be, Todd," Tamara pleaded. "Please, let him alone."

Todd's attitude changed suddenly and he grabbed Tamara's shoulders.

"Did he...did he, ummm, did he rape her?" Tears were stinging his eyes.

"No," Tamara said. She explained that she had heard how Jenny hurt Mark, escaped from him and ran to a nearby house.

"Good," Todd said as he dropped his arms to his side. "Thank you God."

Todd started running toward the barn and Tamara yelled after him but he disappeared past the buildings. Not long she heard him yelling at the top of his lungs. She knew that he would be all right now that he was letting off steam.

On Friday afternoon someone from the Iowa State's Attorney's office called to make an appointment to see Jenny. He had said that they only needed a deposition from her. She told him that she would have her mother drive her over on Monday. After the call she talked to her dad about how she would have to make a deposition. Bob explained to her that the prosecuting attorney would ask her some questions about the incident. He might ask her to describe everything that happened. He told her to tell everything exactly as it happened and do not leave out the smallest detail. Jenny wanted to put the whole incident behind her and couldn't wait until Monday. Bob called the State's Attorney and asked if he could bring Jenny over right away and they agreed so Bob and Jenny left immediately.

After the usual introductions at the office Jenny and Bob were ushered into a conference room with the secretary and a young lawyer. The lawyer informed asked Jenny to tell them exactly what happened while the secretary recorded it both on a tape recorder and on transcription machine.

Jenny recounted the story leaving nothing out. She started from the time Mark had picked her up until the time she was in the emergency room of the hospital. Then the attorney asked her a few questions. After the secretary left the room the lawyer said the he didn't think that Jenny would have to testify since they had enough evidence against Mark to put him away for quite some time. He said that the injuries Jenny inflicted on Mark were enough to convict him alone. Bob thanked the lawyer and they left the office.

On the way home Jenny asked her dad how long he thought Mark would get and Bob said that he figured that Mark would be in prison for about ten to fifteen years on a Class C felony. Jenny figured she would be long gone by the time he would get out and he would never hurt her or any other woman again. She was quite proud of herself at how well she was handling the situation.

Todd hadn't called Jenny the rest of the week and Jenny was worried because he had promised he would. She wanted to find out but was too afraid to call Tamara. What if he found out the truth? Maybe he was just real busy with the farm and the animals? Yeah, that had to be it, she thought.

Chapter Nineteen

Jenny decided to go back to school on Monday although she still had a little color around her eyes. But for the most part, she looked pretty good. Tamara was glad to see her and told her that Todd knew the truth about what had happened and took it real hard. Then Jenny knew why Todd hadn't called her. Walking to her first class Jenny felt that everyone was staring at her and talking about her. She had to keep telling herself that she hadn't done anything wrong. She was OK.

When she walked in to her English class several of the students began clapping. They said that they were so happy to see her back and proud that she was prosecuting Mark for what he had done to her. She knew everyone knew now.

After class someone tapped Jenny on her shoulder.

"Can I walk with you?" A girl asked.

"Sure," Jenny said. "I am heading downstairs, though."

"Me, too," the girl responded. "My name is Julie Hawkins. I just wanted to tell you that we have a peer support group here at school. We meet on Wednesday afternoons. I sure wish you would come."

"I'll think about it," Jenny said.

Julie took Jenny by the arm and stopped her. "Jenny there are so many girls here at school like you. You aren't the first girl that Mark has hurt but you are the first one to prosecute him. Promise me that you will come."

Jenny promised that she would come this Wednesday. She wanted to hear more about Mark. Maybe other girls would testify and put him away longer.

Todd met Jenny at the door of their computer class. He apologized for not calling her and told her that he needed the time to cool off. Jenny understood and asked if they were cool now. He assured her that they were. After class he walked her to the cafeteria for lunch. They sat down at the table where Jenny and Tamara usually eat. Tamara didn't join them though. When Jenny asked Todd where she was he told her that he asked her to give them some privacy today. Jenny grinned and asked him how they could have privacy in a crowded cafeteria.

"Jenny," Todd started. "I am so sorry what Mark did to you. You can be sure that I would never in a million years hurt you. Jenny I really like you. Will you go to homecoming with me? I know it's a little late to be asking but will you?"

"Sure, Todd," Jenny answered with a grin. "I'd love to go with you."

Todd smiled one of the biggest grins Jenny had ever seen. She loved the way his dimples danced on his cheeks when he smiled. They made plans for the homecoming game and the dance. Todd wanted to take Jenny out to dinner before the dance, too. He asked her what color her dress was for the dance and Jenny told him about the light green dress from her cousin's wedding that she was planning to wear. Todd made a mental note of the color in order to get the right color of flowers for her. The rest of the day Jenny was walking on air and she didn't care who was talking about her anymore. Todd would protect her from anything or anybody that wanted to try to hurt her. She felt she had met her knight in shining armor.

Tamara noticed the change in Jenny.

"Well Todd must have popped the question," she teased Jenny.

"Yep," Jenny replied with a huge smile.

"Good," Tamara said. "I'm so glad for you. Jenny he really took the news hard. He was ready to go find Mark and kill him. You will never have to worry about Todd hurting you."

"We had a long talk about it all," Jenny said. "He's the greatest."

"I don't know about the greatest," Tamara giggled. "But, he is pretty special."

After school on Wednesday Jenny stayed and went to the support group. Julie greeted her and offered her a seat. There were about 14 other girls there and Mrs. Davenport, one of the counselors at school. Everyone was so nice to Jenny and each girl introduced herself. After the introductions a girl named Megan said that Mark had hurt her. She said that it was during the summer. He had taken her to a movie then down a back road. She was so afraid of him that she could not fight him off and he raped her. She had kept it a secret until she joined this group in early September.

A small blonde girl named Sally started to cry. She said that Mark had raped her, too. She had told her mother about it but decided not to prosecute because her mom said it would be his word against hers and they didn't want to relive it in court.

Sally and Megan both said that they wanted to tell the authorities about the attacks now. They wondered if Jenny would help them. She agreed to do anything she could to help put Mark away for a very long time. Jenny also said that she would tell her attorney about the other attacks. When Jenny arrived home she went straight to her dad's office to tell him what the other girls had said.

"Are they willing to testify?" Bob asked.

"They said they are willing to do whatever it takes to put Mark away." Jenny replied.

Bob called the Iowa State's Attorney and relayed the information to him. The lawyer told Bob that Mark was going to be tried as an adult and this could get Mark a lot more time tacked on to his sentence and would probably deny his chance for parole. There was also the possibility that his bail could be revoked.

Jenny went to her room and called Sally. When she told her what the lawyer had told her dad Sally assured her that she would testify and said that she was almost positive that Megan would, too. They both wanted to see Mark pay for what they had done to them.

Friday afternoon Jenny promised herself that she was only going to think good thoughts tonight as she was getting ready for her date with Todd. He had seen her at her worst, but she wanted to look extra nice for him tonight. Jenny knew that Todd didn't like a lot of make-up so she used very little. She stood in front of the mirror for over a half an hour trying to get her hair to look just right. She didn't realize that Barbara had been standing in the doorway for the past 15 minutes watching her.

"You look great," Barbara said as Jenny jumped.

"Mom, you scared me."

"Sorry, honey," Barbara smiled. "This is Todd you are going out with, right. This is the boy who has seen you with mud from head to toe. He has seen you with tomato sauce all over your face. And if I am not mistaken, isn't this the boy who you had an egg fight with and got egg in your hair?"

Jenny laughed. "I guess you're right, Mom. Todd has seen me at my worst and he still asked me to go to the game and dance."

About that time the doorbell rang. Grammy went to answer it and welcomed Todd into the living room. Jenny knew she had better hurry down or Grammy would have Todd too exhausted to go to the game from answering questions. When she rounded the corner to enter the living room, Todd stood up and walked over to her. He wanted to give her a kiss but decided to wait. He didn't know how Barbara and Grammy would take it.

When they walked out of the house Jenny noticed that Todd had come with Gary Carson and Michelle, his girlfriend, was sitting in the front seat with him. Todd saw that Jenny looked a little confused.

"Oh I forgot to tell you that we are double dating with Gary and Michelle. Didn't I?" Todd apologized. "It's OK with you, isn't it?"

"Sure," Jenny said. She didn't care who they went with as long as she was with Todd. She waved back to Grammy and Barbara standing on the porch as she climbed into the back seat with Todd.

During the pre-game activities the homecoming candidates were announced. There were king and queen candidates from the senior class and attendants from each class with their escorts. The band had a short program before playing the national anthem. Todd held Jenny's hand all during the program. The first half of the football game was not very exciting and it seemed neither team could score. There was the occasional first down, but for the most part, there would be only four plays before the ball switched sides. Todd slipped away in the middle of the second quarter to get Jenny and him some soda and popcorn before the half time crowd and he made it back to his seat just as the buzzer sounded signifying the end of the first half.

The band marched proudly out onto the field playing the school song followed by Mr. Lowery, the principal, and all the homecoming candidates once again. Mr. Lowery was going to announce the king and queen and their court for homecoming. The freshman attendant and her escort was announced, then the sophomore and junior attendants and their escorts. The stadium crowd went wild when Crystal Peters was named queen and David Churchill was named king. The attendants followed the king and queen to the middle of the field while the band performed a very special homecoming routine around them forming a crown. The band and homecoming royalty had barely left the field when the visiting team came back on to the field to warm up. A few minutes later the Titans came back out ready for the second half.

The Titans had to kick off the second half which meant the opposing team had first chance at scoring. On the first drive, a big senior tackle, Matt Davis, sacked their quarterback and caused a fumble. One of the Titans grabbed the ball and ran 22 yards for a touchdown. With the two point conversion the Titans were leading 8 to 0. They immediately had to kick off again. This time the other team got close enough to the end zone to kick a field goal. But when the Titans got the ball, they ran eight plays for another touchdown. Todd told Jenny it looked like a different team had come out of the locker room for the second half of the game. When the final buzzer sounded to end the game, the Titans had won 15 to 3.

Todd asked Jenny if she wanted to go to the Cardinal Inn with them to celebrate the victory and she said that she would like to go, but she had to call her parents and let them know first. Jenny enjoyed being with Todd, and she liked Gary and Michelle. The two couples sat with a group of other students and the guys talked about the game while the girls talked about tomorrow night's dance. Later on Todd and Gary made final plans for their date on Saturday with the girls. Jenny was glad because she didn't want any more surprises.

Saturday morning Jenny woke up early and took her shower and rolled her hair on rollers. John laughed at her when he saw her and made comments about her being from outer space. Bob also teased her and said he thought girls had quit using rollers back in the 70's. Grammy reprimanded both of them and told them to quit teasing Jenny.

"Let them have their fun," Jenny said. "Nothing is going to spoil my date with Todd."

Jenny got her dress out of her mother's cedar lined closet. She hung it up on the back of her bedroom door. It looked pretty good for being put away for several months and just needed a light ironing before tonight. Barbara said that she would use the steamer on it for Jenny. Everything was going to be perfect for tonight. Jenny couldn't wait but the time just seemed to drag by so slowly all day.

Around 5:00 Jenny put on her dress, finished her hair and make-up and came downstairs for inspection. She walked into the parlor and Grammy and Poppy said she looked like a princess. Bob got a little lump in his throat when he saw that his daughter was no longer a little girl. Barbara ran and got the camera and took several pictures of Jenny with her grandparents, her father and her brother. Exactly 6:00 the doorbell rang. Todd was right on time.

Barbara motioned Jenny to run up stairs while Bob went to answer the door. He invited Todd in and said Jenny would be right down. When Jenny appeared at the top of the stairs Todd smiled and his eyes sparkled as if he had seen this princess for the first time. He walked over to the stairs and reached his hand up to take hers and led her down to where they were standing. He had a very pretty wrist corsage of white roses, baby's breath and small orchids wrapped with a pale green ribbon that complimented Jenny's dress perfectly. After he slipped it on her arm he brought her hand to his lips and kissed it. Barbara and Bob stood back and watched while tears filled their eyes.

"I want to take some pictures," Barbara said as she snapped one.

Gary and Michelle came into the house and Barbara took several more of each couple and the four of them together. Since Gary had made reservations at a very nice restaurant in Keokuk, Michelle reminded the guys that they had to leave. All four of them were thankful for the reminder so they could cut the photo session a bit short....Barbara only taken about 30 pictures not counting the ones she took before Todd, Gary and Michelle came.

When the foursome got to the restaurant Jenny said that she was too excited to eat but Todd said she should eat something even if it is something light. Michelle said that she wasn't very hungry either so she and Jenny decided to split a meal. The excitement of the night didn't bother the boys and they both ordered steaks, baked potatoes and salads. Jenny felt so grown up being here with Todd but on the inside she still felt like a little girl. Every time Todd brushed his hand against hers or when his leg touched her leg under the table, Jenny felt the blush rise in her cheeks. While they were waiting for their meals Todd leaned over and gave her a sweet gentle kiss and released the million butterflies in her tummy again. She really liked Todd but she couldn't figure out why she felt that funny feeling every time he kissed her. After all they had been buddies for so long.

Todd had Jenny by the arm as he led her into the dance. All the girls greeted Jenny and told her how pretty she looked. Todd felt very proud to be seen with her and he led her directly to the dance floor as a slow song was playing. He liked holding her close, too.

"Jenny, you look so beautiful tonight," Todd whispered in her ear. "I never would have thought I could be so lucky to have you for a girlfriend."

Jenny blushed as she laid her head against Todd's chest. She was so thrilled to think that Todd considered her his girlfriend. It was what she had hoped and dreamed for since she met him last summer when he was covered with sheep shearing dust. Todd stood with his arm around Jenny's waist during the crowning ceremony and he didn't even notice that Lori was there with someone else. The only person he cared about tonight was Jenny. They danced almost every dance and they didn't miss a single slow dance. Midnight seemed to come too soon for the young couple.

While Gary and Michelle waited in the car, Todd walked Jenny to her front door. Bob had left the front porch light on and Jenny knew the entire neighborhood could see them. Todd pulled Jenny over onto the whicker love seat that was in the shadows and sat down and had Jenny sit next to him and gave her a kiss.

When he pulled away Jenny said, "Todd, I had the most wonderful time of my life tonight. I hope we can do it again."

"Jenny you are the only girl I ever want to go out with ever again. Will you go steady with me?" Todd asked as he pulled his class ring off his finger and handed it to her.

Jenny swallowed hard to keep from yelling and acting goofy; and also to keep those butterflies from flying out her mouth. Then calmly she said, "Yes, Todd, I will."

Todd placed his class ring on her finger. It was way too big, but Jenny said that she would wear it anyway. Again, Todd leaned down and kissed her and they embraced. They walked over to the door and he gave her one more kiss and said good night and Jenny watched him walk down the sidewalk to the car.

Jenny barely slept at all after the dance. She held onto Todd's ring while she slept and in the morning she found a long chain and slipped the ring on to the chain and clasped it around her neck. If she needed to, she could wear it inside her blouse to hide it, but she wanted everyone to see it. She wanted everyone to know that she and Todd were going steady.

"Oh Mom, it was the best," Jenny gushed as she bounced into the kitchen. "Todd is the best," Jenny proceeded to tell Barbara every detail of the dinner and the dance. She even blushed when she told her mother about Todd kissing her. When she said that she almost passed out when Todd kissed her, Barbara just tittered. Barbara remembered how it was when she was young and had her first love.

Bob had walked in the middle of the conversation but waited until Jenny was finished talking about the dance. He then warned Jenny that she has to be careful.

"You are very young, too young in fact to be going steady with one boy," Bob said. Bob wouldn't admit it that if she must choose just one boy right now, he was very glad it is Todd. He felt that he could trust this boy with his baby girl.

"Daddy, you don't have to worry, about me. I made the pledge at SHOUTfest that I am staying pure until I get married."

"Well, that takes a load off my mind," Bob said and the three of them roared at Bob as he wiped his brow.

Everyday Todd walked Jenny to the cafeteria for lunch. Tamara sat with them now as she had her eye on one of Todd's friends but didn't want to be too forward. She begged Todd to mention something to him and Todd promised to see what he could do for her. Jenny confessed that she had talked to Tamara about Todd before he had asked her to homecoming. Todd smiled and said he knew that the girls were plotting behind his back. He would have asked her to homecoming no matter if Tamara had talked to him or not. He knew he had chosen the right girl.

Chapter Twenty

The next two weeks seemed to fly by. On the day of Mark's trial Jenny wanted to stay home and go to the trial but both her father and the State's Attorney told her she should stay away. Sally and Megan had given their dispositions and were not expected to testify. During lunch, Sally and Megan came over to Jenny's table and sat down. They said they just needed the companionship of someone who understood how they were feeling today. Jenny sure understood how they were feeling and Todd and Tamara tried to give as much support as they could. The small group went into Mr. Hill's classroom and Jenny slipped a CD into his player. They stood hand in hand and listened to By the Tree's *Jesus Washed*.

"That song makes me feel so much better," Sally said.

"Me, too," Megan replied.

The group said a couple of prayers begging God to give them strength to forgive Mark for what he had done to them and the courage to forget what had been done. Just as they said "Amen" the bell signifying the end of lunch rang and the group dispersed to their classes.

When Jenny got home from school, Bob said that he had gone to the trial. The State's Attorney submitted the girls' depositions, showed the pictures of each girl's injuries as well as showing the pictures of the injuries that Jenny inflicted on Mark. Bob said after a very brief recess after the evidence was shown, Mark changed his plea to guilty to two counts of first degree criminal sexual assault. The jury was released and the judge set the sentencing date in one week. His bail was revoked and he is being held in the Lee County Jail.

Jenny immediately called Sally and Megan and the girls were thrilled but sad that Mark had been pled guilty. The only thing about the trial that bothered Jenny is that the charges of rape had been dropped as a plea bargain to two counts of first degree criminal sexual assault. Jenny said that her dad figured that Mark would probably get 12 years for each charge. He hoped that the sentences would run consecutively and not concurrently. He doubted very much if he would be up for parole in less than 10 years.

The next seven days seemed to drag for the three girls. Todd tried to keep Jenny's mind off Mark and the trial by going to a movie on Friday night and going to the farm on Saturday to see Tamara. Jenny even spent the night at the farm so she could see Todd on Sunday at church and spend more time with him in the afternoon. Finally the day of Mark's trial was upon them.

Mark's sentencing was late in the afternoon so the girls made plans to go to the Cardinal Inn right after school and wait for Bob to come with the news. Bob promised he would come there straight from the courthouse and the girls only had to wait about 15 minutes before he walked through the door.

"What happened?" Jenny asked her dad.

"How long did he get?" Sally asked.

"Please Mr. Madison, tell us what happened," Megan pleaded.

"Hold on, girls," Bob started. "Let me sit down first."

Bob sat down, ordered a Pepsi and then told the girls what happened at the courthouse earlier.

"Well, Mark was given 12 years each for assault and they will run consecutively which means he gets a total of 24 years."

The girls started cheering and hugging each other and Jenny hugged her dad. They were so happy.

"Wait," Bob said. "There's more. Mark will not be eligible for parole for 15 years. He is being transferred to Ft. Madison as we speak."

The girls thanked Bob for going to court and telling them the results. Sally suggested that they celebrate and Bob offered to buy supper for the girls. But Sally and Megan said they would buy Bob's supper as a way of thanking him. So they all ordered the best Cardinal Inn burgers and fries they ever had and even had ice cream sundaes for dessert.

The next day at school Jenny noticed that someone had posted the newspaper article reporting Mark's trial and sentencing on the main bulletin board. She wondered who would have put it there. By the time several other students had gathered Mr. Lowery reached in and pulled it down.

"This is a good example to all students, but we do not need to sensationalize it or take advantage of someone's situation," he said. "Mark will be paying for his crime for a very the rest of his life."

Jenny knew that Mr. Lowery was right and she was glad that he took down the article. In a way she felt sorry for Mark. God only knew what he would go through in prison. She would have to remember to pray for him. Now she felt she could go on with her life.

The football team ended their season with a winning record. They didn't make the state play-offs but they were satisfied with their record of 8 wins and 2 losses. Jenny's first quarter report card was very good considering she missed over of week of classes. With the exception of B's in Art and Physics, she made A's in all her other classes. She said she could have gotten an A in Art except she missed two projects while she was out and she did poorly on a test in Physics over the material while she was out. She said she'll get all A's for the semester, though.

Poppy was walking around the house like a caged tiger now. He had gotten rid of the cast on his good leg, thrown away the crutches and was only using a cane for balance. Grammy kept telling him to relax. She was packing their belongings and getting ready to move back to the farm. Poppy couldn't wait.

Jenny and John got home from school about the same time on the big moving day. John ran upstairs to change clothes to go out to the farm and Jenny had to primp a little just in case she might see Todd at the farm even though she had just seen him at school. Bob had already loaded all the bags into the cars and was helping Poppy down the front porch steps.

"Get away, boy," Poppy grumbled. "I can do it myself."

"I already moved the Jack-O-Lantern for you," John said holding up the pumpkin.

Bob just chuckled at the independence of his dad and stepped back. He kept a close eye on Poppy in case he should need a hand. Poppy made it to the car without incident and climbed into the front seat. The rest of the family came outside then to get into the cars. Bob drove the Buick with Poppy, John and Grammy. Jenny rode out in the Taurus with her mom and Barbara even let her drive since she had gotten her white slip. Barbara also let her crank up the radio since she liked the music of *The Mix* and sometimes she would even sing along.

When the cars pulled into the yard, Duke was all over them. His tail was wagging so hard that his whole body was shaking. John tried to help Poppy into the house but he was shooed away. Poppy needed to prove to everyone, including himself that he was well enough to get around on his own. He made it into the kitchen and sat down huffing and puffing. He had done it on his own, but he knew he was a long way from being 100%.

Bob carried the bags up to his parents' bedroom. Poppy had been practicing going up and down stairs at Bob's house for some time and he knew he could do it. But he was going to have to rest a few minutes before taking the trek up the stairs to his own room. The family knew that Poppy would be happier in his own bed, so they decided to let him have his way and just have patience with him going up and down the stairs. John couldn't keep his secret any longer.

"Poppy you gotta come outside," John said with a smile from ear to ear.

"This better be important, boy," Poppy said. "You getting this old man up and outside,"

Poppy just stepped outside the back door when John yelled, "Surprise!"

Bob had bought a golf cart at an auction. It was the perfect solution for Poppy to get down to the barn and check on the animals. It would take some of the pressure off of walking all the way. Poppy actually cracked a smile. He wanted to check this out and asked John to show him how this little "Ditty", as he called it, worked. John jumped in right away and Poppy slid in next to him. John was a very good teacher and explained what the few buttons were for and then they took off toward the barns. As they rounded the corner of the chicken coop Grammy and the others smiled and walked back into the house.

Just then they heard something coming up the lane. Jenny immediately recognized the Kramer's pickup truck. Margie and George were in the truck and she was disappointed when she didn't see Todd. When the truck stopped at the edge of the yard, Todd, Tamara and Terry jumped out of the back of the pickup and surprised them all. Jenny walked over to Todd and he leaned down and gave her a quick little kiss. Tamara had a picnic basket and George and Margie were both carrying big bowls of food.

"We thought you needed a good welcome home," Margie said. "We brought fried chicken, Cole slaw, potato salad, and home made bread. Tamara made a good looking chocolate cake."

"I made lemonade," Todd said as he reached in the bed of the truck and pulled out a 3 gallon thermos jug.

"Yeah, you poured it out of a can and added water," Tamara teased.

They all took the great supper into the house where Barbara got out some plates and silverware for everyone. Bob and Todd set up extra chairs in the dining room, while Tamara and Jenny put the extra leaf in the table. When they finished, Grammy went outside and rang the old dinner bell hanging on the post at the end of the sidewalk. Shortly she saw Poppy and John coming up the lane toward the house in the golf cart.

Although it was quite cozy, everyone fit around the dining room table. Poppy lowered his head and started to say grace. This time he not only thanked God for the food and crops, he thanked God for good neighbors and his loving and caring family. He then asked God to bless them all. When Poppy paused everyone thought that he was going to continue because it was way to short compared to the prayers Poppy usually says. Poppy looked up at everyone and grumbled "Amen". The rest of the family and friends repeated the ending. Jenny and John let out a brief giggle as Poppy started passing the chicken around the table.

After supper Jenny and Todd sat on the front porch swing enjoying the evening sounds. The moon was starting to come up over in the eastern sky. It was definitely a harvest moon and Jenny felt that she could reach out and touch it. When George called to Todd and said that they were leaving, Todd leaned over and gave Jenny a kiss that let the butterflies loose in her tummy. Jenny stood on the porch holding her tummy and waved to Todd in the back of the pickup as they disappeared down the lane.

Inside Bob and Barbara stood behind Poppy as he climbed the staircase. He took one step at a time and made it up to his bedroom with no problem. Grammy helped him change into his night clothes and Poppy went to bed. Barbara and Bob decided to let John spend the night to help Poppy downstairs in the morning. They didn't want anything to happen to either one of the old people and John was big enough now to hold on to Poppy as he came down the stairs.

The rest of the family left and headed back to town. Jenny was so happy that she had seen Todd and wondered why she felt so funny in her tummy every time Todd kissed her. She would have to ask her mother about that sometime when they are alone. They had barely reached the highway when Jenny fell asleep dreaming about Todd.

Chapter Twenty-One

    The next several weeks flew by and Jenny begged her parents to let her go out to help Grammy at the farm for the four day Thanksgiving weekend. The entire family would be here for Thursday's dinner. Bob's brother, Fred, from central Iowa would be here with his family. Grammy's younger sister from Columbia, Missouri, would bring her husband and son. It had been decided that everyone would stay with Bob and Barbara because they had plenty of room and Grammy didn't need the aggravation of house guests when she would be trying to prepare a big dinner and take care of Poppy.
    Bob took Jenny out to the farm after school on Wednesday evening before going to pick up his Aunt Agnes and Uncle Roy from the bus station in Keokuk. Bob never could understand why they would rather take the bus than drive home for the holidays. Aunt Agnes was almost 15 years young than Grammy. Her son, Ray had just turned 21 this past October and he could have driven. He was a student at the University of Missouri studying civil engineering. Bob always said that Ray was a very intelligent boy, but when it came to common sense, he was dumb as a rock.
    Fred, Bob's younger brother, pulled into the driveway, right behind Bob. There was a lot of hugging and carrying on when the three families met. Fred's wife, Mary was a very quiet pretty lady. She was very small and dainty and Bob called her a china doll as she looked as if she might break. Their three children were around Jenny and John's ages. Their oldest child was a son, Joseph, who had just turned 17. He had inherited his mother's dainty features and was very handsome. Joseph brought his girlfriend, Rebecca, with him for the weekend. She

too was very tiny with the perfect figure. She stood out with her very blond hair amongst the Madison's dark hair. The middle child of Fred and Mary was their daughter, Magdalene, who just turned 15 in September. Magdalene was a pretty girl but inherited her father's large build and was about fifty pounds overweight. She was a very sweet and likable girl. The youngest child was another boy, Thomas, who was 12. He didn't look like Fred or Mary. He looked more like John with dark hair but with blue eyes.

Barbara had fixed up the bedrooms on the third floor for the guests. Fred and Mary would have one of the larger rooms, while Agnes and Roy would have the other large room. They would have to share a bathroom, Joseph and Thomas would sleep in one room with Ray in the next room, Magdalene would have to share a room with Rebecca; and Rebecca was not all pleased with that arrangement. She was even unhappier when she found out that she would have to share a bathroom at the other end of the hall with all of the children.

After everyone had settled in and had their things put in the rooms, Barbara called them to the dining room for a light supper of cold cuts and cheese sandwiches. She and Jenny had prepared a huge meat tray and a veggie tray earlier in the day. She also had chips and dip and plenty of drinks available. They had all decided to stay in town tonight to give Grammy some time before they all showed up for dinner tomorrow. Agnes wanted to talk to Grammy so Barbara took her to the parlor where she could make her call in private.

Out at the farm, Jenny was helping Grammy prepare salads for tomorrow. They had two different kinds of Jell-o salads as well as a fruit salad. Grammy had four pies baking in the oven and Jenny had made a cake. All that was left to do tonight was to frost the cake. Grammy said that she would get up around 4:00 and put the 25 pound turkey in the oven. Jenny would have to help peel potatoes and make the rolls. All in all Grammy was ready for the gang. When the phone rang at the farm, Jenny answered it then handed it over to Grammy when she heard Aunt Agnes on the other end. She told Grammy she was going up to her room. Jenny was hoping Todd would call tonight.

Jenny had brought a couple of school books with her to look over during the break. She had set her books in the closet and decided that she might look over her Physics since she had some free time. The books were sitting on an old steamer trunk in which Grammy kept the winter blankets and quilts. When she went to grab her books her only pen slid out of a notebook and fell behind the trunk. Jenny put her books on the bed and then pulled the trunk out far enough to reach behind and get her pen.

What she found behind there was more than her pen. She pulled out a packet of envelopes tied up in a green ribbon. They looked very old. Jenny took the packet, sat down on her bed and untied the ribbon. She fanned the envelopes out across the bed and noticed that the first batch was addressed to Grammy. The postmark was from the late 1960's. Did Grammy have a secret lover? Jenny wanted to read them and find out who had sent them to Grammy. She gingerly picked up the first envelope and slid the contents out. She read the letter.

>Dear Mother,
>
>I have gotten myself a nice little place in Detroit. It is only two rooms but it is big enough for us. I am sorry I hurt you, but you have to understand my feelings, too. Please write to me.
>
>>Love,
>>Helen

Wow! Who was Helen? Jenny had to pick up the second letter now. Her curiosity was really running full speed. The postmark on this letter was only a month later.

>Dear Mother,
>
>I have not received any letters from you as yet. I have found a job at an auto factory. I am working as a stenographer in the office. The pay is satisfactory for us to live on. Give Father my love.
>
>>Helen

Jenny just couldn't figure this out. The third letter was almost a year after that one.

>Dear Mother,
>
>Enclosed please find a picture of your grandson. His name is David. He is a very good baby, and is already sleeping through the night. I have already gone back to work and I have found a very nice woman in my building to care for David while I am gone. I am still waiting for a letter from you.
>
>>Love,
>>Helen

Gee, could this be Grammy's daughter and grandson? Why hadn't anyone talked about her? Was she illegitimate? Maybe she wasn't married when she got pregnant. So many questions were going through Jenny's mind. Jenny needed to know more. The next letter was postmarked 1973 from Detroit also.

Dear Mother,

I want to come home so you can know your grandson and he can know you and Father. He needs to grow up on the farm. The city is so hard on people. Please write and tell me that we can come.

Love,
Helen

Jenny quickly picked up the next letter. This letter had never been opened. It had been addressed to Miss Helen Madison in Detroit. Grammy's return address was in the corner and stamped across the front in big red letters was RETURN TO SENDER! It said that the addressee was unknown. The postmark on this letter was three months after Helen's last letter. Jenny looked at the next letter. It was identical to the last. There were ten unopened letter that had been returned. Jenny had to find out who this Helen person was and what happened to her.

Most of the lights were off in the house when Jenny tiptoed downstairs to the living room. She knew that Grammy kept the family Bible in the buffet drawer in the dining room. She crossed the living room and bumped into a dining room chair before she found the light switch. She opened the drawer and picked up the Bible to take back to her room. As she passed their room she could hear Poppy's deep breathing and Grammy's light snoring. Duke looked up at her from the rug by their bed both times when she passed but didn't make a sound.

Once back in her room Jenny opened the book to where Grammy had written the names of the family. There were Grammy's and Poppy's names at the top. Right under their names was written Robert married to Barbara and below those names were children, Jennifer and Jonathon. On the other side of the page from Robert was written Frederick married to Mary and under them was written children, Joseph, Magdalene and Thomas. To the left of Robert there had been something written at one time but it had been scratched out so hard that there was now a tear in the paper. Who was that person and why was he or she scratched out of the family?

Jenny would have to find out for sure now. She set the Bible on the vanity and tied the letters back up and slid them back behind the trunk. She lay in bed for quite some time trying to figure out this mystery. It must have been something very bad to be scratched out of the family Bible.

In order for everyone to get out to the farm, both of Bob's cars as well as Fred's car had to be used. Barbara had made a green bean casserole and baked sweet potatoes and Aunt Agnes had brought some home made breads and home canned pickles with her. Mary, as usual, came empty handed. They put all the food in the back of the Taurus. Barbara drove the Taurus with Aunt Agnes, Uncle Roy and Ray and her trip seemed twice as long since no one talked along the way. Barbara could only imagine how boring it must be around their house compared to her and Bob's home.

Bob had John, Magdalene and Thomas in his car and John talk constantly about helping his grandfather on the farm. Thomas actually seemed interested in seeing the sheep and cows once they got to the farm. Bob had to remind John that they had to eat Thanksgiving dinner first.

Fred had the rest of his family in his car and followed Bob out to the farm since it had been quite a number of years since he had been to his parent's home. Mary reminded Fred several times that they were leaving first thing in the morning to go back home, so he had better get all his visiting done today.

"Yes, Mary," Fred said. "I know you said you wanted to leave by noon."

"The sooner I get out of this God forsaken dump the better I'll like it. These hillbillies are not our kind of people. I am so sorry you are being subjected to this Rebecca," Mary said to Joseph's girlfriend.

"That's all right Mary," Rebecca said. "All families have a few oddities in them."

Both women began to giggle and Fred was feeling part shame, part anger and part sadness.

Joseph saw how his Dad looked and whispered to Rebecca, "Knock it off. That kind of talk upsets my dad."

Rebecca stopped and gave him an "Oh, poor Baby" look and was quiet for the rest of the ride.

When the entire family arrived at the farm Grammy took turns hugging each of the children and chatting frantically with the adults. The tables had already been set and Jenny had started placing dishes full of delicious food. People were finding their seats and since Jenny helped she was allowed to sit with the adults in the dining room this year. The rest of the children were in the kitchen which also upset Rebecca. After the children had filled their plates and gone into the kitchen and the adults had sat down at their seats Poppy bowed his head and said one of the shortest graces on record. He didn't even wait for the "Amen" before he started passing the dishes around.

Between long moments of silence there were the occasional compliments on Grammy's good cooking, Aunt Agnes's Bread and Butter pickles or Barbara's yummy sweet potatoes.

After the meal the men went into the living room. When Ray turned on the old TV he was disappointed they could only get 3 channels and he had to settle on watching football. Joseph sat with Rebecca, who was bored to death, on the couch; and John took Thomas down to the barn to see all the animals.

Barbara, Aunt Agnes and Jenny started to clear off the dining room table. Mary scraped off the dishes within her reach and stacked them near her. Magdalene had moved into the dining room and was still eating dessert, her third piece of pumpkin pie.

"No wonder you're as big as a horse," Mary criticized her daughter.

Magdalene dropped her fork and ran out of the house.

"Mary you shouldn't talk to the child like that," Grammy scolded.

"I'll raise my children the way I see fit," Mary snapped back. Jenny was shocked. No one in the family ever talked back to Grammy like that. "I just can't understand why that child can't see what she is doing to herself. She is becoming an embarrassment to the entire family."

"Enough!" Grammy snapped. "I will not have you degrade my granddaughter like that."

Mary dropped the fork and plate she had in her hand onto the table, got up and walked into the living room in a huff. Jenny ran out the back door to find Magdalene.

Magdalene was sitting on an upturned 5 gallon bucket in the corner of the tool shed, crying and licking the pumpkin off her fingers. Jenny walked over to her and sat down next to her on another bucket.

"Are you O.K., Magdalene?" Jenny asked sympathetically.

"Please don't call me that," she said. "I hate that name."

"What should I call you then?"

"Maggie or Mags or Ralph," she said. "I don't care, just anything but that."

Jenny paused for a second or two then said, "Well, Ralph, don't you think it is a little cold out here?"

Maggie looked at her and both girls started giggling. Jenny suggested that they go back into the house and go upstairs to her room. Maggie thought that would be a good idea; but how would they sneak past the family?

Jenny knew they could sneak in the front door and go up the main staircase. No one would see them because the door between the living room and the foyer was close. When they opened the front door, Jenny peeked inside and saw that the door was definitely closed. She went in and Maggie followed her up the stairs.

Chapter Twenty-Two

Maggie had never seen that room before. She thought it looked like something out of *Gone With The Wind*. Maggie went over and sat on the edge of the bed across from Jenny.

"I can't believe the way your mom talked to you," Jenny said with tears in her eyes. "Why do you let her talk like that to you? And the way she sassed back to Grammy; that was unreal, and so disrespectful. I even noticed your dad blush a couple times when she did it."

"My mother hates me. She didn't want me to begin with. That's why she named me what she did ~ Magdalene ~ after the bad Mary. You know Mary Magdalene from the Bible."

"But she turned out to be a good person," Jenny reminded her.

"Oh Jenny, I wish I could be as good as you, as pretty as you. My mother doesn't take me anywhere with her and she won't attend any of my school functions. She is so embarrassed to be seen with me. I can't help it that I am fat and ugly." Maggie started to cry.

Jenny reached over and patted Maggie's knee. "Hey Ralph, you aren't ugly at all. You have a very pretty face. All you need is to do something with your hair and put on a little make-up. Let me try something."

Jenny jumped up and pulled the stool out in front of the vanity for Maggie to sit on. Then she got out her make-up bag and started experimenting on Maggie. Jenny put a blanket over the mirror so Maggie couldn't see what she was doing but Jenny thought she was looking good with the little changes she was making already. Maggie squealed when Jenny plucked her eyebrows.

"The unibrow look is out," Jenny said smiling and plucking. Even Brook Shields doesn't have heavy eyebrows anymore."

Jenny stepped back to survey her work and liked what she saw. Now what about the hair? Maggie had very long straight black hair. It was quite beautiful and very shiny. Jenny brushed the hair straight back off of Maggie's face and noticed that she had a very prominent widow's peak. It truly complimented Maggie's face. Jenny just pulled Maggie's hair from the side and top of her head to the back and fastened it with a pretty butterfly barrette and let it fall down her back.

Jenny stepped back and looked at Maggie. She looked like a different person. With her hair pulled back off of her face and the light make-up Maggie looked very pretty. Her eyes were more noticeable without the heavy eyebrows and you could actually see that her eyes were *Elizabeth Taylor* purple. Jenny walked over to the mirror and pulled the blanket away. Maggie's mouth dropped open when she saw her reflection.

"Don't cry," Jenny ordered with a little giggle. "You'll ruin your mascara."

"Oh Jenny," Maggie cried. "I am pretty. I'm really pretty"

Maggie got up and walked over and hugged Jenny. She wanted so badly to show her mother how she looked but knew that her mother would make some crass remark. Jenny suggested that they just go downstairs and see if anyone notices. When they were walking toward the staircase Jenny noticed that Maggie was even walking straighter and with pride.

The girls walked through the kitchen and into the dining room where most of the women were sitting and talking. Mary was still in the living room with the men. No one had paid much attention when the girls walked in because they were in the middle of a healthy discussion. A few minutes later, Ray walked through the dining room and into the kitchen to get something to drink. On his way back he stopped and stared.

"Jenny, who is your friend?" Ray asked. "I didn't see any cars come in the drive."

Jenny smiled. "Oh Ray," she giggled. "This is your cousin, Maggie."

At the moment the other women looked over at the girl.

"Oh my goodness," Grammy exclaimed. "Child you are beautiful! You have been hiding behind all that hair for so long. I had no idea that this beautiful young lady was under there." Then Grammy yelled to Mary. "Mary, come in here. There is someone I want you to meet."

Jenny and Maggie giggled at the remark.

Mary walked into the dining room and her mouth dropped open when she saw her daughter. She couldn't believe the change but she quickly recovered from her surprise.

"Mary I would like you to meet my cousin, Maggie," Jenny said.

With almost no emotion, Mary said, "Very nice, Magdalene. It's a start." Mary then turned and walked back into the living room.

Maggie started to cry but she didn't hide her tears this time. Jenny and Aunt Agnes tried to comfort her. Grammy couldn't believe how cruel Mary had been to the child. She told Maggie that she was a very beautiful girl and that her mother was unhappy with herself and not with Maggie. That made Maggie feel a little better and she stopped crying.

A few moments later Fred and Bob came out to the dining room to check out the new beauty in the family.

"Ray tells us there is a new hot chick out here," Bob said.

Fred took one look at his daughter and his eyes teared up. He walked over and gave her a hug and squeezed her so tight that she begged to be let go.

"Daddy, I can't breathe," Maggie said muffled against Fred's chest.

"Maggie I don't know what to say," Fred started. "You're gorgeous."

"That she is, Fred," Bob agreed, "very pretty."

The ringing of the phone broke the mood. It was Todd and he wanted to come over to see Jenny. Jenny told Todd that her cousin was there and asked him to bring Tamara. By the time Jenny told Maggie all about the Kramer twins the old truck was bouncing up the lane and pulling into the yard.

Jenny introduced Maggie to Todd and Tamara and they decided to sit on the front porch. Todd and Jenny sat on the swing while the other two girls sat in the whicker chairs across from them. The conversation was slow to start with Todd talking about how mild the weather was for this time of year and Tamara complimenting Maggie on her hair. But it didn't take too long before Tamara and Maggie were comparing their schools and Todd and Jenny were talking about, well, talking about slipping away from the girls for a few minutes.

Todd and Jenny got up and quickly and quietly walked down the steps and around the corner of the house. They could hear the girls still chatting as they walked toward the barns. They walked past the sheep barns and down the path to the woods. The sun felt good although there was a little chill in the air. Todd walked with his arm around Jenny's waist. When they got to the woods, they found an old tree that had fall across the creek and sat down on it. Todd put his arm around Jenny and leaned over and gave her a kiss. Jenny put her hand on Todd's cheek and kissed him back. Todd was getting into it pretty heavy when Jenny pushed away from him.

"Jenny," he started. "I love you so much. I don't know if I can wait much longer."

Without saying a word Jenny slid off the log and started walking back toward the house.

"What's wrong Jen?" Todd cried as he ran after her.

Tears were stinging Jenny's eyes. Todd grabbed her arm so she would turn around and talk to him.

"Jenny I am so sorry," Todd said. "It's just that I love you so much and I thought you loved me, too."

"Stop it Todd!!" Jenny screamed at him. "Let me go!"

Jenny pulled her arm out of his grasp and started up the path. Todd ran in front of her and started walking backwards so he could talk to her.

"Jenny, please stop a minute. I am not Mark. I would never hurt you or do anything that you didn't want me to do."

"Then why did you say that?" Jenny said as she stopped and put her hands on her hips.

"It just came out, Jen. I just said it in the heat of the moment. I am sorry." Todd felt like a real heel now. He knew what Jenny had been through and he didn't want to hurt her in any way, shape or form.

"Todd, I think you need to go home now. I think you need to cool off," Jenny said as she started walking again then she stopped and turned around to Todd. "If that is the only reason you are going with me, Todd Kramer, you can have your ring back. Didn't you listen to the speaker at SHOUTfest? I think not! Like he said, this is my body and just because others are doing it, I am not going to do anything with you or anyone else until I am good and ready." She threw his ring and him and started walking again. She stopped once more and turned around again and added, "And married."

As Todd bent over and picked his ring up off the dusty path he cried out to Jenny.

"I'll wait forever until you are ready. I hope I will be the one you choose to walk down the aisle with some day. I'll wait as long as it takes, Jenny, because I love you."

Jenny's anger was dissipating and she was walking slower and slower.

"Those are awful sweet words, Todd Kramer," she said as she finally stopped.

"I mean every one of them," Todd said. Then he added, "Will you please forgive me, Jen? I love you so much."

Jenny knew Todd was very sincere and meant everything he was saying.

"You promise me that you will never try anything like that again," Jenny said with authority.

"I promise, cross my heart," Todd swore.

"And you promise that you will never mention it either."

"I promise," Todd said again. And then he continued, "only if you will take back my ring."

She forgave him then. Todd clasped the chain that held his ring around her neck and they kissed and made up.

As they were walking back to the house Jenny remembered the letters. She wondered if Todd had ever heard about another daughter of Grammy and Poppy. Or, maybe he had heard rumors of a scandal.

"Todd has your family lived here a long time?" she asked.

"My dad was born in our house. Why do you ask?"

"Did you ever hear of another daughter of the Madisons?"

"No, I can't say that I ever have," Todd said knitting his brow in thought.

"Do you know where I could look to find out if there were more children of Grammy and Poppy?"

Todd thought for a moment and then told Jenny she could either check the county records or check old church records. She asked if he could help her search.

"Of course, I'll help. But why do you need to know?"

Jenny told Todd about the letters that she had found. Then Todd suggested they go see Pastor Tom at church tomorrow and see if he has any records. They made plans to meet as soon as Todd finished his morning chores; probably around 10:00.

Jenny and Todd were walking across the side yard when they heard Tamara and Maggie laughing. When they came around the corner of the house they saw Ray sitting on the swing. The girls were in tears listening to Ray telling jokes. Tamara was holding her sides snorting at times, begging him to stop. Maggie couldn't say anything from laughing so hard and just pointed at Ray when Todd asked what was so funny. Ray was imitating some of his teachers and making strange faces and expressions. He looked so stupid that they just had to laugh at him. He mimicked his English teacher with a mock New England accent. His nose was stuck up in the air and his hands were limp at his wrists. Jenny started giggling. Todd had to chuckle at the girls breaking up.

About that time Barbara stuck her head out the front door and told the kids to come in for supper. Todd hadn't realized how late it had gotten. The sun was almost over the hill behind the house and the moon was bright in the eastern sky. Jenny walked Todd to the truck and Maggie accompanied Tamara. Before Todd got in he gave Jenny a hug, apologized once more and gave her a sweet kiss. When Jenny kissed him back, he knew that he was forgiven.

Maggie asked Grammy if she could spend the night with Jenny and Grammy agreed but Maggie would have to ask her mother. When Maggie brought up the subject Mary didn't care. She was happy to be rid of her for the night.

Maggie was going to sleep in Bob's old room and got ready for bed. After it was quiet she slipped over to Jenny's room and the two girls stayed up and talked for a couple of hours. Jenny truly liked Maggie, but she felt sorry for her. She thought that if Maggie would lose weight she would be a much happier person.

"Ralph," Jenny teased. "I don't mean to pry, but…"

"I know what you are going to ask," Maggie interrupted. "Why am I so fat?"

"Well, I wasn't going to put it quite that way." Jenny felt her face blush.

Maggie went on to tell Jenny that she had been on about seven diets already and she starts off doing pretty well then something happens and she figures it isn't worth all the hassle and pain. Maggie said that no one cares what she looks like anyway and she doesn't have any support at home.

Jenny told Maggie that she has to like herself first before anyone would like her. And she reminded her that Jesus loves her and that God doesn't make junk. She had to have confidence and poise and maybe she could join a support group, like TOPS or Weight Watchers.

"There aren't any kids in those groups." Maggie said. "And besides, my mom won't pay for anything like that."

Jenny explained about her support group at school and suggested she check into a peer group at her school. Before the night was over Jenny talked Maggie into cutting back on the amount of food she eats and trying to get more exercise. Jenny also told Maggie that she could call her and let her know how she is doing. Jenny would be her support group. Maggie promised that after the weekend she would really try.

Chapter Twenty-Three

Todd called Jenny at 10:00 the next morning and said he would be right over. Jenny apologized to Maggie and said that she and Todd had a very important errand to run. She said they should be back in a hour. Maggie told Jenny that she was very happy here and would help Grammy clean up from yesterday. While Jenny was gone, Maggie tried to put on make-up herself. She didn't do a bad job, but she definitely needed to practice. She also pulled part of her hair back and pulled it up into barrettes. It looked very nice.

When Todd pulled up in the truck Jenny ran out and jumped in. It didn't take long for them to get over to the church. Pastor Tom was sitting in his office preparing the Sunday's sermon when the kids walked in. Jenny asked Pastor if she could see the records of parishioners from the 1960's. Pastor went over to a large filing cabinet and pulled out two manila folders. One was labeled 1961 and the other was 1962. He explained that these contain the names and addresses of all parishioners of that particular year. Jenny opened the first folder and scanned the list until she found Madison. It had Henry, Ruth, Robert, Frederick and Helen listed. It gave the ages of the children and the address of the family. Jenny asked pastor if he remembered a Helen Madison.

"I'm sorry Jenny," he said. "I didn't come here until 1982. I don't know if Pastor Mike would remember her or not."

"Pastor Mike," Jenny repeated. "Where would we find him?"

They were told that Pastor Mike had retired a few years ago and was living in the Woodland Retirement Home in Hamilton. Jenny looked at Todd and he nodded his head signifying he would take her to Hamilton.

"Wait a minute," Pastor said. "Let's look a few years ahead. Sometimes the records show when people leave the area. They leave a forwarding address."

Jenny asked Pastor to look at the records around 1968 or 1969 and when he handed Jenny the folder she immediately looked at the Madison family. Helen's named had a circle around it with the word "over" written next to it. Jenny turned the paper over and there was Helen Madison's address in Detroit. She got a scrap of paper and copied the address and then she thanked Pastor Tom and told Todd that she would check on Pastor Mike after school on Monday.

When Todd and Jenny returned to the farm they saw Fred's car in the yard. He had come to get Maggie because Mary wanted to go home early. Maggie was so disappointed that she had to leave. Maggie gave Grammy a big hug and through the tears she said that she wished she could stay with her. Grammy thought that perhaps that might be just the best thing for Mags. Mary wasn't giving her what she needed.

Grammy pulled Fred aside and she asked, "Fred, how does Mary feel about Maggie?"

"Mom, Mary is going through some bad times lately. I think she is starting the change. She jumps on Maggie over the smallest things. Mags hasn't said anything but I know that Mary has hit her couple of times." Fred dropped his head then continued. "I don't know what to do about it. She gets along great with the boys."

"Son," Grammy said. "Let her stay with us."

Fred was shocked. He would have to talk to Mary about it. He didn't know how she would handle such a request. If he said okay without asking her, she might go off on him and he knew he had better let her make the decision. Fred decided to call Mary from the farm. If she was going to yell he would be far enough away so she couldn't hurt him. When he made the suggestion to her she very simply said "Sure, Fred, I'll be happy to get her off my hands for a while. Tell Ruth we'll send her things after we get home."

Fred could not believe how easy that was and how easy Mary gave up her daughter. When Fred told Maggie what had been decided she hugged him and then hugged Grammy

"I can't believe it," she cried. "I can really stay here? Oh thank you, Daddy. Oh thank you, Grammy."

Fred told her that she would have to help around the house and not cause Grammy any worry; and she promised that she would be on her best behavior. She hugged her dad once more and ran in the house to tell Jenny the news. Jenny was very happy that Maggie was going to stay with them.

Right before Fred got into the car to leave, Maggie came out and hugged him once more.

"I'll miss you Daddy," she said. "I love you and I'll email you."

"I love you, too, Mags," Fred said as he choked back a tear. He would try to write back to her and would send her spending money when he could. Maggie, Jenny and Grammy stood in the yard and watched Fred go down the lane.

Maggie put her arm around Grammy's waist and just said, "Thanks Grammy, you just saved my life."

Jenny met Maggie and Grammy at school on Monday morning and walked them into the office. Grammy told the register that she was Maggie's guardian and when they ask for transcripts from her previous school Grammy said that they would be sent in a few days. The registrar asked Maggie what classes she had been taking and Maggie said that she had English, Algebra, Keyboarding, Health & P.E., French, Physical Science and Art. Maggie had her report card from the first quarter since she had brought it to show Grammy at Thanksgiving and that was enough to help the registrar assigned classes for Maggie. Jenny asked if she could be put into third period Art and the registrar said that she would check with Mrs. Schneider but she didn't see any problem. Maggie also asked to have the same lunch as Jenny. If she took fourth hour P. E. she would have the same lunch time. Things were working out fine for Maggie.

Jenny had to get a pass for coming into class late and Mr. Hill told her that they were reviewing for a test to be held on Tuesday. Jenny quickly got her work out and paid close attention. At lunch time Jenny asked Todd about going with her to the retirement home to see Pastor Mike and he said that he couldn't go tonight because he wouldn't have a way home afterwards. Jenny said that she would call her mom and see if she would take Todd home after they studied at the library for a major test coming up. He told her to give it a try. All Barbara could say was no.

While Jenny was making a call Maggie and Tamara came to the table with their lunches. Tamara noticed that Maggie didn't have very much on her tray.

"Jenny said I could eat everything I used to eat accept I have to cut the amount in half." Maggie said when Tamara asked what was going on.

"Good idea," Tamara replied.

Jenny walked back then and told Todd that her mom said that she would take him home after studying. She even said that she would pick them up at the library at 4:30 so that would give them plenty of time.

Todd met Jenny at her locker after the last bell to walk over to the nursing home. They would have to hurry in order to get to the library by 4:30. When they were walking out Todd saw Gary and rushed over to ask him if he would drop them off. When Gary said he would Todd motioned for Jenny to come over to the car and they jumped in. When Gary dropped them off at the front door of the nursing home Jenny and Todd thanked him and said they owed him big time.

Pastor Mike was sitting in the solarium when Jenny and Todd came in. He recognized Todd immediately and Todd introduced Jenny to the old man. After some small talk Jenny asked Pastor Mike about Helen Madison.

"Helen Madison," Pastor Mike repeated the name. "I guess I remember her. Why do you have an interest in her?"

Jenny explained that Helen Madison is her aunt and that she wants to write to her but she doesn't have her address.

"Last I heard Helen was in the Chicago area; I believe it was Elgin. She was teaching at the local high school there. Sad thing about her and her family…it was a shame, a real shame." Pastor Mike said and shook his head.

"What happened with her?" Jenny asked.

"I think you should talk to Hank and Ruth about that; it was a bad time for them when Helen left." Pastor Mike changed the subject and asked Todd how he was doing in school. Todd talked to the old man for a few minutes then and thanked him for his help.

Jenny told Todd that they really had to go to the library now. Since Gary had dropped them off at the nursing home they had plenty of time to get over to the library. Jenny would also have time to go in and check out the schools in Elgin. Once they left the nursing home Jenny started running. When Todd caught up to her, he asked why she was running,

"I'm so close, Todd," Jenny said through huffing and puffing.

The two kids ran the four blocks to the library in less than five minutes. Todd and Jenny caught their breath and rested just a minute before they went in and walked back to the reference section and asked the clerk for any books that listed schools in Elgin, IL. The clerk went back and brought an IHSA listing of all public schools in Illinois. Jenny thanked her and took the book over to the nearby table.

She opened the book and quickly looked up Elgin and there were two high schools there. Jenny was excited when she noticed that the book gave a listing of the entire faculty and staff of the school. She read down the list of the first school. There was no one name Madison or Helen at the school. When she looked at the other school she noticed that there was a Helen Douglas who taught English. Jenny copied down the name of the school, address, the teacher's name and phone number of school.

She looked over at Todd and said "Bingo! I found her."

When started a letter to the English teacher at Elgin High School.

  Dear Ms. Douglas:

  My name is Jenny Madison and I am looking for my Aunt Helen from Hamilton Illinois. She is the daughter of Ruth and Henry Madison and has two brothers named Bob and Fred. If you are she, please call or write me.

  Sincerely, Jenny Madison

Jenny signed the letter, addressed it and used her school address for her return address. She asked the librarian if she could buy a pre-stamped envelope and slide her letter inside. After she sealed it, she and Todd both kissed it for luck. She slipped out of the library and ran down to the mailbox at the other corner of the block. Jenny would just have to wait now to hear if this Ms. Douglas is her Aunt Helen.

Exactly one week to the day when Jenny mailed the letter she received an envelope in the mail from Elgin High School. She took the letter and ran up to her room to read it.

  Dear Jenny:

  I received your letter this morning and I'm happy to say that I am your Aunt Helen. I have not been in Hamilton for many years. I would love to talk to you and your father. I miss my family very much.

Should Jenny tell her dad? Should she tell her mom? Should she call her aunt first? What should she do? Jenny sat on the edge of her bed and decided to call Todd.

Todd agreed that she should call and talk to her aunt and find out what happened so long ago. She may be opening up a can of worms that could cause some serious pain. She had better be careful. After she hung up the phone from talking to Todd, she looked at her letter again. Aunt Helen had told her to call collect any time during the evening. Jenny looked at the number and decided to call. She went into her room and closed the door hoping to have some privacy for the call. After the operator asked if the party would accept a collect call from Jenny Madison, Jenny heard the man on the other end of the line say that he would. She didn't want to talk to a man she wanted to talk to Aunt Helen.

"Jenny this is David, Helen's son. Mom will be here in a moment."

"Thank you, David," Jenny said politely.

Jenny could hear David tell his mother that the person on the phone sounds like a very young person.

"Hello Jenny," said the voice on the other end. Jenny thought she was talking to Grammy because the voice sounded exactly like her.

"Hello Mrs. Douglas, ummm, I mean Aunt Helen," Jenny stammered. Jenny proceeded to tell Helen about the letters that she had found behind an old trunk in Helen's old bedroom. She said that there were several letters sent to her from Grammy but that they had been returned to the sender. Helen began to cry. She said that she waited years to receive a letter from her mother. Jenny asked why she had left Hamilton. Helen said she couldn't get into that over the phone right now. But she did say that she and her father had gotten into a terrible argument and very hurtful things were said. She said that it happened a long time ago and she wondered if her father had never forgiven her. Jenny asked her if she should mention Aunt Helen to Grammy. Helen didn't know what to tell Jenny. She said that Jenny could try but to be very careful. She said that it was a very painful time in all of their lives. Helen told Jenny to call her again and let her know how Grammy felt about her. She wanted to speak to her brother, too, but was afraid of what he would say. Jenny said that she would feel out the situation with her dad, too.

Helen thanked Jenny for looking her up and calling her. She looked forward to hearing from her very soon and Jenny promised to call Helen at least by the next week. After they said their good-byes Jenny hung up the phone. She didn't know any more now than she did before she called. She sure wanted to know what happened and she had her mind made up that she was going to find out.

Chapter Twenty-Four

Jenny's mind was far from her classes today. She didn't even say much to Maggie in Art Class or to Todd in Computer Class. During Computer Class Jenny looked up ideas to incorporate her plans into the Advent season but nothing that she found really looked promising. What was she going to do?

She explained the predicament to Todd at lunch but he had no answers for her.

"What are you talking about Jenny?" Maggie asked.

"Oh, nothing Maggie. I'm just trying to solve a mystery here," Jenny answered her cousin as Maggie joined them at the lunch table.

"Did I hear you mentioned an Aunt Helen?" Jenny thought Maggie must have exceptional hearing. "I know I have an Aunt Helen. My dad told me about her a few years ago. He used to send her letters and Christmas cards for quite some time but they always came back unopened."

"You know about Aunt Helen?" Jenny asked in surprise.

"Yes," Maggie said. "They told me the whole story. It is a real shame."

Maggie started to tell the story to Jenny and Todd. "My dad said that Helen had been a very beautiful girl and was very popular in school and had lots of friends. Poppy would not let her date until she turned eighteen but she would go to movies and dances with groups of friends. Grammy adored her and gave everything she wanted. My room at Grammy's belongs to Helen. Anyway, one day she had some friends from high school out to the farm for a party; with both boys and girls at the party. They were all walking around the farm and some of them started to pair off. Poppy walked into the barn and caught Helen with one of the boys making out in the hay loft. He was so angry that he took an old horse whip and beat the boy until he ran from the barn. Poppy grabbed Helen and beat her until she passed out. Grammy saw the boy screaming and he and the other kids left the farm in a hurry. Grammy ran down to the barn and saw Helen lying in the hay bloody and unconscious. She screamed at Poppy to stop and he told Grammy that he wanted Helen out of their house because she was no longer his daughter. Grammy tried to reason with him but she didn't have any luck." Jenny sat spellbound listening to the story. She begged Maggie to continue when the bell rang ending their lunch.

"I have to hear the rest of the story," Jenny exclaimed. "Maggie you got to come home with me after school. I got to hear the rest of the story."

The girls decided that they would call Grammy and Barbara and make plans for Maggie to spend the night with Jenny. Between fifth and sixth hour at school Jenny left a note on Maggie's locker saying Barbara said that it was fine for Maggie to come home with Jenny and between six and seventh hours Maggie did the same. The girls met each other outside the main entrance of school so Maggie could finish the story while they walked home. Maggie wasn't used to walking yet so she was breathing quite heavily as she finished the story.

"Well," she began, "someone had called the sheriff and sent the ambulance. The boy that was caught with Helen was hurt pretty badly and Helen was taken to the hospital. She was still unconscious. His parents wanted to press charges against Poppy. When the sheriff arrested him and was taking Poppy to jail he looked at Grammy and told her that Helen had better not be there when he got home or he would finish the job. Due to some technicality Poppy only had to serve 30 days in the county jail. He yelled loud enough for his sons to hear that he no longer had a daughter…that she was dead to him. After Helen was released from the hospital she went home for a little while. She stayed in her room and didn't talk to her brothers. For all the young boys knew, she was dead. Helen packed most of her things and Grammy gave her some money. Right before Poppy was released Grammy left Helen at the bus station. When he got back home he told Grammy, Uncle Bob and my dad that Helen was no longer a part of the family and they were not to mention her name or they would feel the wrath of his whip, too."

"Wow! No wonder no one talks about her," Jenny said. "Maggie, finish it."

"That's it, Jenny," Maggie said. "That's all I know. Dad said that he never spoke Helen's name since then."

"How long ago did you learn about this?"

"Oh gee," Maggie stammered. "I guess I'll heard about Aunt Helen two or three years ago."

Jenny just shook her head. "No wonder Poppy seems so sad all the time."

At supper that evening Jenny suggested that the family have a Bible verse as a prayer for the Advent wreath she had made today at school. Bob and Barbara thought that was quite a good idea. So after they were finished eating, the table had been cleared and all the dishes were done and put away they walked out into the living room. Jenny and Maggie had everything all planned. As Maggie lit the candle for the first week in Advent Jenny read the scripture of the prodigal's son. Bob and Barbara look at Jenny and thought that was a strange verse for Advent. After the scripture reading was finished Maggie started a prayer.

"Let us pray," she said. "We thank you for giving us a loving family. Please bless those around us and those who are far from us. Amen."

Bob figured she must be talking about her family. Then Jenny and Maggie stopped him from leaving after Barbara and John left the room.

"What is it girls?" he asked them.

"Daddy," Jenny began. "We have something very serious to talk to you about, something you might not want to talk about, too."

"Well," Bob sure was curious now about what was going on; all kinds of scary thoughts went through his mind.

"Jenny you and Todd aren't in trouble are you?" he asked.

"No daddy it's not about me," Jenny couldn't believe he would even think that about her and Todd. "We want to talk to you about your sister Helen."

"What?" Bob exclaimed. "How do you know about my sister Helen?"

"I've talked to her on the phone, dad. I want to invite her here for Christmas."

"Oh Jen, you have no idea what you're getting into here," Bob said as he sat down on the sofa.

"I think I do, dad. Maggie and I have talked about it a lot. That all happened a long time ago and Poppy needs to learn to forgive her. She has forgiven him. Please Daddy, will you help us with this reunion?"

Bob had no idea how Poppy would react to hearing Helen's name, not to mention seeing her again. Bob was so young when all this happened but he remembers the look in his father's eyes when he forbade them to mention her name. He said he should talk to Grammy about it first

"Jen all I can do is promise to think about it. I'll let you know in a couple of days what I'm going to do."

"Okay Dad, just keep in mind that Christmas is coming very soon." Jenny reminded him.

Bob left the room as though the weight of the entire world had been dropped in his lap. Sure he would like to see Helen again. He always got along with her when they were kids. As the girls were going up the stairs Bob paused.

"Hey Jen," he called. "You said that you have talked to Helen?" Jenny nodded her head. And he continued, "Can I have her number?"

Jenny ran back down to give her dad a hug, and then ran like the wind up the stairs to her room to get Helen's phone number. Bob took the slip of paper and turn it over and over in his hand. He held the paper as if it was a hot coal burning his fingers. He then walked upstairs into his office and closed the door behind him.

"Hello," said the female voice on the other end of the phone line.

"Helen," Bob's voice crackled.

"Yes. Who is this, please?" she asked.

Bob was almost in tears. "This is Bob, your brother, Bob," he said.

"Oh my goodness!!" Exclaimed Helen.

They both began to cry on the phone. It had been so long. They had so much to catch up on and didn't know where to start. Bob said that he wanted to keep in touch with her but had no idea where she went. She told him that she wrote to Grammy but never received any answers from her.

Bob told Helen he would try to talk to their mother about her. He also told her Jenny wants her to come home for Christmas. Helen said that she would like nothing more than to be reunited with her family. Bob said he would try to do everything he could on his end. He also said he couldn't promise that their father would come around. Helen understood.

When Bob told the whole story to her, Barbara couldn't believe that Poppy had held this inside of him for so long. Bob had talked to Barbara about Jenny's plan and they decided they would all go out to the farm on Saturday. They would ask John to be sure to take Poppy down to the barn while they talk to Grammy. Jenny told them about the returned letters so Grammy must have tried to write to Helen. Barbara wondered how it would go.

The twenty minute drive to the farm on Saturday seemed to only take a few minutes because Bob was nervous about what might happen once they got to the farm. Grammy met them at the back door and offered John and Jenny fresh homemade cinnamon rolls. John was about to accept when he saw the look on Jenny's face.

"Maybe later, Grammy," he said. "Thanks anyway."

John suggested to Poppy that they go down to the barn and check on the animals and Poppy said the George had been over that morning and went down already.

"But Poppy it has been so long since you and I have been down there together," John begged.

Bob walked in and said, "And it's a beautiful crisp day. There might not be too many more like it this season. Go out and get some fresh air with your grandson."

Poppy finally agreed and went to the porch to get his jacket and cap. When Bob saw John and Poppy take off toward the barn in the golf cart he turned to his mother and told her to sit down. He told her that they had something important to talk to her about.

"What is the Bob?" Grammy started. "Is everyone all right? I feel like you are on ganging up on me."

Jenny started to tell Grammy the story of the prodigal's son and Grammy said that she had heard that before; after all she knows her scripture. Bob told her the real reason they wanted to talk to her. It was about Helen.

Grammy got up and walked over to the kitchen sink not saying a word.

"Mom," Bob came over and put his hands on her shoulders. "Don't you think it is about time to forgive and forget?"

Grammy turned around to Barbara and had tears streaming down her face. She couldn't say anything at the moment and sat down on the nearest kitchen chair. She wiped her eyes on the tail of her apron.

"Bob," She started finally. "It has been so long. You're right about that. But I doubt very much if Hank is ready to let it go. She hurt him so badly. She was his favorite you know. When she was disloyal to him he went crazy. I remember the boy and Helen both were in the hospital with welts and cuts across their backs for over a week. We didn't know if Helen would ever be able to use her hands again. It was such a horrible time." Grammy started to cry again.

Grammy, Bob, Barbara, Maggie and Jenny tried to think of ways to bring Helen's named into the conversation. Jenny had an idea that they would talk about one of her teachers who is named Helen. See if he reacts to the name. Barbara said that she could mention that she needs to call her sister whom she has not talked to in about ten years. Maggie could bring up the fact that her mother doesn't want to have anything to do with her and she will miss her family this Christmas. All of them had good ideas. They said that they would try to incorporate their ideas at lunchtime.

Everyone was very quiet after John and Poppy came back into the house. The women were busy preparing lunch and setting the table. Bob held the newspaper as if he were reading it. When all was ready Grammy called them to the table. When Poppy lowered has head to say grace Jenny piped up and ask if she could say grace today. Poppy nodded and Jenny began her prayer.

"Dear Lord, We thank you for this food set before us and the hands that prepared it. We thank you for our family and pray that we will all be together over the holidays. We ask for your forgiveness and the strength to forgive others. In Jesus name we pray."

Poppy stared at Jenny and then grumbled "Amen." Everyone was so quiet at the table it was a strange and eerie feeling

"Hey, Mags," Jenny started. "Do you like the new art teacher we have?"

"You mean Miss Helen, uh, what is her last name?" Maggie said

"I'm not sure," Jenny said, she just told us to call her Miss Helen."

"Oh yeah, she's pretty nice," Maggie said. "I liked her a lot."

""Me, too," Jenny said as she looked over at her mother who was shaking her head. Poppy had not responded one way or the other to the name.

"Bob," Barbara started. "I got a card in the mail yesterday from my sister. You remember Sherry? She was in our wedding."

"Yes, dear, I remember her," Bob said. "How is she?"

"She sent a nice long letter. She's doing fine. I'll let you read it. It has been over ten years since we've heard from her." Barbara kept peeking at Poppy out of the corner of her eye. "It sure would be nice to have the whole family together for Christmas this year."

"Yes it would," Bob said. Then to Maggie he said "are your parents coming in for Christmas Maggie or are you going home for the holidays?"

"I don't know yet Uncle Bob. My mother doesn't want to have anything to do with me anymore. Maggie pretended to start crying. She basically wrote me out of the family when I moved here. That's OK because Poppy and Grammy are more loving than my mother ever will be."

They were getting no reaction at all from Poppy he just sat there, calmly eating his lunch

"I would give anything to have my whole family together for Christmas," Grammy said. "It would be the best Christmas present in the world."

"You just had everyone here at Thanksgiving." Poppy finally said

Grammy had had enough. She put her fork down on the table with a bang. She looked straight across the table and started in on Poppy

"Henry Michael Madison I have lived with you for almost 51 years and I have never asked you for anything in all those years. Now I have one request for Christmas. I want my family with us for the holidays….my entire family."

Poppy still didn't get it. "Everyone was just here over Thanksgiving and look how that turned out."

Grammy stood up and with her hands at her sides rolled into fists. "Hank you can be so cruel and heartless. I am not going to stand for it anymore. I want my daughter back. I want her to come home."

Poppy's face went pale. He didn't say a word but just looked at the anger and hurt in Grammy's eyes. Then he calmly took a bite of food and said, "Not here, Ruth. Not now."

"Yes here and now," Grammy almost screamed at him. "They have all talked to Helen in the past couple of weeks. Hank I want to talk to my daughter. I want to hold her in my arms. I want to know her children. I will expect nothing less than to have her sleeping in her own room upstairs on Christmas Eve."

Poppy stood up and started to walk out of the dining room. He turned to Grammy and said, "I will not have that girl under my roof. I do not have a daughter." Then he left.

Grammy sat down hard in her chair and began to weep. He had taken away her child so long ago and was too stubborn to forgive something that happened over 30 years ago. Then Grammy wiped her tears and told Maggie to pack her things. They were leaving. Grammy stood up and told Barbara and Bob that they would be in later this afternoon. Then she stormed up the stairs to her room to pack her bags. She was leaving Hank.

Chapter Twenty-Five

Bob, Barbara, Jenny, and John had been home only an hour when Grammy and Maggie pulled up in the old Buick. Bob and John went out to the car to help bring in their bags. John gave up his room so Grammy wouldn't have to climb two flights of stairs. And Maggie took one of the two large rooms on the third floor. Jenny teased Maggie that she would be getting more exercise climbing the extra flight of stairs. Grammy didn't come down from her room at supper time. When Barbara knocked on her door she heard a very quiet "come in." Barbara walked in and sat on the edge of the bed next to Grammy. She had been crying.

"Barbara I am so mad at that old goat," she said. "Hasn't he punished Helen long enough? I didn't dare speak back to him when it all happened. I was afraid he would leave me and the boys. It was hard enough while he was in jail. I begged Helen to ask for his forgiveness. But neither she nor Hank would give in. He had hurt her too badly and she had destroyed his trust." Grammy wasn't talking as fast as she usually did and she was hurt and angry.

"Barbara I want to call Helen. I need to talk to her. She can come here and spend Christmas with us. Hank is the one that is losing out."

Barbara just sat and listened to Grammy talk. They walked into Bob's office and got Helen's phone number. Grammy was so nervous that she asked Barbara to make the call and once Helen was on the phone Barbara asked her to hang on for a moment.

"Helen?" Grammy said

"Mother? Mother is that you? Oh my goodness!" Helen started to cry. Neither she nor Grammy could talk at the moment.

"Helen, I wrote you. I wrote you so many letters but they all came back." Grammy said between sniffles.

"I left Detroit. Mom, I went back to school in Illinois and got my teaching degree. Oh Mother I have missed you so much."

"Come home Helen. Oh, please come home for Christmas," Grammy begged.

"Mom, I can't," Helen said. "I can't come home unless he asks me. I won't come home unless he wants me there."

"Oh my, girl, I'm not asking you to come to the farm. Come to Bob's house. I've left your father. I can't stay there with him like this. I need to see my family, my daughter. I need to feel whole again," Grammy said as she started to cry again.

Grammy couldn't talk anymore so Barbara took the phone and told Helen what had happened at lunch today. Helen felt that it was because of her that Grammy had left Poppy. Barbara told her they had plenty of room for Helen, her husband and three children and she wouldn't have to see Poppy if she didn't want to. Helen said that she would think about it. Grammy took the phone back from Barbara.

"Please Helen, plan to come for Christmas. That's the only thing I want this year. I want to see my baby girl and her family. Please Helen, please come home," Grammy begged.

"I'll call you in a couple of days," Helen said and then hung up the phone.

"Barbara she has got to come," Grammy said as she grabbed Barbara's arm to help her up off the chair.

"Come down for supper, Ruth," Barbara said

"I think I will," Grammy said. "I feel better now after talking to Helen."

Grammy came down to eat supper with the family. Maggie and Jenny had already set the table and were dishing up the roast, carrots, potatoes and gravy that Barbara had made. Grammy sat down next to John. Bob said grace and started passing the plates around. Grammy filled her plate and just stared at it and moved things around on her plate but ate very little.

When the rest of the family had finished their meals Jenny had taken the plates over to the counter. Barbara had made a pie for dessert and asked who wanted a piece. Grammy was still sitting there nibbling at her roast and potatoes. With a mouthful of pie John whispered to his father than Grammy seemed a million miles away. Bob replied that she was only about fifteen miles out in the country. John nodded that he understood. Usually after a meal Grammy would pick up her plate and take it to the kitchen sink and then she would help clean up. But tonight when Grammy got up from the table she just laid her napkin on the plate and walked out without saying a word and went upstairs.

Bob and Barbara were truly worried about Grammy. Jenny felt bad because she had started this whole thing. Bob reassured Jenny that this was not her fault and the two old people had hidden the secret for so long that neither of them would give in to the other. He said that sooner or later one of them would come around. Jenny sure hoped it would be soon, at least before Christmas. Maggie called her dad that evening and told him what was going on and he said he knew something like this was bound to happen sooner or later. He told Maggie to ask Bob if he should come over and talk to Grammy. Maggie just handed the phone to Bob instead.

After Bob said that he didn't think that Fred needed to come over right away, Fred said that he had some bad news, too. After Thanksgiving, Mary started acting strange. After she had sent all of Maggie's things to the farm she pulled the bed, mattress, a chair and the dresser from Maggie's room out onto the front lawn. She got a can of gasoline and poured it over the furniture and she set the pile on fire. A neighbor saw her do it, and immediately called the fire department. Mary fought the firemen who were trying to put it out. Fred said that he had Mary committed to the psychiatric unit of the Iowa City hospital. He asked Bob not to say anything to Maggie about it because he wanted to tell her in person when he and Thomas come for Christmas. He said that Joseph was going to Rebecca's for Christmas. Bob promised not to say anything about it to Maggie.

Bob gave Helen's phone number to Fred and asked if he would call her and talk her into coming home for Christmas. He said that their mother needed to see her and hopefully their dad would come around. Bob hoped it would happen before Christmas and Fred said he would call and see what he could do.

Sunday morning the family was getting ready to go to church when Barbara asked Grammy if she was going to go with them. Grammy said she didn't want to see Hank; especially in church of all places.

"That hypocrite," she called him.

When Barbara said that they were going to church in town Grammy quickly changed her clothes and went with the family to church.

The preacher's sermon was on the importance of the Lord's Prayer and forgiveness.

"Forgive us as we forgive our debtors," he said from the pulpit. "There is nothing so horrible in this life that God will not forgive. God loves each and every one of you and he knows that sometimes we all stray from the right path and He will always give us a hand to lead us home. All we have to do," the preacher said as he reached out, "is to ask the Lord for forgiveness."

Jenny looked over at Grammy who was hanging on to every word that the preacher said. Grammy stood up with the rest of the congregation as the choir began to sing *Show us the way, O Lord*. On the way home Grammy sat the back seat of the car humming the final hymn that was sung at church and then she paused for a second and repeated with a preacher had said.

"Forgive us as we forgive our debtors." she said, "To bad Hank didn't hear that sermon."

"It works both ways, Mom," Bob said.

Grammy just started humming again.

That afternoon Todd called to talk to Jenny and said they had not seen her grandparents in church this morning and his mom wondered if everything was all right. Jenny told Todd what had happened and he couldn't believe something like that could happen to Grammy and Poppy. He said he and his dad were going over to a check on the stock and they would stop in and see how Poppy is getting along. Jenny thanked him and made him promise to call back after they saw Poppy. Todd said he would. Jenny told her mom and dad that Todd was going to check on Poppy this afternoon. Bob was just about ready to leave to do that himself.

"That saves me a trip," Bob said as he walked down stairs to the family room. John came bounding down the steps and plopped down on the seat next to his dad. He wanted to know if they were going today and get their Christmas tree. Bob said that maybe they had better wait to see what happens with the family. John didn't think it was fair they had to suffer for something that happened before he was born. Barbara agreed with John so Bob got up, changed clothes and said they would go out to buy a Christmas tree. Jenny said they wanted a big tree to put the living room. Barbara suggested they put the tree in the foyer but John said he wanted one down in the family room. After lengthy discussion it was decided that they would get a small tree for the family room and a large one for the living room. Jenny, Maggie and John went with Bob to pick out the trees at a lot at the school run by the Future Farmers of America and decided on a big spruce for the living room. John found a smaller free for the family room but it was still over 6ft. tall. Bob told him that it was too big and they would have to get something smaller. Maggie found a full branch tree that stood about 4ft. They all agreed that was the perfect tree for the family room. The boys from the FFA tied the trees on top of the car for Bob after he paid them for the trees and the group left.

"Dad do we have enough lights for two trees?" Jenny asked.

After they took the trees home they decided to take a run across the river to the Keokuk WalMart. Bob gave the girls $40.00 and told them to get as many lights as they could with that. The girls walked out with two huge bags full of lights and big smiles on their faces. When they got in the car Jenny said that the store had lights on sale.

"They were boxes of 120 lights that they were on sale for $2.00 a box so we got twenty boxes," she and Maggie started laughing.

"That's over 2000 lights!" John said.

"Well we got big trees," Jenny said. Bob just shook his head and drove home.

Barbara couldn't believe the size of the trees and she just smiled and shook her head when she saw all the lights the girls had bought. John ran up to Grammy's room and asked if she wanted to help trim the trees but she said that she would be down in a little while.

Bob set the big tree up in one of the larger tree stands that they had while Barbara moved the sofa away from the front window. Bob slid the tree into the open spot. The girls started to put lights on the tree but they had to get a ladder to reach the top. Meanwhile John helped Barbara get all the Christmas ornaments down from the attic. Barbara brought most of the boxes in where the girls were working and John took a couple boxes down to the family room. By the time they were finished Jenny and Maggie had put over 1500 lights on the big tree. They use the gold garland and wrapped it around the tree. When Grammy came, she said that the tree looked wonderful. She helped put some of the ornaments on the tree. Jenny found her "baby's first Christmas" ornament and put it right in front. Barbara found the ornament that she bought on their honeymoon. It was a bride and groom and said "Our First Christmas" and she put it on the tree next to Jenny's. They had put all the ornaments on the tree and Bob was ready to plug in the lights when Jenny noticed they didn't have anything on the top of the tree. Bob reached into one of the unopened boxes and pulled out an angel. She had flowing blond hair, silky sheer wings and a beautiful satin dress with lacey edges.

"Remember this Mom," he asked Grammy.

Grammy looked at the angel. "No Bob, I can't say that I do." she replied after careful inspection of the angel.

"I brought this back from Germany with me when I was in the service," Bob said. "She's Dresden China. We have used every year. She is so pretty."

Bob stepped up on the ladder, leaned over and put the angel on the top of the tree. The girls said that it was the prettiest tree they had ever seen after Bob plugged in the lights, and none of them wanted to go downstairs to help John.

"I think we had better go down and see if we can help John," Barbara said.

The girls picked up all the boxes and put them in the closet in the foyer and went down to see what they could do for John. When they all walked into the family room John and Marble were lying in front of the tree sound asleep. The tree was completely decorated and the lights twinkled softly in the dark room. It was a sweet scene. Barbara went to get the camera and took a picture of her son under the tree. Jenny and Maggie decided to go ahead upstairs to go to bed and Grammy said that she was going to bed, too. It had been a very long and tiring day for her. Bob woke John up and led the groggy boy up to his room. Marble bounced up the several flights of stairs and curled up at the foot of his bed.

On the way up the stairs the phone rang and it was Todd and he wanted to talk to Jenny. He told her he and his dad went over to the farm to check on Poppy. Todd said that Poppy was down at the barn feeding the calves when they arrived. Poppy asked George if Grammy had sent him over to check on the old man. When George assured him that they were just there to tend to the livestock, Todd said Poppy turned in a huff and headed back to the house mumbling something under his breath to George. Todd said his dad had a shocked look on his face and they left right away after that.

"He's doing fine, Jenny" Todd said. "He's just a little steamed at all of you right now. Give him some time."

Jenny said "We don't have that much time. Christmas is only six days away and I hope he doesn't spoil it for us."

Todd said he knew she would have a good Christmas and he would talk to her at school tomorrow. After hanging up the phone Jenny told her dad what Todd had said.

"Stubborn old man," Bob said as he headed down the stairs.

Barbara was checking the doors when Bob came back down to the living room. Barbara was looking at the tree and Bob came up behind her and put his arm around her waist.

"We are lucky aren't we, Bob?" Barbara said. Bob simply nodded in agreement and kissed her cheek.

Chapter Twenty-Six

John, Jenny and Maggie were invited to Christmas parties after school on Monday. Bob and Barbara wanted Grammy to go home and talk to Poppy.

"I'll do you no such thing," she roared at them. "He has to apologize to me first."

"At least call him mom," Bob begged.

"No Bob, you just don't understand or remember how it was back then. I refuse to make the first move." Grammy got up from her chair and walked into the living room. She picked up some needlework that she had been working on for Christmas. All of a sudden Grammy remembered that all the gifts for the family were out of the farm. How was she going to get them and bring them into town? She would have Todd get them. No, maybe Bob would go out and get them. She just didn't know what to do. Grammy went back into the kitchen to talk to Bob. She told him that all of the Christmas presents for the family were at the farm. She can tell them right where they were and asked if he would go out and bring them here. Bob didn't like the idea of going out there by himself. He knew that Poppy would probably start up on him about Grammy being in town and leaving him. But he told Grammy that he would go out tomorrow.

Bob decided to take the whole family with him out to the farm on Tuesday afternoon. As soon as the kids got home from school they piled in the car and left. Grammy stayed home but she had told Bob where the gifts were. That way he would not have to look all over the house. John said that he would try to get Poppy to go down to the barn while the rest of the family loaded the presents into the trunk of the car.

As soon as they pulled into the yard Poppy came out of the house and told them to leave. He didn't need anybody around here.

"Dad," Bob said. "We just came to make sure that you're all right."

"I'm fine. Now get," he said as he motioned toward the lane.

"Poppy will you go down to the barn with me?" John asked.

"John I ain't got nothing against ya boy and I don't need ya ta baby me," Poppy was talking so fast his old Ozark accent came back.

John was getting upset with Poppy's attitude.

"Look old man," John yelled three inches from Poppy's face. "I have been next to you ever since I can remember. I have learned everything I know how to do from you. Now you are teaching me how to be bull headed and stubborn. Get your coat on and let's go down to the barn."

John walked toward the shed to get the golf cart. He had only taken about five steps when he turned around. "One more thing ~ don't be mad at me for something that I had nothing to do with ~ something that happened before I was born. Get over it."

Poppy stood as still as a statue and no one could believe that John would talk like that to his grandfather. Bob was so proud of his son at this moment. Although Bob disdained disrespect, he secretly applauded John's tenacity to face up to his stubborn old grandpa. Under her breath Jenny said, "Way to go to John!"

Poppy grabbed his coat from the back porch and stormed toward John waiting in the golf cart. As soon as they were out of sight the rest of the family went into the house. Bob told Barbara that the Christmas presents were in a wardrobe in Fred's old room and Jenny, Maggie and Barbara hurried up to the bedroom while Bob kept on the lookout for John and Poppy. Sure enough there were several wrapped presents in the wardrobe. Maggie held open the garbage bag while Barbara and Jenny put package after package into the bag. By the time they were finished they had two big bags full of presents.

"Grammy sure went all out this year, didn't she?" Maggie said.

"She always does," Jenny said, while Barbara nodded in agreement.

Bob helped them put all the packages in the trunk of the car. They had to rearrange things a couple of times before the lid would shut tight. Then they went back into the house and waited for John to come back from the barn.

Meanwhile down at the barn John and Poppy were leaning against the fence looking out across the pasture. John was talking to his grandfather.

"Why are you so angry with Aunt Helen?" He asked his grandfather.

"That's none of your affair, boy," the old man replied.

"Don't you love her any more? Did she do something so bad that you don't care what happens to her? In the Bible we are told that Jesus died to forgive our sins. So surely she didn't do anything so bad that you can't forgive her." John was truly interested in the situation that caused Poppy to be in such turmoil.

"Boy, Aunt Helen, as you call her, disobeyed me in the worst way a girl could. She shattered my heart in so many pieces that I just couldn't stand being in the same room with her."

"What did she do that was so bad?" Poppy repeated the question. "She lay with another man just like my mother done," Poppy said almost in a whisper as tears began to roll down his weather worn cheeks.

"Lay with a man ... just like his mother done?" John said under his breath. He was confused. As far as he knew Aunt Helen was not married when Poppy kicked her out. As a matter of fact she was still in high school. But why would Poppy kick her out for making out with a guy? Ground her maybe ... but beat her up and kick her out? And John never knew his great-grandmother or even heard anyone talk about her. He had only seen pictures of Poppy with his father, but never his mother, in old photo albums. Why? What had she done? Where did she go? Had she hurt Poppy somehow? John didn't understand what Poppy meant.

"Never mind boy." Poppy wiped his face with the back of his sleeve. "Let's get back to the house. I'm getting cold," Poppy said as he climbed into the golf cart.

When they got up to the house Poppy told Bob to take his family home because he was tired and didn't want to talk to anyone. He said that he was tired of fighting.

"Then don't you think is time to make up?" Bob ask him.

"Not tonight and not yet," Poppy said as he walked into the living room and sat down in front of the television. "I need to watch the news."

"Poppy, you can still forgive her. Jesus forgives all sins," John whispered over the back of the chair after everyone had walked out of the room. John patted Poppy on the shoulder and then left the old man sitting alone with only the news anchor on the television for company on that cold dark night.

After the family arrived back in town Grammy asked how Poppy was doing and what he had to say. Barbara went in to tell Grammy everything was all right at the farm and Poppy looked all right, too. John pulled his father's sleeve and asked if they could talk.

"Privately," John said with a very serious look on his face.

"Now?" Bob asked as he hung up his jacket on the hook by the back door.

John nodded as he hung his jacket next to his dad's.

"Let's go to the office," Bob said to his son as they headed up the back stairs.

"Dad, Poppy said something I don't understand. Maybe you will."

John then recounted what Poppy had said about Helen laying with another man like his mother done. When John asked if he understood, Bob said "John, I think we have a mystery on our hands. I never knew my grandmother. She had died when Poppy was a small child. I think we need to get a hold of Helen and ask her what Poppy meant by that remark. I wonder if she'll know."

When Helen answered the phone Bob told her what Poppy said to John. He then asked if she knew what Poppy meant.

"Oh Bob, I knew this would happen. I hoped it would never come to surface." Helen took a deep breath and sighed.

"Is there a deep dark family secret I don't know about?" Bob asked almost in a half joking manner.

"Yes, I'm afraid so," Helen said seriously. "When I was in the hospital I just couldn't understand why Dad got so terribly angry when he found us. Pastor Mike came and talked to me. He told me an incredible story about Dad's mother."

When Hank was a small boy his mother had gentlemen callers in the afternoons when his father would be out working in the fields or tending to business. She made Hank sit on a chair, secure him with a belt so he could not get off, and tell him to be very quiet. She would take the man into the bedroom and let him have his way with her while the small child sat and listened to them. Hank would cover his ears and cry when he heard his mother moaning thinking the man was hurting her. A few times her husband would come home and catch her. The man would make a dash out of the house and Hank's father would beat his mother and order her never to do it again. She would promise and all would be well for a short time. But, she would start again. And being the good Christian that he was, Hank's father married for better or worse and would not divorce her. One afternoon Hank's father was coming in from the field and saw a man leaving the house. When he walked in he saw his wife unbuckling Hank from the chair. The startled woman looked up at him and he backhanded her so hard that she fell backwards, falling against the old cast iron stove. The small boy stood there watching the blood flow from the gash on his mother's head. They buried his mother the next day and Hank's father could never look at his 8 year old son the same way after that day, because he was ashamed of himself.

"Bob, are you there?" Helen asked.

"I'm sorry, Helen," Bob couldn't believe what he was hearing.

"Bob, after going to therapy myself," Helen said with a quiver in her voice. "It took a long time, lots of prayer and support from friends, but I have forgiven him."

Bob was sitting with his hand holding his head up and tears dripping onto the walnut desk. John, not even knowing what his dad was hearing, had tears running down his cheeks, just seeing his dad in such pain.

"There's more Bob. No one knows this." Helen paused and wondered whether she should tell.

"What is it, Helen? Can't be much worse than what I've already heard," Bob said, wiping his eyes with his sleeve.

"Bob, when I was in the hospital they found out that I was pregnant. The doctor was surprised that I didn't miscarry from the beating. Bob," Helen paused again.

"Don't tell me anymore, please," Bob said. "I don't know if I can handle anymore. I just don't want to hear it."

"Bob, I'm sorry. I have to say it. I came this far," Helen's voice cracked. Bob could tell she was crying. "Bob, I had George's child. I had his son."

"Oh Helen," Bob said. "I didn't know who the boy was. Does he know?"

"No, I never had the courage to write to him. And Bob," She paused. "He looks just like him. I am sure if we come home, there will be no denying of him."

"Well, that will be a bridge we will cross when we get there," Bob said.

John was sitting on the couch listening to his dad's half of the conversation and seeing his father's tears. He couldn't imagine what had gotten his dad so upset.

Helen told Bob that she would try to come home on Christmas Eve. She didn't promise anything but she would call Friday and let them know what she had decided. She thanked him for calling and caring and hung up the phone.

When Bob put the phone down John asked what was wrong. Bob figured in this day and age John was old enough to know what really happened to Helen so he told John the whole story. John sat in complete awe. He had heard about this happening to people and had watched the talk shows on television. But he couldn't believe that his idol, Poppy, would ever do anything so horrible. John and Bob went down to the family room to be with the rest of the family but they were not interested in anything that was going on.

That night while they were getting ready for bed Bob told Barbara what he and John had learned today. She sat and stared at Bob in complete disbelief. That news would kill Grammy so they decided to keep it to themselves for now. They would tell John in the morning that he shouldn't tell anyone what he knows, not even Jenny or Maggie.

The next couple of days were quite routine for the family. The kids went to school and Bob worked in his office. Barbara and Grammy made Christmas cookies and candy and Grammy made some pies for Christmas dinner. Barbara had a hard time holding her tongue when Grammy brought up Poppy's or Helen's names. This was the hardest secret that she ever had to keep. Friday afternoon Jenny and Maggie had placed Grammy's presents under the tree in the living room and were wrapping some final Christmas presents when the phone rang. Jenny hopped up and answered with a chipper holiday greeting.

"Merry Christmas!" She said into the phone.

"Well, Merry Christmas to you, too," Helen said.

"Oh Hi, Aunt Helen," Jenny said. "I'll get dad, just a minute."

Bob came down into the living room after talking to Helen. "Well we have got another present for Grammy," he said.

"She's coming," Jenny said in a whisper.

"Yes! She'll be here tomorrow around the 11:00 and let's keep this a secret from Grammy. OK," he said.

"Our lips are sealed," Jenny and Maggie said as they locked their lips with imaginary keys.

There had to be some rearranging in the sleeping arrangements. Maggie would have to move in with Jenny. John would go in to one of the smaller rooms on the third floor. Helen and her husband would take the large room. Helen's son, David, and his wife would take the other large room and their baby will sleep in their room with them. Bob called one of the neighbors to borrow a baby crib. Helen's daughter, Janet, would have one of the small rooms and her son, Eric, would have the other small room. Although it was hard getting everything arranged for Helen and her family so they wouldn't spoil the surprise, everything was all set now. All they had to do was wait until 11:00.

Grammy was sitting in the kitchen helping Barbara with Christmas Eve dinner. She had remarked that Barbara had enough to feed an army. Barbara said that her kids ate like an army. Jenny and Maggie were sitting in the living room waiting for Aunt Helen to get there. John was watching out the front window while Bob was pacing back and forth. Bob looked at his watch. It was 11:15. Where were they?

All of a sudden Jenny jumped up and ran to the front door. A van and a car pulled up and stopped in front of the house. She didn't wait for them to ring the doorbell because that would spoil the surprise. She greeted the family and ushered them into the living room. Bob hugged his sister as she introduced her family. Her son David looked so much like his father that even John could see the resemblance.

Jenny stood in the foyer and hollered at Grammy that they needed her help in the living room.

"Grammy, can you come right now?"

"What on earth?" Grammy said. Barbara told her to go ahead to help the girls as she had everything under control in the kitchen.

As soon as Grammy was out the door on the way to the living room Barbara ran through the other rooms because she wanted to be there for the surprise. When Grammy turned the corner into the living room she almost fainted. It was a good thing that Barbara was there to catch her.

"Oh my goodness!" Grammy exclaimed as she walked to Helen with arms outstretched. "My baby girl has come home." Grammy started to cry.

Chapter Twenty-Seven

Grammy sat on the couch in the family room with Helen almost on her lap. The family really liked Aunt Helen's husband, Rodney. He was an architect in Elgin and he was really very taken with Bob and Barbara's house. Grammy liked all of Helen's family.

David was in his final year of residency at a Chicago hospital and he planned to go into private practice next year. His wife, Paula was a teacher at the same school as Helen. Janet was a senior at Northwestern. She already had a job waiting for her at a major corporation in Chicago as a computer software specialist. Eric was just starting at Northwestern and hasn't decided what he wants to do yet. Grammy was so proud of her children and grandchildren. Bob was somewhat uncomfortable at the resemblance of David to a young George Kramer. Bob wondered whether David knew that George was his father. All he knew is that he wouldn't be the one to tell him.

The entire family stayed up talking after a wonderful supper until almost midnight and it was decided that they would all go out to the country church for Christmas morning services. Helen hoped that her dad would be there. She was ready to forgive him and she hoped he would forgive her during this joyous season of the year. Grammy walked all the way up to the third floor to say good night to Helen and her family.

"Mom you use to tuck me in bed every night when I was a kid. It was the one thing that I really missed when I left home." Helen leaned up on one elbow and kissed her mother goodnight. Grammy patted Helen on the cheek and walked around and gave Rodney a goodnight kiss on the forehead, too.

The next morning the family gathered in the living room to open up their presents. Grammy had crocheted each of the girls a beautiful sweater. Bob got a new cell phone and John got new game for his computer. Helen had brought gifts for the family, too. By the time all of the presents had been open there was a mountain of discarded wrapping paper all over the living room. Jenny and Maggie picked up the paper and put it into a bag Janet was holding. When they came back to the room Janet noticed that there was one more present under the tree.

"Dad, look," Jenny said as she pointed to the small package.

Bob walk over and picked up the package, read the tag and then handed it to Grammy.

"This has your name on it, mom."

Grammy took the present from Bob and looked at the tag. It was from Poppy. She sat the package on the coffee table and said she was not going to think about him today.

"Grammy," Jenny said. "Who put that present under the tree? We didn't bring anything that small in from the farm?"

Grammy didn't know. She looked at Bob who looked at Barbara who looked at John. None of them had any idea. This was a mystery that would have to be solved after they all came back from church.

Grammy rode out to church with Helen and Rodney. She still couldn't believe that Helen was here and she hoped that Poppy would stay home from church today.

The small country church was very crowded when they walked in and squeezed into pews as close to each other as they could find. The choir was singing Christmas hymns and the altar was adorned with several poinsettias. Soon Pastor Tom came out and greeted the congregation and invited them to stand and welcome the baby Jesus into the world with song. Grammy sang her heart out as she was so happy. Nothing was going to spoil this Christmas Day. Jenny look around to see if Poppy was in church but she didn't see him. When she saw Todd she smiled at him and he winked at her. Tamara waved to Jenny and Maggie. Pastor Tom kept his sermon short this morning.

After the service everyone felt so full of joy and happiness. As always after every service the youth group had coffee and treats set up in the fellowship hall. During service George had spotted David and knew his past had come back to haunt him and Margie had seen him, too.

"I see an old girlfriend of yours has come home, honey," Margie said to George as they both looked across the room to Helen and her family. "I just didn't know how close you two were," she added jokingly.

"Margie, I'm sorry," George said looking down at her, breathing heavy as if he was on the verge of an attack of some sort.

"Honey, settle down. It's OK. George, sit down," Margie ordered as she pulled a chair out for him. "Are you all right?"

Margie sat down next to George and his breathing became easier. It had been years since he had seen Helen and he had no idea that she had his son. They weren't even high school sweethearts back then. They were just fooling around…and she has a son! He started breathing heavily again.

"George, settle down," Margie ordered as she put her arm around her husband.

Bob noticed what was going on and walked over to the couple.

"Are you all right, George?" Bob asked as he sat on the other side of his friend.

"Bob, I swear I didn't know," George said in all sincerity.

"I know, buddy. I just found out a couple days ago. As a matter of fact, I just found out that Helen was still alive a couple days ago. It's a long story." Bob looked at Margie and asked, "How are you with this?"

"Hey, it happened long before I was in the picture. I'm fine," Margie replied in her trooper sort of way. "But that kid has more of George's DNA than our kids have." Margie added with a laugh.

George began to feel a lot better once he knew Margie was OK with the situation but he was still terribly nervous to go meet David and Helen. As he was walking over he was thinking this might be a good lesson for Todd.

"Helen," George started as he walked toward her. "It's nice to see you again after all these years."

"And under such joyous occasions," Helen said as she reached out and gave George a hug.

Tears were running down both of their cheeks and neither of them wanted to let go first.

Margie tapped George on the shoulder and said, "Introduce me?"

George stepped back wiping the tears from his eyes as he introduced Margie to Helen. The two women embraced.

Helen had previously told David about George and she wanted him to know his biological father.

"I want you to meet our son, David," Helen said as she looked directly at George. Todd, Tamara and Terry were surprised at the news, but knew who she was talking about when she said "our" because David looked so much like their father.

"So, this makes you our half brother," Terry said almost as a question. "But you're old enough to be my dad." Then to his father he said, "Gee, dad, you must have been my age when he was born."

Everyone started laughing.

"Out of the mouths of babes," Margie said.

"Well, not quite," George said with a little rose glow in his cheeks. "But that's what I keep telling you boys about waiting until you're married. Get it, now?"

Looking over toward Jenny, Todd said, "Definitely, I'm waiting until I'm married. I've made a promise."

"We're glad to hear that, son," George said, as Margie gave Todd a little squeeze.

Todd walked over to talk to Jenny and pulled her away from the families.

"I have a present for you, Jen," Todd said as he pulled a small package out of his coat pocket.

"I have something for you, too," Jenny said, "but it's at home. When do you think you can come and get it?"

"Maybe tomorrow," Todd said. "Open yours now."

Jenny pulled the wrapping paper off the small package. She was holding a small jewelry box and the butterflies were turned lose in her stomach. She gingerly opened the box to reveal a pair of ruby earrings. They were beautiful.

"Oh, Todd," Jenny gasped. "These are the most beautiful earrings I have ever seen. I love them. Thank you." Jenny reached over and gave Todd a big hug. He leaned down and gave Jenny a very sweet kiss. She had to put the earrings on right away so Todd helped her with them.

"They look even better on you," Todd said.

Just then Bob called Jenny and told her that they were ready to leave. The fellowship hall was almost empty as the families were headed to their homes for Christmas dinners. A few kids promised they would come back tomorrow to put the tables and chairs away so Pastor Tom let them go and locked the doors.

Bob was just getting ready to get into the car when he saw Poppy's truck turn into the church parking lot.

"Oh no," Bob said aloud shaking his head, "not today."

Barbara saw the truck pulling in and was afraid that Poppy would make a scene and ruin their Christmas. Jenny was still standing next to Todd and grabbed his arm. Maggie and John were just getting ready to get into the car but were standing there as if time had stopped them. The tension was as tight as a too tight wound up mantle clock.

Grammy told Rodney to go ahead and leave but Helen said that it was time to settle this once and for all; and what better place to settle it than in front of church; and what better time than on Christ's birthday…Christmas morning.

When Poppy got out of the truck he just stood there behind the open door. Helen stepped out of the van and looked over to her dad. Bob and Barbara were holding their breath waiting to see what was going to happen.

"Merry Christmas, Father," Helen said breaking the ice first.

Poppy stepped away from the truck, closed the door and then walked over to the van. He stopped a few yards in front of it.

"Merry Christmas, Helen," Poppy returned the greeting.

Poppy lowered his head as if he was about to say grace but when he looked up there were tears in his eyes. He had a piece of paper in his hand at his side.

"I got this here note saying there is a Christmas surprise for me at Church and I should come. I thought it just might be Ruth coming home." Poppy looked at the note then shoved it in his pocket. "It ain't signed but I know who left it." He looked over toward John.

John looked over at Todd and Todd winked back at him. John knew that Todd would slip the note in the house while Poppy was either doing chores or upstairs.

Todd put his arm around Jenny and gave her a little squeeze.

"I guess I am supposed to be your surprise," Helen said. "It's been a long time, Father."

"Daughter," Poppy started, "I am so sorry. Can you forgive me?"

Helen walked over to Poppy and gave him a hug but his arms hung limp at his sides. Grammy got out of the car and walked close enough to hear what was being said, but she didn't want to interrupt the reunion.

"Daddy, I have forgiven you a long time ago. I love you and I want you to be part of our lives," Helen was crying now, too. "It's time you forgive yourself."

Poppy reached his hand out to Grammy. "Ruth, I'm an old fool. Do you think you can live with an old fool again?"

Grammy walked over and took Poppy's hand. "I couldn't handle training a new one," Grammy said. "I guess I'll have to take you back."

Poppy stepped back from both women and looked over to Bob's family and then to Helen's family and then walked over to John.

"Son," he said, "You may have learned a lot from me over the years but you taught me the most important lesson the other day." He took Helen by the hand that still showed the scars that were inflicted all those years ago. "We all do things that we are ashamed of. I did more than my share." Poppy brought Helen's hand to his lips and gently kissed it. "I am so sorry, daughter. I ask forgiveness from all of you. I want my family back."

Bob and his family walked over to Poppy. Maggie hugged Poppy. Barbara and Bob patted him on the back. John went over and stood there looking at him and simply reached out and shook his grandfather's hand. Jenny kissed Todd good-bye and thanked him for helping John and went over and hugged Poppy with the rest of the family.

The entire Madison family met back at Bob's house. Fred and Thomas arrived later in the afternoon and told Maggie about her mother. She was a bit upset but said she was happy that her mom was getting help, and would have to pray for her.

The family celebrated Christmas day as if they had never been separated. The past has not been forgotten but all was forgiven. Poppy took Grammy into the living room, picked up the small package on the coffee table and handed it to her.

"This is just a little something to remind us how things should be," Poppy said.

Grammy took the ribbon off the flat box and opened the lid. Inside was a beautiful cross on a gold chain.

"It's a lovely, Hank. Thank you," she said as she pulled it out of the box to put around her neck.

"Wait a minute, Ruth," he said as he took the cross from her hand. "Look through the crystal of the cross. You can see the *Lord's Prayer* inside the cross."

Grammy looked through the crystal and inside, sure enough, every word was there. Poppy took the cross from her again and put the chain around her neck. He leaned down and gave Grammy a sweet kiss on the neck. She smiled and knew everything would be all right.

"Forgive us as we forgive our debtors," Poppy said with a crooked smile and a tear in his eye.

Grammy put her hand to her heart where the cross now lay but where the love for Poppy was bursting more now that it did over 51 years ago when they were newlyweds. She nodded in agreement and they both walked arm in arm into the dining room to join the rest of the family for the best Christmas ever.